Fae Wars

Volume IV

Tales from the Occupation

Created by Lucas Marcum and J.F. Holmes

Edited by Michael Morton

1. J.F Holmes   Hearts and Minds
2. Alex Shaw   One Man's War
3. Michael Craig   Forget me Nots
4. John Olsen   A Wing and a Prayer
5. Cedar Sanderson   The North Way
6. James Copley   Hopper Station
7. R. Kyle Hannah   Where There's Smoke …
8. Brian Gifford   Tukor and the Iron Maiden

Hearts and Minds

By

J.F. Holmes

Prelude

"Better a jail cell than a dungeon, right? I mean, no Iron Maiden or thumbscrews, and it's dry."

Sheriff Bannerman tipped his hat back and leaned forward. He was old but tough like me, though to be honest, sixty-six felt like a hundred sometimes. "Mike, I don't think you're taking this seriously enough. The elves are going to be here in a few hours and then you're going to wish for a torture chamber."

"Fred, I don't have to remind you, but back in '70, we got drafted and sent to that hellhole we called Vietnam." I didn't like to think about that time, matter of fact I had buried a lot of those memories.

"Yeah, and I spent a year in an air condition warehouse at Cam Rahn routing material to guys like you out in the bush," said my friend, a guilty look on his face.

"Can't help it if you scored higher on the tests than I did! I got sent out there because I'm a dumbass, as you can see," emphasizing my point by waving my plastic MRE spoon at the cell bars. "This, though," and I held out the field ration, "is a hell of a lot better than a C-rat. Not as good as your wife's steaks though."

"Not anymore, they came and took over Paulson's this morning, gave all the prime beef cows to some orcs, slaughtered them on the spot," he said bitterly. "Yeah, we get plenty of food for nothing at the market, but it's not exactly the good stuff."

It's started already, and he hasn't been dead more than a day. I grunted and then said, "Doesn't matter to me now."

"I suppose not. Gonna tell me why you did it though? Me being the law and all, such as it is." As he said that, a look of disgust ran across his face. Fred Bannerman had, before the Invasion, taken the job of policing our small town, and the bigger county, seriously. Even if we were in the middle of nowhere, the wrong side of the Catskill mountains in New York, with more cows than people.

I sighed and said, "You're gonna be mad when I tell you, Fred."

"Try me, Mike."

***

It was, I think, about two month after the Invasion when I met Lord Bilarien Tavor. That was his title, but eventually I just called him Billy. He was a fifth nephew once removed or something of THE Tavor, the shithead ruling New York City. The one in the video, where he got taken down by some special operations guy in a damned sword fight. He showed up that week, about time the son was in charge, I guess, same one that's ruling the City right now. Bilarien had been 'given' our valley up here in the back side of the Catskills as 'reward', meaning being sent out to the middle of nowhere for being too nice a guy to his prisoners. His troops loved him, though, both Red Arrow and White Hand. He had a platoon of each, tasked to keep order in the county, but like I said, it took them a while to get here.

No one had really bothered us up here in the sticks. There was a National Guard armory in Binghamton, an engineer unit, that got mobilized on Day Two, and none of them had ever come back. All five soldiers from our town gone just like that, and the State Police barracks over in Cobleskill was empty too, apparently. Well, Chrissy Somerston, a Spec Four in the Guard, showed up two months later, but she wasn't all there and ate a pistol a week later. I think on the third week a convoy showed up, a bunch of humans driving semi's and escorted by a troop of elven cavalry. Good thing because food was getting pretty damn short. I did notice, though, that the drivers were scared shitless and one of the trucks was running on a flat and another was smoking badly from under the hood. That and bullet holes in the cabs and trailers, as well as a few empty saddles. Good, fuck 'em. At least someone hadn't stopped fighting.

As for the locals, well, the panic of a small town running out of food had pretty much taken the fight out of us before it started. Seriously, what were we going to do? New York had for the most part, with their stupid gun laws, stripped us of anything to fight with. We were a thousand people scattered across a small town and a bunch of dairy farms in the middle of the mountains. Most of the roads were two lanes that ran between the narrow valleys, one farm to the next, with our town being the biggest. We actually had two stop lights.

Plus, I think we were in shock over how fast everything happened. I know I was. Recently retired from the state, working for the DEC managing state lands. Not the best paying job, but it kept me out of doors like I wanted. And we had made it work, me and Anna raising three kids who had all jetted out of here as soon as they could. Can't say I blamed them, because I was a bit of a dick for quite a while after I got back from 'Nam. How she put up with me for as long as she did, I don't know, but she was a better woman than I deserved. I think she was in California last I heard.

Me, I just hung out at the Hamlet. It was a diner slash coffee shop, and I had one or two other old timers like me that met occasionally to argue about politics, but mostly I read the paper. Even that last one from the Albany Times Union, three pages of complete confusion and bullshit. I was kinda amazed they managed to get that printed and out, since I heard the Fae went after the Watervliet Arsenal and the NY Guard HQ at Albany airport hard. We had some refugees but honestly the city folks just stuck to what they knew, running from one urban area to another. Didn't matter, the fighting upstate was over in a week.

So, I sat and drank my coffee and shot the shit with the other old guys, flirted with the waitress who, if my kids had stayed, probably would have gone to school a little bit before my granddaughter. That is, I did until a Friday morning, a week after the Fae had rolled into town and left a squad of orcs to despoil the local library.

I never sat with my back to the door, a habit I learned almost fifty years ago, so I saw them come in. My coffee sat untouched as I watched first a big bruiser of a White Hand orc, though I learned later that their tribe ran small compared to the Red Arrow. Shit, I wouldn't have taken him on if I was forty years younger. He cleared everyone out from a couple of booths with gestures that easily conveyed his threat, then went back and opened the door again, the entrance bells jangling in tune with his chainmail.

In stepped three elves, the first two, well, knights I guess you would call them. They wore swords and well broken-in plate mail, and they looked like some seriously dangerous fuckers. I learned later that they were the landless nephew and niece of Lord Bilarien, a brother and sister named Ashut and Lathy. I learned to like them, in a way, because having been a fighting man myself, I could respect their skills and, to be honest, they said what they meant and meant what they said. Not a lot of humans lately that were into that.

Behind them stood another elf, similar in features to the first two but wearing a shiny ass chainmail shirt under a hand tooled leather coat that looked like it cost a million bucks. This dude was, I'm not afraid to say it, beautiful. Even the scar on his face just made him more rugged looking, like a model for western wear or something. The waitress and the other two women in the diner just stared. Now I know that pretty much all elven nobility, and even the 'commoners', have that effect.

I picked up my coffee and took a sip, trying to play it cool, like a dumbass. I wasn't sure what to expect; I had seen videos of people getting killed for not kneeling fast enough or somehow pissing them off, and I realized that maybe I had just given myself a death sentence. Well, I should have died fifty years ago in that bamboo cage. Lord Bilarien looked at me, the only one doing anything other than staring, quietly gave an order and nodded in my direction.

Jack and Jill, my private names for his two retainers, moved quickly towards me and pinned my arms in grips of steel, no screwing around. Like I said, I've been an outdoors kind of guy my whole life so I'm in decent shape for my age, but these were, well, fighters. I'd say young, but who knows with elves?

Then the brute squad, their orc, gave me a professional once-over that was the most intimate contact I've had in years. He immediately found the Colt 1911 that I carried every day for the last, well, almost fifty years. Never used it once, but then again, my house never burned down either and I still had a fire extinguisher. He laid it on the counter, just out of reach of anyone, and proceeded to finish his pat down, ending with a grunt of "he's clean" or whatever it was in orcish. The two Fae forcefully sat me down on my stool at the counter and stood behind me, no doubt ready to cut my head off.

The head elf walked and pulled up a chair, turning it around to sit on it backwards, taking off the leather coat and handing it to another creature I hadn't seen come in, kind of a cross between a monkey and a dog. The thing, which I later learned was an honest to God demon servant, growled at me, took the coat and disappeared. Not beat feet, literally disappeared.

Seeing the look of discomfort on my face, Bilarien said, in perfect American accented English, "Sorry if Grau disconcerted you, he's perfectly harmless. This, on the other hand," and he took up my Colt and started examining it.

"Careful with …" I started to say, but he dropped the magazine, racked the slide, snatched the ejected round out of the air, slipped the round into his pocket then field stripped it faster than any Drill Sergeant I had ever seen, laying the pieces out on the counter. Then he smiled, closed his eyes and put it back together just as fast. Last, he put the magazine back in the well and then handed it to my, butt first. No round in the chamber, of course. He wasn't stupid but he wasn't scared, either. Of course, he was in no danger at that point, I'm sure my head would have been separated from my shoulders before I even started to pull the slide back, never mind cocked the hammer. I took it and put it back into the holster on my belt, my heart racing.

"Thank you," I said, kind of awkwardly. What exactly do you say after that?

"One can't be too careful, there are bears in these woods," he said with a smile, then leaned forward and continued with a wink and conspiratorial tone, "and in the case of dashing men and elves such as us, jealous husbands! Just between us, it is very hard to be this good looking of a rogue, is it not?" Then he turned and shot a dazzling smile at the other waitress, who was almost my age. Sally blushed fearfully.

I laughed. That was how I came to meet the new boss, very different from the old boss.

***

We all expected Bilarien to jump in with both expensive boots and rule the way we had seen things going all around the country. Occasionally people came up from New York City and told us about the fighting still raging in the suburbs, and we saw it on the internet. Apparently, remnants of the military were giving them hell, but all was quiet here. We were mostly a farming community, the town being a hub for supplies like tractor parts and tools and honestly, we were an older population. Kids had been leaving here for decades, and most of us just wanted to live our lives.

    Instead, the guy was a good leader. He treated everyone with respect, set himself up as a judge for criminal court and was pretty damn fair. A lot harder on people who had been getting a free pass, like Willy Johnston who had been beating his wife for years. He got forty lashes and was banned from the community, his wife getting a job at the once vacant casino & summer resort that had become Bilarien's estate. Other disputes, the Fae took the time to listen to both sides and his judgment was, well, fair. No one was ever completely happy with what he pronounced, but as time went on people learned to either be right or not complain. He was often harder on false complaints than on losers in legitimate cases. A few hours in the stocks did a great deal to put people into a less litigious mood, and once word got around that whippings were a thing, whatever petty crime we had disappeared.

    What sealed the deal for the county was when a group of, I don't know, bandits, gangbangers, refugees, whatever, drove down from Utica. It was stupid shit that had been happening a lot more often even before the Invasion, mostly car theft. They attacked a farm and, well, raped and killed the couple living there. One of Bilarien's flyers saw the smoke, investigated and sent some kind of message to him. Next thing we knew his cavalry troop of a dozen elves were hauling ass down main street, whatever kind of magic they had moving their horses faster than a car. When they came back, a couple of hours later, he had a bunch of heads tied to his saddle and three kids with his riders. The heads were stuck up on spikes at the off ramps leading up into the mountains with a proclamation from the elves that they basically weren't fucking around. That kind of thing put a dead stop to anyone coming into our quiet countryside again, and Bilarien's stock went way up.

I kept waiting for the other shoe to drop, because it always does, and it kind of did. I was sitting having my morning cup of weak coffee and Bilarien walked in through the door. He had shown up several times since our first encounter and Jack and Jill now only stood on either side of the doorway. The orc, Grishna, stood outside the diner and probably scared the shit out of anyone who tried to come in. The owner didn't care because gave him a five-gold piece tip every time he ate there, and dollars were rapidly becoming useless. He sat down across from me at the counter and Sally poured him a cup of the real thing, strong. A nod from him and she poured me one, too.

We had talked several times since he had first shown up, mostly him asking me questions about humanity in general, never any specifics on local people. What the hell, the better he understood us, maybe the better he would treat us. Coffee between us had become a regular thing, a couple times a week. Crap, I even taught him how to play spades, and he picked Grishna of all people as a partner. That lasted for only a few games until I caught Sally giving him hints as to what cards she held. The dude couldn't help his effect on women, and I had fun, more than I had had in a long time.

Now, though, he had a troubled look on his face. "Tell me something, Michael, son of Giovanni. I have a human problem and I seek your advice."

Human problem? I took a moment before replying, "Uh, I don't know if human medicines work on elves, but we have this thing called 'penicillin' if you, uh, caught something from a woman."

He seemed amused, chuckling as he said, "No, we Eldorai aren't subject to the same ills and diseases that the weaker races are. And even if I were, I would just go to a healer." Then he grew more serious. "I need to know how to deal with some humans."

"I'm not going to rat on anyone here," I said emphatically.

"Rat?" he replied with a raised eyebrow. "What an interesting word, but I understand. No, I have been ordered to do something that is … distasteful. I'm being given a group of prisoners who have been sentenced by Lord Tavan to life in slavery. They were warriors who were captured during the Battle of the Bridge."

"I've heard of it." Dangerous ground. Had to be careful what I said. The fight at the Brooklyn Bridge had become almost legendary in the few months since the Invasion, with the Golden Harp being spray painted by insurgents at the scene of their attacks.

He snorted and said, "The sooner we get rid of your 'social media' the better off this entire land will be."

"Every young person in America will rise up against you!" I wasn't exaggerating.

He smiled at that one and said, "Thank the gods I have avoided having children so far. But we digress. These men fought honorably and extracted an enormous toll on our forces, for which I have a great respect. All my life I have trained for this war and though my part in it was minor, I saw enough to understand their sacrifice."

"If you don't mind my asking, where did you fight?" I asked, genuinely curious. "I mean, you're of House Tavor, probably one of the most powerful if they were giving New York City to rule, so I think you would have seen action there."

"I ... I do not follow my uncle's creed. I am ... I was a boon companion of my cousin Elarissa. We believed in a different way, especially when it came to being a liege and the way to rule. The way of the fist may be how most of the Eldorai think they should deal with their subordinates, whereas Elarissa and I think ... thought ..." He paused and took a deep breath. This man, well, elf, was in pain and I felt for him. I had lost buddies back in 'Nam who were closer to me than family, but I hadn't lost any actual relations. I had heard of Ellarissa and seen her statue.

I waited and eventually he began again. "There is a school of thought that duty goes both ways. If you are a ruler, you are under an obligation to provide for those you rule over. My uncle believes that rule should be through strength, not persuasion or example. I believe differently."

"You didn't tell me where you fought," I said.

"No, I didn't. As I said, I trained for this war my entire life, but I have been studying humans in general for just as long. I knew we would win, so when I learned that our House was going to attack this country, the one you once called the 'United States', I learned the language, studied your armies, your weapons, what we knew of them."

I let the 'once called' thing slide. "No translating ring for you, huh?" I asked, looking at his hand.

"As I said, rule by example. You, all you humans, along with my Fae retainers and the Uruks, are MY people, so I needed to speak your language."

"Fair enough, and pretty smart." Still, I pressed him.

"And what part did you play in the war?"

"None," he finally said. "I was in the second wave, tasked with pressing the fight once we had broken the lines. My ... what is the word? A group of riders."

"Cavalry."

"Yes. That. We started up across a bridge, the one named after your first president, to flank your forces in the ... the Bronx, who were putting up a fierce resistance. Your 'Mountain" division troops. Excellent fighters."

"Ha, my unit would have kicked their asses," I grumbled. I had told him of my service in Vietnam and he had immediately gone to our library and gotten out a book on it, quizzing me endlessly.

"No doubt, no doubt! We all think our comrades are the most valiant," he laughed. "So, there I was, about to order a charge across this mighty bridge, into the teeth of the defenses. A glorious ride! And we found that the defenders had been overwhelmed by crowds of refugees. We had a clear path if we but trampled the civilians fleeing. They saw us coming and laid down, cowering in fear. We only had to take their surrender and move them back to the rear, and slaves are always prizes of war, even in your culture. It would have taken us ten of your minutes and we would have been away to the real battle, seizing the Bear Mountain Bridge and opening the door to an assault on your fortress at West Point while sending troops into the Bronx defenders' rear areas."

"Sounds like a plan," I said, biting down on my bitterness. It was a textbook cavalry mission, and if you could ignore the dying, well worth the risk and so-called glory.

He saw the look on my face and said, "Well, those

were our orders. I asked for the time, but I was told instead by my commander to slaughter them. I argued, he drew his sword, challenged my honor, and I slew him in single combat. I am of high nobility, though young, and he was of a lesser status family, so to avoid a deadly feud, my uncle sent me here. I am in exile, but I'll do my best for all the people and the land that I am charged with."

"Single combat, huh?" I said, impressed. "Like a sword fight? That's badass."

He smiled that dazzling smile and pointed to his face. "Females are attracted to scars,"

Shit. I liked this guy. Guts and honor.

"So your problem. These prisoners. How many?"

"Twenty males. All of fighting age."

"No women?" Dinosaur that I was, I knew that more and more females had joined the military, especially the Guard and Reserves.

"No," he said flatly. "Any women captured were ... taken away."

OK, stay away from that one. I thought for a moment and then said, "Do you keep records of who you have? Name, social security number?"

"Of course, we have their names, who their fathers are, whence they come from, what unit they were assigned to." He said it very matter of factly, I could almost hear the "duh" in his voice.

"Well, what are your choices?" I asked.

He pondered for a moment, then said, "My uncle would have them become thralls and work in the iron mines that are being reopened -"

"I said your choices," daring to interrupt him. "Haven't you been given this land and the people to rule? Backwater corner of the world that it is, a Lord is a Lord, am I right?"

Belarian looked at me for a long time, and I'm pretty sure his decent nature was warring with his elven upbringing to decide if he should kill me or not for being uppity. He went so far as to draw his poniard and twirl it in his fingers, as he sometimes did when making a decision. I had seen it in court, and I had also seen him throw it in the blink of an eye through the leg of a man who was arguing with the Sheriff. He could cut my throat before I could blink.

"Michael son of Giovani," he finally said, "sometimes I tire of hearing the word 'yes'. I give you leave and right to say no to me, at any time, if you think my course of action may be unwise. Would that you had been there when I disobeyed my orders! You might have convinced me to go forward and continue my attack and shared in my glory!"

"I might not have counseled you to obey. I am human, after all, and I doubt I would have told you to ride down innocent civilians," I told him.

He grinned and said, "That means nothing on the balanced weights of good and evil. What you mistake for 'evil' in the Fae is not the same as your human concept, but there are 'good elves' and 'bad elves'. Though I must admit, we do lean towards the latter. I would call them shortsighted instead of bad. No, it was more a matter of honor than good versus evil. The humans had surrendered, and I was loath to kill those who had yielded."

"Well, call it what you will, I appreciate it." And I did. I had seen too many die in a senseless war just for expediency. Napalm sticks to kids as well as commies.

"I was tempted," he said, "It is hard to think of you as anything but the ancient enemy who sent us into exile. Had I been of my father's generation, who experienced the war with your ancestors, I probably would have."

"Are we all beholden to the sins of our fathers?" Shit, I was starting to talk like him.

He laughed at that. "Of course we are. Doesn't your Bible say so, unto the seventh generation? And yet I am only of the second."

"Sucks to be you. Now about your prisoners. You can do magic, right?" I had assumed so, didn't all Fae?

"I have some talent, but I have not explored it. Few do, and I prefer the blade to the Ways."

Well, that was good to know. "I was going to say that you can send them home with some kind of tracking spell on them. Here we use what's called an ankle monitor. Maybe you can come up with something similar? After all, most probably have families, and the word might get around about maybe you all might not be so bad after all."

He snorted at that. "And let twenty trained angry fighting aged males back into the population? Hardly."

"Well then, keep them here and have them send for their families. Give them some of the vacant farms, split them up around the county. We could use some new blood around here and they would be in your debt. Besides, if most of them are not full-time military, they'll probably have a lot of civilian skill sets that will help you run your estate. And with their families here, their good behavior will be guaranteed."

"You know, my cousin Elarissa would have liked you, Michael, and that is a high compliment. I shall name you my counselor."

"The hell you will!" I blurted. "Do that and eventually you'll find me strung up from a telephone pole with a golden harp nailed to my forehead. I'll give you advice over coffee if I think it benefits everyone, but the second someone thinks I'm actively helping you rule this place, I'm a dead man."

The mention of the harp cooled his expression; we hadn't had any attacks here but the supply convoys on the Thruway, across the mountains, were getting hit on a regular basis. "As you wish, Michael. Though, may I call you Mike? Isn't that what your friends call you?"

"If I can call you Billy, why not?"

"Belarian, Billy, Billyrian," he said, rolling the sound on his tongue. "You may."

And then he surprised the shit out of me by holding out his hand. I took it and he shook it awkwardly. "Until the next time I need coffee."

***

They came for me, as I knew they would, but it took a while. Though I never went to see Belarian at his estate, of course our conversations at the diner were noted. Hell, I expected them to be. I didn't know the other three, but they didn't move military and looked young. They had one regular army with them, probably a Green Beanie. They did slip a few times and call him Sarge, but he ignored it. It was him that did the talking while a driver sat behind the wheel of the battered, blacked out Jeep Cherokee and two more stood guard, one looking down each direction of the road.

"I understand your position, Mister D'Mateo. I really do. Thing is, collaborators have been attacked. I'd hate to see that happen to you." The soldier said it calmly, but it was a threat nonetheless. He knew it and I knew it.

"Don't blow smoke up my ass, son. I spent more than a year in a NVA POW camp way before you were born, getting my ass tortured. Don't you fucking question me or my patriotism."

He was a cool customer, I'll give him that. "I know your record, corporal, and I respect your service. I'm just saying that others might not see it that way, and this is a different kind of war. We all must do our part, I'm just not sure what yours is. Informer? Collaborator? Servant of the New World order? How did you last a year in that camp, anyway?"

"Fuck you."

"Think about your actions, that's all I'm saying. We could use some information on your friend Belarian. His habits, schedule, whatever."

"He's not my friend. We talk, I give him advice on how to deal with the people in my community to keep them safe. So far, it seems to be working. No slavery, no torture, our women aren't being sent through portals to God knows where. We have food and our animals are still alive."

"And yet the rest of the country is suffering under the bootheel of these Fae bastards. Ever hear of Kingston?" Sarcasm through and through.

"Of course, and I know what happened there," I answered. "The elves hung one out of a hundred in the city when they rebelled. You aren't helping your position."

"And generated a hundred times more enemies," he said.

"Is that what you want? Martyrs? Again, go fuck

yourself." I was as calm as he was, on the outside. On the inside my heart was racing.

"Ever read the book 'Watership Down'? You're in danger of the silver wire." he said, and I knew damn well what he meant. Rabbits who were fat and happy as long as they occasionally gave up a member of the community to the farmer.

"Yeah, a lot of my friends," I shot back, "were drafted as unwilling sacrifices to fight in another war and didn't come back."

I was angry now and he saw that his remark had hit home. "We'll be back. I want any kind of information you can give me about Belarian. Have a good night, Mister D'Mateo. If you want to talk, paint a harp on a bridge support on Route 23," and he handed me a small can of spray paint, white, not yellow. He stood up and walked back to the Jeep, whistled to call his security in. They sped off into the night in a cloud of dust and I went back into my trailer, lit a cigarette with a shaking hand, took a deep drag and blew it out. Shit. Then I went to a cabinet, dragged out a bottle of Jim Beam, and drank until I passed out.

***

The next day I drove into town, only four miles, but I took it slow. Gas was getting kind of scarce and the Stewarts had started asking for payment in gold. All I had was my cash and my debit card, but the bank kept saying that they would open again tomorrow, always tomorrow. My VA check was direct deposited, my retirement from the State, well, same thing. I was OK for now, but I had no income and I'd have to start looking for a job. Maybe Billy ... no. And I slammed on the brakes.

Jesus Christ. On the side of the road lay headless three corpses, spilled from an arrow pierced Cherokee. There were dozens of expended rounds littering the ground in a long trail and then the body of the guy I had been talking to the night before, about thirty feet away and facedown. He was the only one who still had his head, though it was cut through with a nasty sword stroke and his brains had spilled on the road. A suppressed M-4 lay on the ground next to him and there was a large knife gripped in one hand. The body looked small, like the dead always do. Further on were two dead orcs getting picked at by crows.

The local ambulance was parked on the side of the road and I pulled up next to them. "Hey Jed," I said to the guy filling out a clipboard. "What the hell happened?"

"Lord Billy and his sidekicks killed these gang bangers last night! Probably on the way to raid another farm. Ain't that the shit! I know I've seen how bad the elves are on the internet, but hell, half of that is made up propaganda shit. Billy's OK in my book."

I drove away with a troubled mind, still thinking of the whole incident when I sat down to drink my coffee at the Hamlet. They would be back, and what the Green Beret had said bothered me. Were we just being fat rabbits waiting for the slaughter?

"Ah, Michael!" said Balarien, throwing the door open with a bang. His armor was covered in dried blood, even had a cut across his cheek that looked nasty. Aside from the gore he was the picture of happiness. He took his customary seat across from me at the counter and had to ask Sally for a cup of coffee. I guess even she was grossed out enough to overcome her lust.

He drank it in one long pull then sat back, banging his fist on the counter. "It is good to see you well, I had feared that the bandits had stopped at your, um, moveable house, before heading to richer pickings. No doubt you showed them off with your own martial skills! I sent Ashut and Lathy to check on you but there was no answer. No signs of violence either, so they left you to your rest." He peered a little closer at me and said in a quieter voice, "You do not look well, friend. Are you OK?"

"I had a little too much to drink last night with dinner, I'm fine," I said, as politely as I could. Truth be told, my heart hurt and my head was pounding.

He smiled at that and said, "Ah, well humans are far more fragile stuff than the Eldorai. Though I need to tell you of a most respectable warrior, even for a bandit! Do you see this?" and he pointed to his face. "Another scar of honor! A few inches or a second earlier and I might have been in actual danger!"

"Where's your Uruk?" I asked, not seeing the orc. Lathy had a raw wound on her arm, what looked like a through and through 5.56 hit and a bright scarred place on her armor, center mass. I also noticed that Belarian had a long metal score on the side of the helm that he had set on the counter.

"Died in my service, may his name be remembered by his tribe!" said Belarian. "They were skilled fighters, maybe deserters from the battle. Their leader challenged me to personal combat! We fought with knives in the darkness, and he almost had a chance with that final thrust!"

Then he leaned forward and, in a conspiratorial tone, "Do you think it would be a good idea for me to employ a human servant to follow me around and record my exploits for your social media?"

I had been taking a sip of coffee and it shot out my nose as I started coughing. After a minute I finally managed to gasp, "Jesus Christ, no! Are you insane?"

"Why? What do you mean?" he asked, a bit taken aback.

"Because maybe the Harps will learn a hell of a lot more about you and make you a target? Didn't operational security figure into your training?"

"Bah!" he said dismissively, "let them come! My people, my humans, have already been informing me of any stranger who ventures within our borders! They love me, unlike my cousin Jayrn. He has put the boot to the people of 'Syracuse', and he has nothing but insurgent attacks and work stoppages. In fact, he has had the impudence to ask our Lord Tavan to give my lands to him! Claims I am too soft and weak, but he fails to see that our peoples can learn to work as one."

"Does he have any right to your land? Can he do that?" I asked, and I was sick to my stomach over it.

"Well, yes, were something to happen to me, he is my closest relative. I have never had time for children. But who is to say what may take place over the next year? With peace here, I can perhaps turn my attention to wooing a maiden from the Land Beyond." He smiled at the thought, and I can't say I blamed him. The elven women I had seen made even my heart race at sixty-five.

"Well, whatever I can do to help keep the peace. You know that I hate war and violence."

"I do, my friend, even though you 'carry' a weapon

with you. I have learned that it is ancient, maybe you wear it only from tradition? You did say your father used it in your 'second' world war, and his father before him in the Great War. Tell me, what glory did you ancestors cover themselves with in this Great War?"

Glad to divert him, I delved into what was to him his favorite pastime, listening to stories of our wars. Of course, I always embellished them, and never mentioned the sick disgust I felt at violence, even though I knew it was sometimes a necessary thing.

Finally, after a while, I told him I had to go, but asked, "Do the people of the Land Beyond ever engage in recreational fishing?"

He looked puzzled. "Recreational? What does this mean?"

"Hmm. Well, like bear hunting. I know you have hunts for sport." They did, I had seen them ride out and come back with deer and the occasional boar.

"Yes, but that prepares us for war. A struggle to catch a fish? What good is that, and how hard can it be?"

"Oh, you have no idea what it feels like to land a trout after a tough fight. That and getting it to take the bait is an exercise in patience and intelligence. Plus, they taste great, too."

"Can you show me how?" he asked. "After the long years, new diversions are always welcome."

I nodded. "Of course. I'll even provide the gear."

"And," he said, without a hint of his usual inbred arrogance, "it is good to go with a friend who you can speak your mind to."

***

We headed up into the mountains where the water was cooler and the trout still ran. Late summer they stayed way up, out of the heat and deep in the pools. Instead of riding a horse I drove in my old Nissan Pathfinder and they followed on their weirdly magical mounts. Fine with me if they choked on the dust, but instead they kept pace with the truck, just off to either corner.

When we reached my favorite spot, a sun dappled forest stream that rushed its way downward and over the edge of a set of falls, I pulled over and went to the back to get my favorite fly rod and my tackle box, and of course one Billy. Ashut gave me the once over, rather less invasive than his orc underling, and seemed satisfied when he didn't find anything other than a fish cleaning knife. Not a threat, really, against a trained swordsman. He knew I wasn't stupid and Belarian was in a hurry to get to it. "Wait here with the horses," he said to Ashut, and when his knight objected, he barked at him in Fae. I only caught the word "friend". The elf had even left his chainmail home and was wearing, of all things, a fishing vest that looked like it came straight from a sporting goods store, almost a match for the one I wore. Underneath was a Bass Pro Sho t-shirt.

"You look ridiculous," I told him.

"I feel glorious!" he replied, "to be able to spend time with a boon companion and engage in warfare with a fish that is undoubtedly smarter than both of us!" Then, no shit, he laughed and lightly punched my shoulder.

As we made our way up the stream, I started to teach him the rudiments of casting a fly rod, the subtle flick of the wrist, the teasing of the dark shape under the water. He was quick to pick it up; great reflexes and incredible patience. In no time he was landing the lure right where he wanted it and teasing a large brownie to the surface, laughing as he did so. I thought back to those golden moments when my son was young and I was sober long enough to take him fishing and my chest started to hurt. He got the bite, set the hook and with a shouted battle cry, went to land the struggling fish. I let him walk it back slowly towards me, and when it finally tired, he reached down and grabbed it by the gills, lifting it up in the air in triumph and turning towards me with a huge smile on his face.

I had pulled the .45 from the tacklebox, and I should have shot him when his back was to me but I couldn't. Where was the honor in that? He deserved better. Instead, I looked at him, tears running down my face and said, "I'm sorry, but I must. It's a war, you understand. Your way is … the right way for you to win, and I can't let that happen."

I don't know if I was asking for his forgiveness, but I think he did get it. He knew that the way his uncle and cousins abused the conquered would stoke the fires of rebellion, and he had the key to defeat it. Belarian was the perfect ruler for a defeated people, ones who would trade safety for peace, and if that peace never came …

Finally, he said, "It's inevitable, but I still call you my friend."

He was fast and I was shaking like a leaf. If he hadn't been holding the fish in his good hand, I would have been dead. The thrown knife whipped a cut in my cheek just as I fired, the big pistol hammering back into my hands. A round went into his chest from ten feet away and he spun and fell with the impact, my second shot catching him in the side as he crashed downward.

Elves are tough bastards, and he took a bit to die. I sat down and cradled his head in my lap as he wheezed his breath out, blood starting to fill his lungs and spraying as he coughed. He gripped my hand and managed to whisper, "You will have ... a great scar ... and I will see you ... someday, Michael son of Giovanni, and we will fish together in ..." and then he died.

Epilogue

"So you see, I had to. If his way of doing things had spread, well, eventually we would become a slave race, subordinate to the Fae. He held the key. Now his cousin is going to come in here and be a complete asshole, and we'll HAVE to fight." Telling the whole story was exhausting; Ashut had known exactly where to beat me to leave me in one piece for the elven authorities to torture.

"Who the hell are you to make that decision for the entire county, Mike?" My old friend was pissed because he finally understood what was coming.

"Me? I guess I'm the only one who saw it. If we lose, no matter how nice the elves are, we'll be slaves and at their mercy. If humanity eventually wins, and I'm sure we will, then how do you think the people who rolled over and gave up are going to be treated? Hung from telephone poles if they're lucky."

"Goddammit!" was all he said. He knew I was right. "So now what? They have magic and shit. They're going to keep you alive for a long time and make an example of you."

"Not if I get killed escaping," and I nodded to where

Lathy stood up against the wall, watching me like a hawk, not understanding a word we were saying. She wanted to kill me, I could see it in her eyes, but I was sure her orders had been to deliver me safe and sort of sound to the new ruler of the county.

"Are you sure?" he asked. I just looked at him until he turned away and walked out of the room.

I engaged in a staring contest with the elf until I heard the electric lock go snick, then gave her the finger. "Fuck you, you piece of shit," I said. That she understood, the tone and gesture if not the words. The warrior strode closer, sword lifted, and my shoulder hit the door, slamming it into her. I grabbed at her belt and ripped her short knife out, stabbing ineffectively at the chainmail.

***

It was a green place, with golden light and a faint breeze that rippled across the tops of the trees. I walked forward towards the glinting waterfall where Beleriand stood, a smile on his face, and I felt better than I had in decades. Coming up with a fly rod in his hand, he put his arm around my shoulder and said, "Come, let us enjoy the forever peace, my friend. This morning we fish, this afternoon we fight, tonight we feast."

"Sounds like a plan ... my friend."

J.F. Holmes is the owner and senior editor of Cannon Publishing. Along with Lucas Marcum, he created the Fae Wars universe and is the writer of the first book, "Onslaught." Mr. Holmes has over twenty books in print and is a two-time Dragon awards finalist.

One Man's War

by Alex Shaw

Steve Sim's eyes fluttered open. He struggled to comprehend what he saw. Above him an open distant sky twinkled stars but something else too, flames. A sudden shout to his left made him jerk his head, and daggers of pain pierced his temples. He remembered.
Ten feet away sat the Ukrainian oligarch he'd been hired to protect. He was still strapped into the hugely padded, leather seat of the executive jet. The oligarch's crisp, cream suit was stained with blood across the chest.
"Steve, get me out of here!"
Sim reached for his own belt release and clicked it. Head protesting, he hauled himself out of the seat. Moving towards his boss, his arms reached out when suddenly spike-like objects penetrated the bulkhead, and the entire side of the fuselage folded inwards before being torn away. Sim stumbled back as he saw something he could not comprehend, something he could not believe…
A giant mouth had taken a bite out of the plane, and that bite included his boss. He was still strapped to his seat, waving his arms, and screaming, as whatever it was that had grabbed him rose and flew away from the wreckage of the jet. Giddy, Sim felt himself fall forward as blackness enveloped him…

Sim dry washed his face with his hands and then took in a large breath of salty, sea air. How many times, he wondered, would he have to relive the attack which had put him out of action for weeks and prevented him from getting home to his daughter and ex-wife? He wasn't a religious man but prayed to whoever, whatever may be listening, that Debbie and Kim were safe.

Marcel clamped a hand on his shoulder, "Soon you will be back in England."

"If some mythical sea monster doesn't attack us first."

"Oui, that is a risk, however we are bringing over fresh French cheese and wine for the elves. I do not think they would be happy if it were to be, how do you say, 'gobbled up'?"

"Gobbled up by a goblin."

"That is not possible, my friend, Goblins do not swim."

Sim continued to gaze at the English Channel and the ever-nearing British coastline. There was nothing to remind him of the Fae's brutal and bloody attack on the world he knew. No smoke, listing hulls of blackened ships or even a single dragon in the sky. As a kid growing up in North Wales, he'd been a fan of myths and Arthurian legends, and of course he'd started playing 'Dungeons & Dragons' after that time he'd run away from home and hid in the woods imagining all the creatures were real. He'd always been an elf with an enchanted dagger yet never for one minute had he ever envisaged all those he fought in the game were living creatures. He'd counselled against his boss fleeing Dubai when news of the first attacks happened, but the man was determined they should relocate to his French chateau with its meter thick stone walls, wine cellars and black-market RPGs. But they'd never made it that far…

Sim pulled out his UK mobile phone and tried again to call Kim. Now as they reached the coast, he had coverage, and her phone rang but there was no answer.

It seemed odd the Fae had kept the networks and the internet up, but then they were an odd adversary and scared of technology.

The container ship Newhaven docks. In the time since the Fae had taken over, Marcel's contacts had explained, the town had been designated a 'regional import port' by the local occupation authorities. Sim noted Newhaven fort, which stood on the cliffs overlooking the sea. The WW2 fortification was built to defend against the Germans. Now it watched over a land enslaved by a supernatural force.

"Remember the plan," Marcel said, "When we draw alongside the dock, drop into the water on the sea facing side of the ship. The goons on guard won't check. They have not the brains to believe anyone would jump ship."

"I hope you're right."

"So do I, my friend," Marcel replied, "otherwise you'll be dead."

Sim smirked at the former Legionnaire, whom over the past two months he had come to regard as a friend. Marcel had found him wandering in the wreckage of the Learjet. He had been coordinating the local resistance to the Fae, and then offered to travel with Sim across occupied France before finally arranging for this boat ride home. Their journey however had been anything but simple.

Minutes later, the container ship came into port and slowly, guided by a pilot vessel docked. Sim, now wearing a dry-suit and shouldering a waterproof daypack, was on deck but hidden in a walkway between the stacked containers. He heard a tune whistled on the breeze, Marcel appeared and silently mouthed, 'Go.'"

Sim was up and over the gunwale in seconds. Hands

clamping his mask in place, he pencil-dived into the sea. The cold gnawed at his hands and head. Sim broke the surface, shielded from the dockside by the hulking hull of the container ship. To the immediate left of this was the marina with its small yachts and powerboats. Sim let himself drift as his ears attuned to the sounds of the port. The current took him away from the ship and afforded him a wider view of his surroundings. On the dockside cranes moved unloading heavy shipping containers, and amongst these were grotesquely large figures with whips. Sim shuddered, he had to get to Debbie and Kim, and get to them fast.

He swam in the direction of the marina, keeping as low as he could in the water. It was an overcast day, and he was thankful for the shadows that made him a dark speck in equally as dark water. Finally, he grabbed the ladder attached to the stern of a small yacht. He bobbed in the icy water for several minutes, making sure he hadn't been spotted, before climbing onboard. He lay on the oiled decking, listening. The constant keying of gulls overhead and the clinking of the masts and lines as the boat rose and fell in the gentle swell were all he could hear. Shivering, Sim removed his fins, shuddered to his feet, and shouldered the door leading into the cabin. The wood around the lock gave way on his third strike. Hearing no alarms or shouts, he entered the cabin. Immediately out of the frigid air he struggled out of his dry suit. He found a towel, dried his damp hair, and wet feet. Shaking, he took his trainers and jacket from the daypack and dressed. Sim raided the store cupboard and found the remains of a bottle of Lamb's Navy Rum and a packet of custard creams. He emptied the inch of booze into a tin mug and drank a slug. The sweet, fiery liquid warmed him from the inside. He munched on a biscuit. During his time in the SAS, Sim had been taught to eat and sleep whenever the opportunity arose. He glanced longingly at the bed in the far end of the cabin but knew he had to move on. He ate three more biscuits and drained his mug. It was time to go.

Going top side, he walked to the edge of the boat, and stepped off onto the quayside. There he strode as casually as he could towards the exit. He'd made it back to the UK and now he had to get to the two people who mattered the most to him in the world, and that meant getting along the coast from Newhaven to Brighton.

***

Sim was the only person out on the narrow, residential street, and this made him stick out. A light rain had started to fall which along the already gloomy sky however meant that visibility was cut down. And this was good for him. As he took the steep A259 coast road up and out of the small town, traffic was light and was mostly trucks transporting goods from the former ferry port. This was his first time back in his homeland for a year, he allowed himself a smirk, no this was England, not Wales, but still home. He was Welsh but the houses lining the road here were still the same. Small, dark, and Victorian. He'd seen the same thing in France, the population living either by candlelight because of the loss of power or cowed by fear of the Fae into darkness. In fact, the only lights he could see were those of the trucks pulling past him.

He continued to walk, and the rain intensified. There was a flash of light in the sky. A dragon. Flames exploded from its open maw at something much smaller flying in front of it. Sim watched on, angered, as the light aircraft spiraled downwards towards the distant hills. As images of his own plane crash abruptly filled his head, he grabbed a concrete streetlight for support.

"You wanna lift mate?" The voice was coarse and local.

Sim blinked; he hadn't seen the taxi arrive. "Sure."

Sim checked the driver was the only person in the car before climbing in the back and placing his day sack on the seat by his side. He knew from experience in France that the Fae had let taxis and public transport continue to function.

"Where to?"

"Whitehawk," Sim gave the name of the notorious Brighton council estate.

"Where exactly?"

"I'll show you when we get there."

"Right you are." The driver put the car back into first and slewed away from the curb.

Sim remained tense, ready to dive forward at the driver if he needed to. His experience in operating in combat zones made him wary of everything and everyone, and this included the overweight lump in the driver's seat. Sim's nose twitched. There was an odd smell, it wasn't bad just out of place - almonds. He mentally shrugged, it was better than day-old sweat and week-old takeaway.

"Where you from then, that's not a Brighton accent? You a Scouser?"

"Yep," Sim lied. He wasn't from Liverpool, he was from Prestatyn, North Wales but it was a common mistake and both accents were similar and miles away from the Sussex coast.

"So, what are you doing here?"

"Same as you, living."

The driver nodded but kept facing forward. "I know mate, it's all we can do now, since Lord Dalrymple took over."

Sim said nothing. He didn't know the name of the local Fae occupiers or which house they were with. Information from the UK whilst he had been in France had been scarce. He knew the British military had been overwhelmed and what remained of it had retreated to Ireland, taking King Charles with them.

The driver got the message Sim didn't want to chat, so they continued in silence until a lorry blocking the road caused him to slam on the brakes and swerve. They skidded to a halt on the wet tarmac. A pair of burley figures appeared, bathed by headlights as they blocked the road. They were as wide as they were tall. Sim recognized them as orcs. Their dark skin was part-covered in chainmail, and both held axes. It was 'Dungeons & Dragons' come to life again, they were dangerous, even deadly, but unlike him they were not elite. And he knew how to fight them if he had to. He slipped his right hand into his bag and wrapped his palm around the grip of his Beretta.

The driver turned and Sim saw something he hadn't encountered before, something new and unknown. The driver's eyes became red, in fact they glowed, and his shoulders and torso started to grow, to inflate. Sim heard the springs in the seat complain as the driver grew larger and larger until he was no longer a man but a humanoid creature with skin of a pale green pallor. A shapeshifter, is that what he was? Whatever he was, he was glaring at him.

"Now, Scouser. The boys are taking you away for a little, rigorous questioning!" The shapeshifter started to laugh, but Sim had the last laugh, as angling his hand up, he fired a double tap. The silver-filled, hollow point rounds tore through the exposed neck of the shapeshifter. The thing was dead, all but decapitated, before it had time to realize what had happened.

The last time Sim had been stopped by an aggressive roadblock he'd been in Iraq, and then it had been local militia, but the principal was the same. Maximum speed and maximum aggression. Opening the door, he came out behind it, weapon up, firing. A pair of double taps hit each of the orcs above their dwarven hardened armor. Four rounds, four impacts, and two dead orcs. Sim advanced, towards the truck. He peered in the cabin. The driver was lolling to one side, a large, jagged wound in his chest. Sim seethed; these bastards had no idea how to govern.

He retraced his steps and opened the driver's door of the taxi. The dead shapeshifter fell out onto the road, his body having deflated like a giant swimming pool toy. A vision of a blow-up 'Incredible Hulk' Sim had bought his daughter for their holiday in Greece flashed before his eyes. Sim moved to the passenger side, shut the door then back to the driver's side and got in. He depressed the clutch, put the gear stick into first, released the handbrake and squealed away from the scene. He swerved past the truck and continued along the A259. He had no way of knowing what, if any, means of communication the Fae had, if they were the same as those he had encountered in France they would eschew all forms of electronic communication for telepathy or physical written forms. But he certainly wasn't going to hang around to find out if anyone had been alerted to his handy work. The shots had been muffled by the fog and it was late at night, so he chanced his luck.

The road continued to climb before flattening out. On his right there now were undulating hills and on the left the cliff edge and the sea. Traffic continued to be light, and the only other vehicles he saw were trucks or taxis. The road narrowed and he continued past the sleepy seafront communities of Peacehaven, Saltdean and Rottingdean, these were overflow and retirement towns. The stores were closed and there was no one out on the dark, wet evening streets. There were still no visible signs of the Fae's invasion and conquest as here there was nothing of military or civil importance. That changed however when he passed a large, Victorian building atop a rise. On the roof of the ultra-exclusive 'Roedean School for Girls,' sat a dragon looking like a bird of prey on its nest. Every part of Sim was on edge as he passed, and then the road split into three. Straight ahead went to central Brighton, left arrived at Brighton Marina and the right fork would take him past an area of affluent nineteen-thirties houses before reaching the ghetto like Whitehawk estate, where he prayed his family were.

***

On the estate he parked behind a disheveled looking Ford transit van, took his day sack, and left the taxi. He'd make his final approach up the hill to his house on foot. Sim knew he should have waited until full dark to move, but he had come so far that he was compelled to continue. When Kim had chucked him out, he'd agreed she could have the family house. Since then, his new job in Dubai had paid extremely well, yet she refused to take anything from him except the agreed allowance for their daughter. However, he had opened a savings account in Debbie's name and transferred over the course of two years almost sixty thousand pounds into it, but now? Was his daughter's money still there? Did anyone's savings exist? The Fae only believed in what they could touch and feel, or what existed in their supernatural realm. Anything digital was nonsense for them, as much as their magic was to man.

Slowly, in the shadows, Sim continued up the hill. Not much had changed in the time he'd been away; the estate was still a miserable windswept looking place. Gulls called overhead and cars that were at least a decade old sat outside homes built in the late seventies. What was different however was the lack of life on the streets and the occasional scorch mark on the tarmac, evidence at least of some fighting. Resistance or military? There was a reservist army training base several miles away but that was just boy scouts with berets, no he reasoned this had to have been either the Brighton Police Armed Response Unit or who? He remembered there'd been a street gang running the estate a while back. What was their name? Sim wracked his brain, 'The McCarten Crew' that was it, led by Kirk McCarten. Now they had been from Liverpool. Perhaps the shapeshifter had thought he'd been one of them? Sim didn't know and he didn't much care, overgrown kids who thought they were gangsters were the least of his worries.

Sim turned his head back to stare at the sea. A distant

container ship was passing, new routes now bringing it closer to the Brighton coast than ever before. His mind wandered back to Marcel, and the other free Frenchmen who had helped him. He said, quietly in French, "Bon Chance."

Sim abruptly froze. A head appeared over the brow of the hill. It was that of a giant bear, and he knew where large animals were, elves were not far behind. Sim darted to the left and vaulted over a hedge into a front garden. He commando crawled across the damp lawn to the edge of the house and scurried around the corner. Retrieving his Beretta, he waited. From his viewpoint he watched as a monstrous bear, ridden by an elf warrioress, proceed down the hill. It was followed by a troupe of twelve armored orcs. A banner fluttered from a pole one of them carried, a symbol for a house Sim didn't recognize. He knew the House of Trelain, commanded by Lady Azra, oversaw France, but not who now controlled Britain as apparently it had changed. Was it the name the shapeshifter had said, or was that just to catch him out? He continued to eye the orcs. The armor was unusual, almost delicate, almost filigree. Like on the two he'd shot earlier, gone were the bulky, flat black US Football 'linebacker' type panels in favor of form fitting chainmail. Yet the wearers still looked the same, large, and muscular like wrestlers on steroids. If pushed, Sim knew he could take a couple by surprise, but traveling with an elf meant some type of enchantment had to have been cast to protect them all.

"We have met before, you and I."

Sim spun, surprised to see an elderly woman standing behind him.

She continued, "The last time you were with a pretty

girl and her mother. I may be ancient, but I never forget a face."

There was a noise. The bear stopped across the street. It was sniffing and its rider pointed at the garden. Two orcs, looking in Sim's mind like Rick and Scott Steiner but forty percent larger and uglier, lurched towards him.

The old woman said and pushed past him to stand defiantly on the lawn.

Beretta raised; Sim looked on from the shadows in amazement. The elfin warrioress and the woman exchanged words, and then the invaders marched away.

"How?" Sim managed to say.

"They know me. Lady Tiguan and I have an understanding."

"Tiguan, isn't that a Volkswagen?"

"It is indeed. The Fae takes that as a personal slight. Tell me, have you seen any Volkswagens here?"

Sim shook his head, "No."

"Exactly. I'm an old woman, I am no threat to them, and as such they are pleasant enough to me."

"Stay safe," Sim said. He had to go. If the months of fighting his way across France had taught him anything it was that nothing was what it seemed. And suddenly meeting this woman was one of those. He started to walk away.

"Your family is not there. Unlike I, your wife and daughter are of a breeding age."

The words hit Sim like a punch in the gut. "What?"

Sim started to shake with fury and fear. He'd seen civilians led away in France and had dark thoughts about the fate of his family, but now had those become a reality?

The old woman took his free hand. She held it tightly

as her eyes rolled back in her head. Sim felt a jolt of energy, as though he'd been shocked by faulty wiring. "They have been taken to Arundel Castle. The younger elves like to play with human women. I can sense them. They remain healthy, untouched and unharmed."

Sim tried to pull his hand away, but her grip was vice like. "Who are you?"

"We met first when you were just a child. In time you will remember. I am just one who has always believed in the old ways, and one who has always known you. Go to the house. There is one there who can help you." She let go and walked away, disappearing around the back of the building.

Sim had never been big on 'mumbo jumbo' as he called it, crystals, scented candles, chakras, and David Copperfield, yet since the arrival of the Fae he no longer knew what was real and what wasn't. The only concrete fact he had was the location of his house, just over the rise.

Sim jogged back onto the street. He crested the rise and saw his house; it was the end of terrace and bordered directly onto the rolling countryside behind. Eyes scanning the street on both sides yet seeing nothing he continued past the house taking the road that led inland over the hills. He angled left, onto the grass and in a dip, the dead ground, not visible by anyone watching from either a house or the road, worked his way back to the rear of his family home and climbed over the wooden fence into the back garden.

The house was dark and quiet. Sim crept up the grass to the patio, left hand in front of his eyes ready to shield them from the security floodlight he'd installed. It didn't go off. He lifted one of the patio slabs and reached underneath for the key. It was still there. Now he stepped to the backdoor and opened the house.

The stale air filled his nostrils but there was something else too. Something that was familiar to him but something that had no right to be in his family kitchen. Gun oil.

"You took your time, Simo!"

***

Sim lowered his Beretta and let a smile across his face. At sixty-five Dave 'Danger' Smith was a former SAS armorer, a Regiment legend, and an old friend. He too had made Brighton his home.

"It's good to see you, Danger." Sim shut the door. "Are they here?"

"No. Simo. Look, I did what I could. They're like family to me – you know that. When it kicked off, I came over. But then we couldn't get out. Anyone on the streets was being stopped or, well, eaten," Danger shook his head, "so we stayed here. And then the orcs started to round people up. It was the women they were taking away...." Danger stepped forward and, in the twilight, Sim noticed his left leg was heavily bound. "We ran off through the fields, but they caught up. Some bear took a swipe at me. We only survived because Lady VW stopped them in time."

Sim nodded, the intel confirmed the old woman's words. "She has them?"

Danger nodded, "She's set herself up in Arundel Castle. Living it large as a robber Baroness."

"So, we make a plan, then we go to Arundel." Sim pulled out a chair and sat at the kitchen table. "How long ago was this?"

"Two weeks," Danger slapped his leg with his hand, "I was out of it for days - must have caught something from that dirty bastard bear. I wanted to go, to bring them back but my leg just wouldn't work."

"I understand," Sim rubbed his face with his hands as the fatigue threatened to overwhelm him. "Is there anything to drink in the house? Or have you finished it all?"

***

"Look, Simo, I've been working on something, a plan to get them both back, but you won't like it," Danger said as he lowered his glass.

Sim frowned, "If it gets my family back, I'll like it."

"Right," Danger nodded, "Debbie is eighteen now, she's not a little girl anymore."

"Meaning?" Sim knocked back the last of his whisky.

There was a tap on the window, Sim snatched his Beretta, but Danger raised a hand in a 'stop motion'. The backdoor opened and a figure wearing a hoodie entered then froze when he saw Sim.

"Who's this?" the figure asked.

"This is my house," Sim said, "who are you?"

The figure pushed his hood back to reveal a shaved head and a hard face. "Sammy McCarten."

Sim nodded, "Brother of Kirk?"

"Eldest son. And my little brother Mikey is engaged to your daughter," he extended his hand, "so that sort of makes us family."

Sim hesitated then shook the proffered hand. "She's too young to have a boyfriend, let alone a fiancé."

"How long does she have to wait?" Danger said.

"Until she's thirty-five," Sim replied, deadpan. "And you're here because you want to help me rescue Debbie and her mum?"

"Yeah, but no offense mate, I'm more concerned about rescuing my brother, he was taken with them."

"Lady Tiguan has needs too," Danger stated.

"So, the scorch marks on the road, is that your handy work?"

McCarten nodded, "I make a mean IED."

"Sammy served in Afghanistan." Danger said.

"I did, but I wasn't a mad SAS lunatic like you two."

"Which regiment?"

"Tigers," McCarten replied, using the nickname for The Princess of Wales's Royal Regiment.

"Good man," Sim stated.

"I've brought most of my toys with me, by the way." Danger said, tapping his nose. "I thought they may come in handy."

"Ok Danger, let's hear your plan."

***

Sim shivered in the cold, thankful the lorry's refrigeration system was off otherwise he and the others would have risked hypothermia. Empty crates had been stacked at the end of the truck nearest the driver to form a false wall and it was behind this that the three of them sat. Despite the vacuum pack and cling film the stench of cheese was overpowering, Sim wondered if this was purposefully so. In theory the journey to Arundel should have taken no more than forty minutes but since being let into the truck by the driver, who owed McCarten a favor, they had been sat in the lorry amongst mounds of imported French cheese for the better part of two hours as it passed through checkpoints that had sprung up.

Danger sat opposite Sim, his back resting against a crate of Camembert and an AK74 SU held across his chest. Next to him sat McCarten, who cradled an Ingram Mac-10. Sim knew where the AK was one of Danger's mementoes from the Regiment, a souvenir from overseas, but he hadn't asked the providence of the Ingram. McCarten had assured him it worked and that was that. Sim himself had an HKG3 KA4. It was a weapon he knew well. In the months since the Fae had attacked, Danger had not been idle and together with McCarten and his crew studied the Fae and worked on plans how to combat them. In short it had been a classic SAS insurgency plan, guerilla warfare. Danger's toys had included several pairs of NVGs, and stash of weapons and ammunition – each piece given to him for safekeeping by a member of the Regiment 'just in case.' Like the fighters in France, Danger had realized that normal rounds did not have the same impact on the Fae, so the crafty armorer had been using his munitions training to adapt them by manually filling hollow points with silver. This was sourced by McCarten's crew who had knocked over several local jewelry stores. The fact the Fae had already trashed these – stealing all the gold and gems but fastidiously leaving the silver, encouraged Danger he was on the right track. These adapted rounds, together with weapons stolen from the Fae and made of an unknown metal which cut and pierced enemy armor, had enabled McCarten's crew to fight back. But then the Fae started to randomly kill civilians, and the McCarten crew either scattered or defiantly died. And this was when Danger tried to escape with Debbie and Kim, and when the women were taken.

"Tell me about Dubai," McCarten asked, "I've always wanted to go."

"It's what you see on TV - Dubai Bling. But there's a quieter side too. Residential. My boss had a huge, posh villa on a golf course, with a pool and green parrots in the garden."

"Tell me about the birds?"

"There was also a type of grouse that roamed around."

McCarten smirked, "I meant the woman, mate."

The driver banged on the panel separating them from the cab. The conversation immediately stopped as the three men listened. The truck slowed to a halt and then what sounded like heavy chains rattled outside. They proceeded forward again but this time there was an incline.

"The castle," Danger stated.

Sim had visited the place several times since moving to Brighton and had a picture of the terrain and layout in his head. If he was right, they had just passed through the gatehouse at the outer walls and would now be taking the snaking drive up towards the castle itself, past the manicured lawns previously enjoyed by day-trippers and picnicking families.

***

As the lorry lumbered on, they could now hear the raucous noise of the Fae outside. Loud laughs, shouts in unintelligible languages and even the heavy clank of metal on metal as though giant axes were being struck together, which Sim reasoned they probably were.

Danger checked his watch, "We've got two hours to sunset. Then we wait till three a.m."

Sim said nothing, it had already been agreed. Three in the morning the time when generations of assaults had started, a time when the enemy's awareness would be at its lowest ebb, a time long enough before dawn to ensure most would be asleep. Yet these were the Fae, and anything was possible.

The driver banged on the divide again, to signal they were coming to a halt. The three men pulled large dust sheets over themselves to further obscure their features and scent from the Fae. Moments later they heard grunted instructions in heavily accented English and the rear doors of the truck opened. Hiding behind a wall of cheese, Sim and the others were invisible but equally as important was that fact that both orcs and elves alike could not detect their scent. The orcs were repulsed by the odor of the fromage whilst the elves were intoxicated by it.

The cargo began to be removed, and through a hole in his sheet and gap in the crates Sim saw a human arm and then a hand grab hold of a box. The face of a woman became visible. Her eyes met his. Her mouth dropped open, and she silently said 'Help,' before there was a piglike grunt, and she was jerked backwards. Sim remained immobile as through the gap now he saw another human, this one male, drag away a crate.

The unloading done the lorry started to move again before coming to a halt minutes later. The driver banged on the dividing panel again and then Sim heard the cab door open and close.

"Davey's a good boy," McCarten said, talking about

the driver. "He knows what to do. The truck stays here overnight, as per usual."

Sim nodded. If things went noisy however, their back up plan was for Danger to blow the truck by remotely setting off an IED to cause a diversion. McCarten had made it and hidden it next to the fuel tank. In addition to this Danger carried a pair of grenades.

"Right, get some kip," Danger said.

McCarten frowned, "You think I can sleep with them bleeding monsters milling about outside?"

***

Sim woke with a start, images of giant fangs vivid in his mind. He looked up, reassured to find the lorry was still very much intact. The temperature had now dropped, and he was stiff and cold. He listened and heard nothing but the rhythmic breathing of Danger and McCarten. Checking his watch, he saw that it was five to three. He woke the other two. Without words they slowly, and as quietly as they could, pulled back the modified panel which separated the cab from the load space. Sim crawled forward. Outside he saw a cloudless, dark sky with a waxing moon. It gave off little enough light to conceal their presence, and enough to enable their night vision equipment to operate.

Sim was the first into the cab and pulled down the NODs over his eyes. The dark of night changed to a multitude of greens as the ambient light cast by the moon enabled the nightvison goggles to turn night if not today then at least to a salad-colored twilight.

Sim noted the lorry had been parked on the stretch of hardstanding just outside the main wing of the castle but well within the castle grounds. To his immediate right the castle soared above him on a high grass mound. A couple of flames flared atop the battlements, but he could see neither movement nor any lights from inside.

A wide, winding path led away from where they were parked towards the rear grounds and the private wing inhabited by the Duke and Duchess of Norfolk, which he could never understand as they were in Sussex.

Left was one of the castle's lawns, which led to the small museum, tea rooms and the fortified side gate of the historic property, an addition which allowed additional access to the castle. He'd never seen it open, and tonight was no exception. Shapes littered the lawn - tents, and the bodies of what were once believed to be mythical beasts. It was as though he had been transported back in time five hundred years and was watching an army slumber behind the sturdy castle walls. He realized that's exactly what he was seeing.

Gingerly, Sim pushed the door open and dropped down to the ground. His feet made the slightest of crunches on the gravel as he landed, and he brought his HK up ready to engage. He hoped the 'Danger special' 7.62 rounds worked better than the 9mm ones in his Beretta because if things went noisy he'd need the stopping power.

McCarten appeared at his shoulder a moment later joined by Danger who let out a muted grunt as his bad leg took his weight. According to the lorry driver, the prisoners, including the women, were kept in the canteen on the ground floor which had been converted into a large dormitory. Sim knew the place and had eaten an overpriced plate of fish & chips there. But to get to the canteen they had to take the steps up the hill and then pass through a portcullis and a set of centuries old, thick, wooden doors, and if either of these were closed, they had problems.

Sim estimated their chances of success were slim to none, but he had no choice and no other option. He had to gain entry to the castle, extract his ex-wife and daughter, or die trying.

Skirting around the lorry, the three men used the dead ground between it and the castle mound to move as quickly as they could towards the steps. They reached the bottom and ducked down behind the wall, now completely obscured from any onlookers below.

Sim made the hand signal for 'OK', McCarten nodded, and Danger gave a thumbs up. Sim pointed to his own chest, then pointed up. The other two understood. Danger and Mccarten took an arc each, one pointing up and the other down.

Sim ascended the stone steps, slowly, silently. Eyes feeling as though they were on stalks behind his NODs. Apart from the flaring flames atop the battlements, Arundel Castle was dark, and still. Sim reached the top of the first flight of steps where from memory he knew there was a small terrace before the steps dog-legged left. Lowering himself to his haunches, he slowly extended his head around the corner. He heard snoring...

In the green gloom he saw a body propped up in the corner. Its legs were apart and between them were what looked like two wine bottles. There was no way Sim could continue forwards without passing the elf. Keeping his HK trained on the sleeping creature he advanced until he was no more than two meters away.

He could now see that the elf was a warrior, like the orcs he too wore chainmail but his was complemented with ornate plate armor. But his neck was unprotected. Sim knew he had to dispatch him; he was an enemy combatant however inoffensive he may look. The former SAS soldier remembered the first elf he had been forced to kill, it was slight, and he thought it could cause him no harm but then it had attacked with the strength of two men. He'd shot him in the face. Sim pushed his HK backwards on its sling and was about to reach for the elf's neck when he saw a glow coming from his side. Sim smiled, it was a dagger and the glow meant it was enchanted. Holding his right fist up ready to strike the elf in the face if he stirred, Sim placed his left hand around the hilt of the dagger and gently tugged it out of its sheath. The glow intensified as the blade was exposed and Sim had to close his left eye to guard against the flare in his NODs. His right eye now saw the eyes of the elf snap open. Instinctively Sim punched him in the face, rocking his head back against the cold, castle wall. And then with his left, Sim struck the exposed neck in a savage swipe. Eyes still wide with shock, the Elf's helmeted head was freed from his body and clattered onto the floor. Sim pushed himself into the dark corner of the terrace and waited for anyone or anything to approach.

 A minute's pause reassured him that their incursion was still clandestine. Sim searched the body, found nothing more of use so just removed the sheath and placed the knife back inside and put it in the large pocket of his jacket. He retraced his route and slowly let himself be seen below by McCarten who now followed him up, trailed by Danger.

Together they took the last flight of steps and slowed as their heads, and the business ends of their assault rifles, rose above the top step. The portcullis was raised, doors were ajar, making the entrance look like the maw of some gigantic beast. Best of all, it was unguarded. Again, Sim went ahead as the other two stood in the shadows on either side of the door. Sim was immediately confronted by a long hallway, lined with various suits of armor from the place's historic legacy. With the scene illuminated in a green glow it reminded him now more than ever of a scene from Scooby-Doo. He immediately moved to his left and crouched, weapon up and ready to engage any possible threats. He cocked his head, to tune into the sounds of the ancient fortress. Ahead and off to the right he could hear water running and an irregular clanking of metal on metal, both sounds were low, and almost inaudible but enhanced by the echoes of the flagstone floor. Sim knew the toilets were to his immediate right, but the sound was too far away to be coming from there. No, someone was in the canteen kitchen. He knew he should clear each room, to make certain that no one could creep up on them or engage them but with a team of three this was not a viable option. Their intelligence, from the lorry driver, said the women were held in the canteen, and getting in and out of there was his only concern. McCarten would have to ask the women if they knew where his brother was being kept.

Sim retraced his steps; all the while keeping his focus on the corridor and beckoned the other two inside. He pointed down the hallway at the door he knew was the entrance to the canteen, then at each of them in turn. They were going to enter it together. With Danger acting as 'tail-end Charlie' they tactically moved towards the canteen.

Footsteps, heavy and with an irregular cadence, suddenly sounded behind them. Sim silently cursed. Someone, or something, had been in the toilets. Danger was the nearest to the threat, and as each of the men took cover in the shadows behind suits of armor, the veteran SAS man took aim. A figure staggered up the short, twisting flight of stairs off to the side, which led to the bathrooms. His left arm was held out, bracing himself against the wall whilst in his right he clutched a bottle. It was another elf. His helmet had dropped to obscure his eyes and he hadn't seen them. The three men remained motionless. It was movement that attracted attention rather than noise, and the elf was making enough of that to be oblivious to their breathing. He wobbled sideways as his hand ran out of wall and took three adjustive steps to stop himself from falling. He collided with the nearest suit of armor, sending it toppling, then tripped over the end of a long spear that the suit had held in its gauntlet.

"Move!" Sim hissed. Things had gone noisy, but not in the sense that Sim had imagined.

Leaving the elf face down and dazed, the trio scampered towards the canteen door and spun into the room. Each of them 'cutting the pie,' taking an arc of the enclosed space. In the gloom Sim could see three rows of mattresses and shapes underneath blankets. He left the other two scanning the room and advanced into the kitchen. Moonlight came in through a narrow, high window and it glinted off something metallic, something knife-shaped. An orc, wielding a meat cleaver, charged at him with a growl. Sim's finger took second pressure on the trigger when he abruptly swung his HK off target as another shape, this one smaller and holding a round shaped object appeared behind the orc. Sim's eyes widened in disbelief as his ex-wife Kim slammed a large iron skillet into the back of the orc's head. The creature stumbled forward, dropping its weapon as its eyes rolled back and up. Sim stepped aside as the creature fell. Kim had the skillet raised again, her eyes wide with fury and was about to swing it at him again.

"Kim!" Sim grabbed her wrists, "It's me!"

The skillet dropped, and Kim's jaw became slack, "But...but you're in Dubai..."

"I took a plane. Where's Debbie?"

"Debbie?" Kim seemed confused.

"Where is Debbie?"

Kim blinked, "Upstairs, with Lady Tiguan and Mikey her –"

"Yeah, I know."

"How did you find us?"

"We've no time for talk." Sim took her hand and dragged her into the canteen. By now Danger and McCarten had roused the slumbering women. There were twelve in all, and with two empty beds – for Debbie and Kim that made fourteen. Fourteen women they had to somehow get out of the castle and away from the Fae.

Sim's head swan as he suddenly realized the magnitude of his task and he beckoned Danger over. "Take Kim and the others and get them into the back of the lorry, it's their only chance of getting out of here."

"No way!" Kim jabbed at Sim with her index finger, "I'm coming with you! Besides, I know which room they are in."

Sim knew there was no time or point in arguing, "Fine. McCarten, I guess you want to come too?"

***

Sim edged back into the hallway. The elf was still on the floor. Dead, or sleeping off the booze it made no difference to him, if he remained down. Kim pushed past Sim and took the lead; she guided him and McCarten to the bottom of a grand staircase. She cupped her hand, placed it against his ear and spoke softly. "It's the first door up the stairs. The room is the Queen Victoria room."

"Ok." Sim nodded, he remembered the ornate décor and the wide yet short bed. The room had been used over several days by the monarch on her visit to the castle and preserved as a shrine ever since.

"Tiguan is expecting me, I was preparing food for her. She likes to play 'house' with Kim and Mikey."

In the darkness Sim frowned, he didn't understand.

They advanced up the stairs, their feet registering the slightest of sounds on the plush, carpeting. They encountered no one else before they saw light spilling out from under a closed door. Once the two former soldiers had taken up positions by the door and pushed the optical tubes of their NODs above their eyes, Kim knocked on the heavy, wooden door. It was answered by a man in his early twenties, wearing a suit and tie.

"Mikey!" McCarten was unable to hide his surprise.

Sim pulled his future son in law out of the room as he burst inside, his eyes and HK in unison searching for his daughter. Without the night vision equipment, the room had a golden glow which suddenly seemed to intensify. Sim felt his arms growing heavy and falling away as he dropped his rifle. The bed was in the middle of the room and sitting atop it, facing each other with a child's tea set between them were two women. His daughter was on the left, her raven black hair betraying her Welsh roots whilst on the right and looking for all the world like a negative image of her, was a woman whose hair was so bright it was almost white. She turned to face Sim as the glow intensified.

"Hello Steve, well didn't you grow up."

Sim's mouth attempted to move, to make words as before his eyes, forgotten memories flashed. He was once again the eight-year-old boy who had wandered off in the woods and was lost for a week. Although he hadn't been lost. He'd been with the fairy folk. He'd been with his new friend, the pretty lady who lived in the woods. That lady he now knew had been Lady Tiguan, and in the thirty years which had passed she hadn't aged. Her name appeared on his lips, "Lilith?"

The elven noblewoman smiled and reached across the bed to stroke Debbie's head, "When I laid eyes on her I knew she was part of you, and I knew you would come here for her."

Sim blinked and finally managed to break out of the trance, "Debbie, has she hurt you?"

Debbie frowned, "Dad, Lilith is my friend. Like she was your friend. She would never hurt me, or mum, or you. She brought us here to save us from the others."

Sim thought back as to how easy their ingress into the castle had been, and how little resistance they had met. Had she made it so?

"You took me by surprise at how quickly you arrived here, Steve. The Trojan Cheese was most amusing, and delicious."

His mouth dry, Sim swallowed. "So, what happens now?"

"Now?" The elf stood. "If any of my guests wish to leave, they are more than welcomed to do so, however Steve please be aware that those of my kind outside of my direct control are loyal to my father. Even many of the orcs, here in the grounds, I cannot control."

"If you are so fond of helping humans, why don't you fight for us?" McCarten said.

Lilith's eyes narrowed, "Ah, the other McCarten. I will not turn my sword against my father, or my brothers for anyone, or anything. I believe in a peaceful integration, and taking up arms against my own house would be the opposite of this."

"Kim, are you happy working in the kitchen?"

Sim's ex-wife glared at him, "If the alternative is being hunted down outside then I'd rather stay here."

Debbie stood up from the bed and hugged her father, "Dad, I've missed you so much. And Lilith has told me all about the time you two spent together."

"Your grandparents went crazy with worry; they thought I was dead." Sim said, looking into his daughter's eyes and not understanding what he saw.

"Time has a different meaning to us Fae, Steve. I still regret the pain I caused your parents, but I was here to find out your ways before the invasion. How better than to speak to the open mind of a child? But I meant you no harm."

"Thank you," Sim said, thinly.

"Steve, please stay here with us, with your family. There is another war coming, not between man and Fae, but Fae and Fae and I need somebody I can trust as a military adviser and tactician. I will make you a Lord."

Now Sim frowned, as he tried to process the offer. "What about all the innocent people outside who have died because of you?"

"What of those I have saved from our own savages? My house is a good house, my father – our High Lord, is a good man. And because of that he will be targeted by those hardliners who believe human and Fae cannot and must not coexist. They view humans as animals, at best replaceable slaves. I am different, and I know eventually my father will come to accept and embrace my view. What say you Steve Sim, will you join me? Become my Lord?" Lilith moved towards Sim, and as his daughter stepped away, the elf gently clasped his face with her hands.

Sim's nostrils flared and it was only then he made the connection. Unseen by Lilith, he drew the elfin blade he had taken earlier and thrust it upwards, under her ribcage. Instantly the elf let go and staggered, her shape changing and growing she collapsed backwards onto the bed. No longer the most beautiful female he had even seen, but a humanoid abomination with skin of a pale green pallor, a shapeshifter.

"Dad? Dad, what are you doing here, how?" Debbie wrapped her arms tightly around her father and this time when he looked into her eyes, they were bright, and he saw the love she had for him.

"Christ!" McCarten shook his head. "How did you know?"

"The real Lilith called me Stephen, and she didn't smell of almonds."

"That's nuts," McCarten said, dryly.

***

There was a glow in the room, it seemed to come from the walls and then it grew into a ball of light which formed into a human shape. It was the old woman Sim had met in Whitehawk. "There are many of this creature, you have now encountered three. The real Lady Tiguan needs your help, Stephen Sim. Her father's men have incarcerated her in The Tower of London. Please help her. The elves of this castle will be loyal to you, of this I can assure you."

Sim nodded, not because he had accepted the quest rather because he now knew where he had met the old lady before. She had been the woman who had led him out of the woods, all those years before, and into the arms of his distraught parents who had been waiting at his favorite tree. One who still remembered the Old Ways. He said, "And the Orcs?"

"Alas no, they are happy to remain here pillaging and plundering." The woman faded away as quickly as she had appeared.

"This is too much for me," McCarten said. He moved to his brother and grabbed him by the shoulder, "Mikey, let's move!"

The younger McCarten rubbed his head, "I can't remember anything... Sammy? Sammy? Is that you?"

"It's me bro," McCarten said, "I'm taking you home."

"Debbie?"

"She's coming too."

The dull boom of an explosion from outside reached Sim's ears, making those in the room flinch. Sim exchanged looks with Sammy. Danger had used a grenade. Whether that meant he and the woman were safe or not he didn't know. There was footfall outside and through the doors appeared a pair of elves, in full armor. Sim raised his HK to take a shot, but the lead elf raised his palms.

"Wait! The Spirit Protectress sent us!"

The second said, "We are here to lead your escape! You must come with us!"

Sim glanced around at the others, what alternative did he have?

***

Kim grabbed hold of her daughter as the two McCarten's left the room first. Sim swept the room once more and then followed, now he was tail-end Charlie and forced to place his faith in the pair of elves leading the way ahead. The train of escapees turned right out of the room and took a corridor which led to a flight of stone steps. Narrow and worn smooth with age they wound upwards following the wall of the tower. Sim realized he was being led to the roof and the battlements. Sim could hear guttural noises from behind and slowed. He turned and aimed his HK back in the direction he had come from as he sensed movement. A hideous head loomed into view. An orc. Its scaled shoulders almost too wide to negotiate the space, soon followed. Sim fired two rounds, a double tap into the orcs' fanged face. The creature's head jerked backwards, but its body remained jammed in the space, backing up those Sim could hear behind. Turning once more, Sim hurried up the stairs and reached the opening to the battlements. The cool, crisp air whipped around his face, yet it brought with it the sound of gunfire. Danger, the only other gun in the otherwise medieval castle.

"Steve!" It was Kim, and she was waving her arms at him.

He pushed down the optical tubes of his NODs and only now saw where she was. Sim froze, unable to move, unable to think as a set of giant fangs approached him. And then a set of yellow eyes, each as large of tractor tires lowered and glowered at him. Past this was a scaly body and just where the shoulders of the monstrous creature started was a harness and a saddle. Three figures sat on this, one of the elves and behind him Kim and Debbie. Before Sim was able to fully comprehend what was happening the dragon turned to its right and dropped off the edge of the battlements. Seconds later it soared into the air and flapped its mighty wings as it powered away from the castle.

There was a second dragon, further away along the walkway, balancing on the top of the battlements, and another elf was running towards it.

"Quick! Come on!" McCarten shouted back at him.

Sim started to jog but then there was a roar from behind and something heavy hit him in the middle of the back. He crashed forward, his HK flying from his hands. The strap sailed over his head, and it skittered across the floor. Gunfire erupted above him as McCarten engaged whatever it was that had attacked him. Sim felt something grab his ankle and lift him into the air. He found himself hanging upside and looking back at a scene he had never once imagined he would see.

Two orcs fanned out across the battlements. They held crossbows. They opened fire, their bolts whizzing past Sim and hitting what he now saw was a second dragon. The dragon reared up and became airborne. Its rider slipped from his saddle and fell screaming over the side of the castle wall. Sim swung his arms wildly still not knowing who or what had hold of him and then he saw. The giant troll was armored. It had one huge hand clenched around his ankle whilst the other held the largest battle ax Sim had ever seen.

McCarten yelled as he fired a burst into the giant's chest. The rounds impacted the creature's breastplate and Sim felt its grip on him loosen. He crashed to the ground, landing heavily on his left shoulder. A white pulse of pain shot through his entire body as he tried to roll to one side.

"Sim, C'mon man –" McCarten's words were cut short as a heavy, crossbow bolt lodged in his chest.

Mikey moved forwards to grab his brother, only to meet the same fate.

Desperately Sim reached for his Beretta in his pancake holster. He scrambled away, loosening off rounds at the crossbow wielding orcs. The first spun sideways and then the second dropped too, but the giant stomped towards him. Dizzy with pain, and jerky from adrenalin, Sim failed to find a kill shot, his rounds either missing or hitting the troll in its huge extremities. And then his handgun clicked on empty. He hurled it at the creature who let it hit his chest and unperturbed carried on. Sim pushed his back against the parapet and levered himself to his feet. The troll swung his ax. Sim ducked and it sparked against the centuries old castle wall. The troll took a step forward and this time changed his angle of attack, swinging the ax down. Sim sidestepped and as the ax struck the floor he leapt up and thrust the enchanted, elf dagger upwards, under the armor and into the stomach of the still advancing nightmare. The creature shuddered, stumbled, and then fell forwards against battlements, its chest coming to rest against Sim's head.

Sim crabbed away from the dead giant as more yells and grunts were now audible. In his peripheral vision, figures were advancing on both sides, brandishing vicious looking melee weapons. Pulling himself to his full height and adopting the stance of a knife fighter, Sim roared at the top of his voice, "Who wants it next!"

Talons appeared above his head and grabbed at his torso, Sim shrieked silently, his vision starting to gray out as the dragon lifted him into the air.

A voice sounded in his ears above the screams of battle. It was a voice he had been desperate to hear for months. "DAD! Dad! We've got you!"

And then he was above it all, above the castle and above the orcs who were now streaming onto the battlements from two other entrances. Below the orcs had reached his spot and were angrily waving their weapons and their fists. It was comical. Bolts now were fired from crossbows but arcing up and coming short raining back down on those below. The pain in his shoulder subsided as another kick of adrenaline surged through his system, Sim searched the grounds below for the lorry, but it was no longer in the castle grounds, he spotted it crossing the bridge out of Arundel town center a mile away. As the sky started to lighten on the horizon heralding a new day, Sim knew for the moment at least, his family was safe.

ALEX SHAW spent the second half of the 1990s in Kyiv,

Ukraine running his own business consultancy before being head-hunted for a division of Siemens. The next few years saw him doing business for the company across the former USSR, the Middle East, and Africa. Most recently he has spent several years in Doha, Qatar.

Alex is an active member of the ITW (The International Thriller Writers organisation) and the CWA (the Crime Writers Association). He is the author of three international bestselling thriller series featuring AIDAN SNOW, JACK TATE and SOPHIE RACINE, and the standalone 'Delta Force Vampire'. His writing has also been published in several thriller anthologies.

Alex, his wife and their two sons divide their time between homes in Kyiv - Ukraine, Sussex - England and Doha - Qatar. Follow Alex on twitter: @alexshawhetman or Instagram @alexshawthrillerwriter or BookBub @AlexShaw or find him on Facebook.

Forget Me Nots

By Michael Craig

"Well, that's not fucking creepy," Specialist Howl groaned, but after a tour of Afghanistan, I was familiar with how enlisted men whined. After two days of evading the Fae through dusty back roads, everyone was tired. Riding in a produce truck wasn't much better, but it was our ride into town.

I just didn't care. Some things never changed. War would be war. People would be people. And Specialist Darrel Midnight Howl would always be at my side bitching and whining because that is what enlisted soldiers do.

My focus was on the high-desert farm town. A strong enough force could get past the blockade, but no one was doing it stealthily. Which was how we found ourselves on a produce truck, hauling potatoes and day laborers.

"This is a significant Frago, Terrill. Are you sure we need to do this?"

"It's Doctor Katherine Terrill, Sergeant Pict. I am the lead researcher on this project for the Idaho National Laboratory, and the top researcher in my field, so please show a little respect.

And please tell this private," she sneered in Howl's direction, "not to refer to my daughter as 'creepy'."

Howl rolled on his side and pumped his fist at hip level a few times.

"Sarnt she's playing with a dead scorpion, and my K-Bar, and chanting or something."

"Sarnt isn't a word, you hill-billy fuck, it's Sergeant."

Kate glared at us both. "She is reciting a prayer her grandfather taught her, it's part of her Nez Perce culture."

"Bullshit." Howl muttered, "I'm Navaho, and that's some other shit. And what the hell is up with the flowers?"

The little girl looked up. The dark rings under her eyes gave her a wasted look, but at least she'd put on a little color instead of the lab rat pale she had been when we picked them up.

"Some call the flowers scorpion grass, but I like the name forget-me-nots. It reminds us to never forget those who have passed, and where we come from." Kaya placed a small blue flower in the hair of her doll, then stroked it lovingly.

Howl scooted away from the girl, his movements kicking up that earthy smell that clung to the potatoes we were hauling. "I don't care what you call it, kid. Keep that voodoo doll away from me, or I'll have to shoot it."

"It's a totem." Kate said absently.

"Dialogue doesn't always include a 5.56 round, Howl," I said, glad the wind was in our faces so our voices wouldn't carry.

"I can also speak nine-millimeter if you don't let me ride up front, Sarnt."

"Sorry Howl, maybe next time. Besides, I think she likes you," I laughed, but Howl's face pinched up in disgust.

"Will you just listen? This research is vital to our struggle against the Fae!" Kate Terrill demanded.

I shot the pompous bitch my coldest glare, "I hear you, Kate."

"Okay then, good." Kate cleared her throat.

"Once we get to the research facility, we won't be able to skip down to the drugstore. You want my research. You'll have to accept that without my daughter, you've got nothing." Kate Terrill was one of those people who couldn't get past years of deferential treatment because of her position, money, and status.

Trying to keep the annoyance out of my voice, I said, "I got it, you get what you want, or we get nothing."

Kate stared at me for a moment. "Close enough, Sergeant."

Ahead, several Orcs in light armor were lined up on the road, and one, larger than the others, waved us down and pointed to a place he wanted us to park. As we did, , we saw the other crews being ushered toward a tall cement building that reminded me more of a bunker.

Most of them didn't look like they had enough to eat in a while. they had that hollow wasted look that I was used to seeing in videos of refugee camps. Young or old, they marched obediently in line, waiting for their chance to have their work passes inspected.

One man in line was hyper-vigilant like he'd just come out of combat. His head jerked at every little noise, and he gulped air like a fish on the shore.

"Not eligible!" a small Gnome-like creature, a Waldzwerge according to our OP order, was shaking his small finger at the twitchy guy in line.

"There must be some mistake. I am supposed to be on this detail," the man whined.

"Not eligible. You stink of sickness," the Gnome said, his pointed gray beard quivering.

"It's just a cold," he pleaded, "you don't understand. I have kids. I need the rations."

Tears were leaving muddy trails on his dirty face, but

the man pressed forward with an urgent expression.

"Gnome said NO!" The large Orc used the buttstock of his crossbow and sent the man cartwheeling into the gravel.

A small squeak escaped Kaya, and she clung tightly to her mother.

"Looks like we're up next."

"Work passes. Present your work passes," the Gnome said, as if the last guy wasn't bleeding in the parking lot.

"Mitchell family, a work party of four." I presented the work passes to the stern-faced Gnome.

"For ages we stood in line," Kaya muttered. In a glance, I knew the violence had shocked her.

Dressed in new jeans and a wrangler shirt, an older man, lean with a high and tight haircut looked on with a neutral expression, and stepped up next to the Gnome.

"The kid okay?" he asked.

Kate pulled her in protectively. "She's fine."

"Packing sheds! You, you, and you." Pointing to each of us he made a mark on his sheet, then paused and looked at Kaya.

His gaze lingered, then like a dog on the scent he walked around her sniffing the air and assessing her. It was unsettling, but something about her had set him off.

"Not eligible! She's too small, and she stinks of illness."

Howl perked a brow. "What?" He motioned with his chin toward Kaya. "Did she bust ass again? We had SOS for dinner last night and–"

Kate cut Howl off with a raised hand, as she spoke to the Gnome. "My daughter is nearly fifteen, she can work."

The Gnome crossed his arms and glared at Kate. "No, too small. My contract expressly states I need appropriate, suitable personnel. Send her home."

The Orc, seeing the pair squaring off, decided to intervene. "GO HOME!"

Involuntarily, all of us stepped back as the rank breath and spittle rained down.

"You go home, freak!" The voice was filled with rage and despair and something new, something unhinged.

The crowd broke under waves of anger, and there standing in the parking lot was the twitchy dude holding a small nickel plated .380 semi-automatic.

"Don't be a fucking idiot!" Howl screamed.

Twitchy wasn't listening, and he fired four rapid shots at the Orc. "Screw off you damn monsters! This is our world!"

El Dori shields flared around the Orc and in the crowd, someone screamed. A woman in line pressed a hand to her now-ruined cheek.

The Orc slowly began to chuckle. It reminded me of choking more than mirth, but a grin spread on his face as he unslung his crossbow.

Seeing the Orc's reaction, Twitchy's face went pale, and shrieking he yelled, "No! I didn't mean it. I have a family!"

As I watched, the twang of the bolt registered just before it slammed into Twitchy's throat. Blood sprayed out like a sprinkler, and he went cartwheeling in the dirt until the dust obscured him.

"Flipping idiot." A gravelly voice jerked my attention to the man with the high and tight haircut behind me. The man noticed me at once, and his cold dark eyes locked with mine for a moment. There was real anger in his eyes, not just outrage, "He should have come back tomorrow. Now those kids will miss every meal he could have provided."

The sound of pen scratching on paper drew both of our attention. The Gnome was busy scratching names off his list, his head shaking ruefully.

"No good, not good at all," he sighed, like the administrative details were the important thing. "Mr. Shank, Mr. Hyer, pick new permit holders."

Anger burned in my chest at his casual behavior. "You're a real son of a –"

The man with rocks in his throat, Shank, stepped forward and cut me off. "The two men are already mine. The two women will make up for…" A puzzled look came over his face as he tried to remember Twitchy's name.

"Mr. Janson accounted for one slot, not two. The woman can work the produce sheds, the child needs to step back."

A panicked look crossed Kate's face, but the labor boss cut her off.

"The woman doesn't count as a full worker. Besides, if the family is kept together, they'll work harder."

Red-faced, the Gnome pulled at the straps of his overalls. "I have a contract! I fill the work assignments. I don't make them."

"Then, I'll stay with my daughter," Kate said louder than was helpful.

"This is not acceptable! Workers were counted, we are already short."

Kate's voice went up to a near screech as she stepped close, "Kaya can't work on her own! She needs supervision. You don't understand, she's not like other girls!"

The Orc uncradled his crossbow, and stepped forward as well, that little gleeful smile starting to re-emerge. "Stand away," he grunted in heavily accented English.

"She can't be on her own," Kate hissed and moved forward again.

Howl grabbed her, an easy smile appearing on his lips as he made some distance between Kate and the Orc. "It's nothing, boss. She's just a protective mother, is all."

"Maybe I can ease your mind." Hyer used an affable used car salesperson voice to draw everyone's attention.

The man was tall, and thickly muscled like he knew what a hard day's work looked like. However, I could see that his nails were clean, and he was a bit soft around the middle, and I knew his kind.

"The girl whose face was shot off was supposed to be mine, so the girl can fill a servant position at the kitchens."

Shank's worn look hardened and something about his jutting chin, or pinched brows made me wonder what he was trying to keep from saying. Every second or so his jaw would work a little, and he'd nearly step forward, but he held back.

"She needs medicine. That's why we came here to work." I said uncertainly, and Hyer put on his best cheesy smile.

"That won't be a problem." Hyer spread his hands wide like he was presenting the answer to all life's problems, "After your shift, bring them downtown, I will see that she gets them."

"Talk over!" the Orc bellowed. Coarsely, he grabbed Kaya and shoved her at Hyer.

"NO!" screamed Kate, but I held her back, and whispered through clenched teeth, "We'll get her!"

The doctor struggled against me, then seeing Kaya being shoved into a waiting truck, she melted into tears. "This isn't safe."

"Later," I cautioned and darted a glance toward the Orc.

"Get your man, and come with me," Mr. Shank growled, and I realized he was looking past me, and out toward the crowd.

"It's time to go!" I called, just stopping myself from calling him by his rank. Howl glared at me in response.

"There's nothing we can do right now, my friend," I said to Howl, but his jaw muscles bunched as we fell in line.

The town looked a little better than the people looking for work. Complete subdivisions had been plowed under. And my guess was that the residents were stacked like cordwood in the high school gyms and classrooms. I was so distracted I almost didn't hear Mr. Shank when he started briefing the new workers.

"You get rations in the morning and evening. Right now, there are a lot of canned goods, so you might get a can of chili if you're lucky or stewed tomatoes if you're not. Throw nothing away, there is a strong barter system among residents."

We'd loaded from the emergency door to the rear, and he'd held us back from getting on the bus till last with a warning to keep our mouths shut and heads down. With a conspiratorial tone to his voice, he mumbled, "Wait a minute before you get off. We need to talk."

Howl and I had sat at the back of the bus and looked

out the windows like everyone else. Trees that looked several years old were lined up in rows in what had been a hometown market's parking lot less than a year ago.

"How did they do it? Did they raid every nursery in the state?" Howl's voice was full of wonder, and a bit too loud.

"Fucking Fairy magic!" someone yelled.

Shank stood up tall, and in his best Gunnery Sergeant voice bellowed, "Listen up, newbies! You never call them fairies! They have different clans and castes; trying to lump them all together will cause problems. And believe me the last thing you want is a highly offended Warg."

Glancing down the row, his eyes went hard, and I knew that look in an instant, "Looks like we have an old Marine on our hands."

Howl leaned over and looked down as he spoke, "Yeah, but is he a friend or collaborator?"

"Good question," I said just as Shank started to speak once more.

"Listen up! Early farmers brought in Apples, cherries, onions, and potatoes. Thanks to their efforts we are lucky enough to grow the food the elves are going to share with us, and all the other humans in the area. You work hard, you just might get enough food to feed your families."

Once more he scanned the now silent bus, "You don't work hard, they'll feed you to their Wargs."

Kate suddenly stood up and struggled to get the aisle, "They can't feed Kaya to Wargs! She is too important to my…To me."

Kate's fingernails looked clean, and I was glad of that as they pierced the skin on my right biceps. She struggled to get past me for a moment, till Howl pulled her back down into the seat and whispered harshly in her ear. After a moment, she calmed down, but I had no idea where the cold-blooded scientist had gone.

"Is she going to be a problem?" Mr. Shank demanded, and I raised my hands placatingly and shook my head.

Howl cut in coolly, his Texas drawl soothing understanding. "No, sir, she can work. She's just afraid for her kid, that's all."

Shank explained more as we rode. There was some talk about exit inspections and warnings about eating the produce. But other than trying to keep Kate calm I didn't pay much attention.

Once we'd made our way into town, and down by the river, it became clear we were headed toward the old cannery. It was a relic, something right out of the thirties.

Now that the town was being returned to that former...Glory I guess you'd call it, the place was reborn. I say reborn in that it stunk to high heaven, and heavy trucks raced up and down the streets hauling logs and produce in and out of town.

"Get off the bus!" Shank bellowed, and like cattle, we all stood and started to shuffle toward the front.

I watched the yard, trying to get a sense of my environment, and I wasn't shocked at what I saw. The workers were working, but they did so in silence and with a defeated look in their eyes. Most of them looked underfed, which made sense considering they were likely burning more calories than they were getting.

Remembering Shank's words when we loaded up, I paused and let the group get ahead of us until the last were off the bus. After a few seconds, Shank's head popped up from the stairs and he looked down the length of the bus at us.

For a second, he just stared, then as if deciding something he raised his hands and patted the air, before nodding once. Then I saw him drink in a full breath just before he bellowed, "What the hell are you doing? I said get the hell off my bus! Are you daft? Do you need a special invitation? Do I need to say please?"

Jumping like it was my first day in boot camp, I shuffled forward while Kate was mewling like a calf, behind me. "I don't know why he wasn't moving. I was trying."

"I don't need your excuses. Excuses are for officers and slackers!" Shank was roaring, but his eyes were darting toward the windows as he watched the orcs lining up workers into groups and hustling them away.

"Well, I have just the place for slackers. You are goddamn right I do! Come with me!"

Once we were off the bus, we were dogged by Shank who screamed, "What the hell is wrong with you? Did you have an English Nanny? Did she shake you?"

 His vitriol was steady and practiced, and we found ourselves in a stumbling half trot as we made our way inside past conveyor belts ladened with fresh cherries.

Line workers dressed in stained paper smocks, and hair nets that had seen better days, watched fearfully in furtive glances. They had the look of people who'd seen this kind of thing before and expected it to end badly, and even I had to admit the thought was growing increasingly alarming.

We were herded into a dark hallway, and I found myself facing a dark cement wall, condensation dripping down over dark moss, and no idea where to go.

"Down the stairs, genius! There on your right," Shank screamed and to my surprise there they were, metal and rusted with their stability in doubt.

Descending, we dropped to a small landing, then turned and went down more stairs only to repeat the process four more times. By the time we reached the bottom the stairs were shaking and creaking, and the smell of moss, moisture, and decay was everywhere.

"What's happening? Why are we down here?" Kate's voice was near panic.

"You can stop acting a fool now, we're secure down here," Shank said. But I was pretty sure nothing Kate had said or done had been an act.

Reaching out, I offered him a hand. "Thank you, Sir, I thought our goose was cooked up at the blockade."

"As unfortunate as it was," Shank took my hand and gave me a knowing nod, "if that Tweaker hadn't freaked out, it would have been."

Kate looked between us, her jaw working like she was chewing over a response. "What's the meaning of this?"

With a lazy grin slipping into place, Shank turned to the frail-looking woman and bowed his head a little in contrition. "Gunnery Sergeant Crandall Shank, US Marine Corps, Retired Reserve, at your service."

Kate's mind suddenly seemed to grab a gear and her eyes narrowed, "You're part of some kind of resistance cell?"

Just like that, the Doctor was back, making me wonder if it had all been an act after all.

"Those are dangerous words, Ma'am. Just consider me an old soldier who knows two young operators when I spot them. Hell, anyone would except those damn Orcs. The only differences they see in humans are male and female, young and old, or skinny and fat."

Leveling a skeptical gaze, Kate said, "And you just picked these two out of the crowd and decided to just help?"

"Let's go with that," I interjected and turned to Shank. "Can you fill me in on our current situation?"

Shank smiled and jerked his head down a corridor. "You and the lady can stay down here till you're ready. I've got bunks, MREs, and an operations kit."

"You sure had me. I was convinced we were headed into Satan's boot camp on the way down here." Howl grinned and shook Shank's hand, "what is this place, anyway?"

Shank looked around and smiled sheepishly, "It was a bulk root vegetable storage area. When Y2K happened, the local Mormons asked me to store some survival stuff down here, later the kids got me to set it up for paintball. Now, "he huffed, "It's kind of a makeshift armory or will be if we ever get enough people I can trust. Heck, there is even an old laptop back there if you're into gaming."

"I don't know what anyone is laughing about!" Kate cut in and glared at each of us as if daring someone to smile.

"My daughter is being held by that collaborator!" She shouted. "And did you forget she needs those medications? That was why we came here in the first place!"

Howl grabbed her from behind and put a hand over her mouth. For a moment, we all froze, eyes scanning the stairs and listening for the sound of someone descending. Above the sound of the conveyer's running was ever present, and the rumble of the carts moving produced sounded a little like thunder in the distance. On the stairs, however, we still seemed to have no movement.

Shank got up close to Kate's face and quietly growled, "I realize you are worried about your daughter. I know you're scared to death, but I have people, too. If you make me lose even one of them because you're a self-important admin POG who can't keep her mouth shut, I will feed you to the Wargs. Do you understand?"

Kate's eyes went wide, and fitfully she nodded her head. There was real fear in her eyes as if she was realizing that she wasn't immune to death. I'm not sure how many people upstairs knew what this man was, but I knew it, Howl knew it, and now Kate did as well. He was a professional Marine. And killing was a Marine's profession.

After Kate had calmed down, we were ushered further into the depths of the storage area. We hid in makeshift rooms hidden by industrial equipment that on the first look was too heavy to consider moving. Fortunately, Shank was aware of the service doors. He used the hiding spaces before Y2K to store less conventional supplies for the local Mormons.

"You know, Sarnt," Howl said as he chewed an MRE 'Redcon1' protein bar. "I have to hand it to these Mormons. They're like militia preppers, with a national organization and sophisticated leadership.... And guns."

"I guess part of their survival training includes a little strategic offense." I looked over the sand table that was supposedly for planning "paintball" battles around town.

Shank lobbed a white paper bag to Kate. "Here, these are the meds for your kid. They were all out of olanzapine, but they had risperidone and the pharmacist said it would suffice. There is also some midazolam in there, but be careful, that stuff will take down a horse."

Snatching the bag out of the air, Kate eagerly dug into the bag, inventorying the bottles one by one. Once satisfied, she set the bag down and resumed her focus on the screen in front of her.

Looking up, I saw the lean man assessing Kate. He didn't like her much and I couldn't blame him. She was demanding, selfish, and goal focused. She'd sell us all out if it got her what she wanted and where she wanted to go.

Kate, on the other hand, had made use of the laptop computer. With her external hard drive plugged in, she accessed her research and appeared to get lost in the data.

"You sure the meds are for her daughter? She seems kinda off to me," Shank asked suspiciously.

"Computational Biologist." Eric made air quotes with his fingers.

"She studies Fae bioinformatics using computational tools. I think it's some think tank big brain bullshit."

Shank raised both eyebrows and then rolled his eyes, "Okay, sure."

Eric grinned and motioned to the sand table, "I think we can map out a proper egress route after we extract the target. But it would help a lot to know our logistical capabilities."

"I am afraid there isn't much time to plan. From what my people tell me, we need to get the kid tonight. It's Lady Elida, and Sir Elias, of one of the El Dori Houses, are scheduled to inspect the farm tomorrow afternoon. You can expect security to be ramping up."

Kate closed the laptop with a snap and stared up at Shank evenly. "What does that mean?"

"It means we have about four hours to plan, or we are here another two days," he said, lifting his hands in the air like he was about to weigh something. "That would be outstanding for operational planning, but we risk the kid the longer we wait."

"Then we need to go now." Kate started stuffing things into her pockets. "She needs her meds. There are cultural considerations for a girl Kaya's age."

Howl raised a brow. "Lady, you know I'm Navaho, right? Just because your kid is like, thirty percent Nez Pierce doesn't make it her culture, and even if it did, that really doesn't matter anymore."

Kate froze, her glare enough to turn a person to ice. "My daughter is fifty percent native. Her grandfather was the last shaman of the Samtiak people."

"I never heard of them." Howl scoffed.

"There are a lot of tribes you have never heard of! Atfalati, Chepenafa, Luckiamute, Santiam, Yoncalla, but what do I know? I'm just a woman with four PHDs. I'm sure your Commando School taught you more about it than I learned in 18 years of college, Private. Now can we get going?"

"Are you trying to tell me Kaya is insane, or some special tribal endangered species?"

Kate took a deep breath but didn't open her eyes. "In her tribe, when they are blessed by the Wéeyekin they get trained to be Cúukwenin'. Spiritually adapt."

Howl's eyes went wide. "She's too young to have completed the-"

"She's never even started the training. When she started hearing voices and seeing things, I assumed the medical doctors were correct."

"Schizophrenia." I nodded.

"Exactly, but her people think that those are the voices of the great spirits, the ancestors speaking to her. Which I found completely insane."

"What changed your mind?" I asked, but the cold stare was my only answer.

"We'll go soon enough," I said firmly, which made her pause. "Until then, sleep, eat, do whatever you need to because once we kick this off, there will be little time for rest till we get to safety.

***

The footage on the laptop was the best intel we could get given our current situation. The second-story loft, above a building that still had "Drink Coca-Cola" in weathered paint on the side. It was transformed from a print shop in the sixties to the 'Black Canyon Brewery & Smokehouse' in more successful years. Now, it seemed to be where Mr. Hyer held court.

Howl turned the screen so we could all see it, then looked at Kate apologetically, "This is about all we got to work with. Drones are out, and any satellite footage would be impossible. So, we are down to good old human intelligence."

Howl had become the de facto caretaker of Kate, but his loathing of her became more apparent. Maybe it was a white lady talking to a native like he was the ignorant dog about his culture, or maybe he just didn't enjoy being around a pompous ass. In the end, I didn't care as long as he kept her from screwing up.

"That's her!" Kate said, as she pointed at the monitor.

On the screen, a pair of men, perhaps in their late twenties, stalked into the room and grabbed one girl sitting against the wall. Several of the others appear to object and one, a redhead older than the rest stood defiantly and tried to intervene.

Savagely, one man backhanded her into the arms of several of the others. As she writhed in pain, the one they grabbed tried to go to her, "Sally!"

"No, you don't!" laughed a chubby guy whose hand was exploring the folds of her blouse as he held her.

"Oh my god, they are going to rape her," Kate realized out loud, her hand going to her mouth.

"If they did, they didn't do it there," Howl said in a flat tone, and on the video the girl was pulled away as the others wailed.

Howl's accent seemed thicker as he briefed us, and I put that down to stress. "The way I see it, Sarnt, the girls work the floor downstairs, serving the damn Fae collaborators during the day. Then at night…"

"They can't do that! This isn't some third-world savage country," Kate said in a disbelieving voice.

"Bad people are everywhere." Shank shook his head, "But there are things we can do about it."

One corner of his mouth tugged up in a smirk as he pulled a hard case off the table and handed it to Howl.

Popping it open, Howl whistled. "McMillan Tac-50. Five-round magazine, fluted match grade Lilja barrel, and an adjustable buttstock made of lightweight materials."

Shank nodded in approval. "You know your guns."

A lazy grin slipped over Howl's lips as he checked

out the weapon. "Sniper school in 04. I did a little time with the Rangers hauling something similar around Iraq."

"Well, once you fire that thing everyone in town will know you're up to something, so even if you're not a Marine, you better hit what you're aiming for," Shank warned.

"Yes, but they won't know where I am if I use the topography of the area correctly."

Turning his head to me, he pulled out a much smaller weapon. "Silence is your friend, so this should work."

The weapon he held up was a crossbow, but nothing I was familiar with. It looked like an AR. A collapsible buttstock, pistol grip, and a forward assault grip, just what you'd expect, except for the larger-than-normal upper receiver and bow struts on the side.

Shank smirked manically as he motioned to the weapon, "AR-6 Stinger II, repeating crossbow."

"A crossbow? I know we've been talking about native tribes, but I'm too old for cowboys and Indians," I said deadpan.

"Yes, it loads from the top, and I have a few speed loaders for it. You cock it," he broke it at the stock and the action drew back the string, "From here. Disarming is simple enough, hold the string firmly and slowly release. It's no joke, it has enough power to put down a boar, so it should be fine on an Orc if you don't hit bone and you use the Bodkin hardened steel tips. Practice with that thumb safety. It has to be depressed just right, or it can hang up."

"I'm not hunting Orcs, but that's good to know."

"Good, but just in case I also have a tomahawk for you."

Shank handed me the long-handled weapon and watched me heft the weight, "Seriously? Where did you get this?"

"My nephew got me some stupid gift box thing that came with scotch, cigars, this damn thing, and aluminum free deodorant. Made use of the rest, but this thing is meant to kill people or hang on a wall, and I don't need wall art."

I grinned a little. What soldier doesn't like a new toy once in a while? Sure, it wasn't my Sig, but I didn't want every Orc to come running if I had to shoot something. As it fired bolts not bullets, it would take someone a little smarter than an Orc POG to realize the killer wasn't one of their own.

"Shank, do your people know the extraction point?" I asked, but we all had been present during the operations order.

"Sure, but even with the fires in the north orchards being set as a distraction, I still think you going in alone is a stupid idea," Shank admonished. He didn't like the idea of trying to do it as quietly as I was planning, but we didn't have a squad of trained operators, so an extraction by force was out of the question.

Kate stood, her bright blue eyes fixed and hard just like the lines of her mouth. "I think I should be there. She will need her medication injected immediately once we have her, you don't want her to miss her medication twice, it could be a real disaster."

Gritting my teeth, I nodded, "I can give her meds on-site if it's that serious."

"She doesn't really know you, Sergeant Pict, and I would be more comfortable–"

My temper flared, "I don't give a shit what makes

you comfortable, Kate. This isn't a democracy!"

Howl stood and put a hand on my arm, "Easy Sarnt, she's a bit extra, but we need her alive."

Kate glared at me, and venom dripped from every word as she said, "You have no idea what will happen if she doesn't get her meds! I told you, there are cultural considerations!"

"I know that you're a pain in my ass," I growled, then looked at Howl and saw the disappointed expression on his face and sighed.

"Okay, you explain it to her, then gear up and get in position."

"Cross the parking lot, skirt around to the side of the first building, and make your way up the side. Then cross five rooftops till you come to an alley, there should be a semi-truck there. Basically, it's a little hop, skip and jump and you're on the first level roof of the building where she is being kept."

Howl's instructions had been dead on, at least until I reached the alley, "hop, skip, and jump, my ass."

The promised Semi-truck was missing. The space between the two buildings was at least two cars wide, and I was loaded down with gear. Not to mention I'd never been a track and field kind of a guy, so the long jump was out of the question.

Below me, a sudden yell made me press myself closer to the roof. The crossbow hadn't been the only toy Shank had given me, the cold steel tomahawk. I didn't want to go hand-to-hand with these guys, but an ax to the face would give me a little time to ready a bolt.

"Orcs," I thought and listened as they passed. The pair were clearly on patrol, but way too comfortable in their environment. I didn't know what they were saying, but it wasn't going to be much different from two bored infantrymen, bullshit stories, and boasts. Of course, that was great for me, it meant they weren't focused.

It would have been smart to lie low and learn their route, but I didn't have time. A power pole near the building was my way down, and I didn't spare my knees for the last four-foot drop. "Tuck and roll," I said to myself, before popping back up on the other side of the street.

Above the rear door, a small awning had been constructed to look old-fashioned. Its supports were flat iron which had been bolted to the brick. Grabbing it, I pulled myself up, then found a hold on the ledge of a transom window that was just wide enough for a toe hold once I'd grabbed an overhead light. With a risky little hop, I pulled myself up on the roof.

"Get it together, Eric." Smoothly, I extended the stock of the AR 6 and took a quick check of the holographic sights.

I smiled as I saw the radiance of a new fire painting the evening sky dirty orange.

"Good man, Shank."

Taking my time, I climbed a steel ladder up to the next floor, then paused just at the edge.

"Who's there?" a gruff male voice called.

Pivoting to my right I saw two men standing near the skylight. One was peering down, eyes wide and face red, the other was holding a rifle and moving his head like he was trying to spot someone in the darkness.

"Perverts, or guards?" I wondered, then decided it didn't have to be mutually exclusive.

"Jared, there's someone up here with us," the first man hissed, and as he turned around a bolt sunk into the soft tissue of his eye and lodged in his brainpan. The way the blue fletching stuck out reminded me of the flowers some people wore on their lapels at funerals, and that reminded me of Kaya and her stupid doll.

"They call them Scorpion Grass, but I prefer the name Forget Me Nots."

"No, that little psycho is just doing that voice thing again. I think she's just trying to make people think she's psycho, so they won't see what kind of woman she really is." The one named Jared laughed, unaware of his friend's demise.

Before he could slump, Jared looked over his shoulder, then stunned, watched as his friend crumpled to the ground making little gagging noises.

"Ted!" Jared said a bit too loudly and while he was distracted as I crept forward, cocking the AR-6, before driving a bolt into his throat. The shot silenced him, but it wasn't a killing blow. As I moved to the skylight, the wounded man grabbed at the bolt and kicked at the ground, trying to regain his footing.

Pulling the tomahawk from my belt, I swung hard down into the side of Jared's head and felt a satisfying crunch. Like the man at the checkpoint, his blood spurted out and painted the ground, but I didn't feel bad for his family.

Staying back from the edge of the skylight, I flipped open the top breach of the AR 6 and rammed the quick loader in place. Glancing down, I was unsurprised at what I saw. The room had been turned into a little whore house. The bed was curtained off by multi-colored blankets hung on cords. From above, there was nothing hidden, even the stuff that would give me nightmares later.

One woman, the redhead from the video, lay on the bed, clearly brutalized. "Fucking animals," I growled, then saw two girls no more than eighteen trying to treat another who looked pale and sweating. I guessed she had internal bleeding and my heart was screaming for me to do something for her, but there was nothing I could do.

"But where is Kaya?" I asked myself, then spotted her sitting in a corner off by herself with a dreamy expression on her face. She'd gathered scraps of paper and other detritus around her, but her focus was on the old brick walls.

"There she is!" bellowed a loud voice followed by a few laughs from his buddies.

"I think the new girl is ready to party!" the man laughed high and twisted, a cruel grin on his mug.

"Oh, come on, Justin," a female voice complained, "She's just a kid."

Inside the curtained-off sections, the girls all started to move like scared chickens fleeing to the corners of their pens, but Kaya didn't seem to notice. Instead, she stayed on the floor and started to hum, or sing, I couldn't tell for sure.

"Shut up whore!" A male voice roared, then a meaty thump and a cry told me the man didn't like being challenged.

I'd like to say I reasoned out my best approach, but it's more likely I just instantly ruled out jumping through the skylight. Things like shooting through a half-inch of reinforced glass didn't make sense either, so instead I ran for the ladder.

Skipping the rungs, I locked my heels against the outside of the ladder and slid down to the first-story roof. My left hand screamed in pain, a vivid reminder of the glass I'd impaled it on earlier, but there wasn't any time to worry about that. I needed to get inside.

At first, there didn't seem like there was an external entrance, but after a frantic few minutes I found a trapdoor. It was locked from the inside, so I knew I'd have to go through the ground level, and anyone that got in my way.

Scurrying around the edge, I came to the front of the building and saw a truck and leaped into the back, then swung down to the ground and rushed inside the front door. To my shock and horror, people were everywhere.

Diners, drinkers, and socialites found a home at the Black Canyon Smoke House. The place was filled with everyone from clear collaborators eating brisket in curtained-off booths, to workers at a communal table silently drinking under-aged ale. Unfortunately, all eyes were immediately on me.

"There's a Dragon in the North orchards!" I screamed, and the room erupted.

A few things happened then. Most of the room rushed to their feet, eager to look out the window for a glimpse of the dragon, then seeing the orange glow frantic cries went up and people rushed out. I ignored them all and located the stairs, while they worried about Shank's distraction.

One of Hyer's goons must have heard the commotion, because I met him on the stairs when he rushed to investigate.

"Move, mother fucker" he screamed, as blue fletching sprouted out of his chest reminding me of Forget-Me-Nots, again. He slid down the steps as he pawed at the bolt, but I kicked it in deeper as I passed, and hurried up the stairs.

From upstairs, an enraged roar speared through me, and I knew Kaya was pissed. In my head, I could see Hyer's goon tearing at her clothing while she fought ineffectively against his size and weight. I needed to watch each corner as I climbed the stairs or risk another surprise.

I reloaded AR 6 before I came off the roof. Six shots weren't much, and I knew I'd need every shot. Rounding the corner, I saw the leering man, and he saw me.

"Who the hell are you?" he shouted, and I fired from the hip. My Forget-Me-Not inciting a deafening howl of pain. Enraged, he lunged at me, a knife appearing from nowhere.

Together we rolled back to the landing, breaths bursting out with each stair we slammed into as we cartwheeled down the stairs. With a little luck, I kicked off the wall and slipped his grip, but there was no way I could gain the mount as we fell.

At the bottom, we were both up fast, but he was faster. The AR 6 was hooked to a retractable sling, but I couldn't bring it to bear fast enough. The big fellow wasn't just size and strength. Skillfully, palm and hammer strikes fell into some kind of rapid stick fighting technique, and it overwhelmed me.

Upstairs, another scream also raged filled, and I knew whatever was going on up there was getting serious. With no other choice, I retreated to the ground floor, and the big man pursued drumming blows down on me the whole way. Once at the bottom, I turned, falling forward into a roll, trying to make space. But space was just what he wanted, I realized as he grinned through bloodied teeth.

"Now you die, asshole!" he chuckled. In his head, he was seeing a Bruce Lee moment, but I was seeing something else. Behind him, a woman in a sexy corset, and a rapidly bruising eye, lifted a cast iron frying pan and brought it down soundly on the back of his head.

The crack of bone was sickening, but as the man fell the red-headed woman from upstairs looked at me with a feral snarl, then crushed his skull with it again.

"Save the girls!" she yelled and fled to the kitchen, even as I rushed up the stairs. She was the woman from upstairs, I realized, the one who'd tried to help Kaya.

At the landing, girls were scurrying everywhere, some grabbing clothing, others any possessions they could as they hurried past me. This was their chance, for what it was worth, and they were taking full use of the opportunity. Unfortunately, that left me struggling to get past them and the blankets to find Kaya.

"What did you do, you little whore?" roared Hyer, then a snap-crack went through the room, and I zeroed on the sound.

Pushing away a blanket that hid her corner, I found Hyer standing over Kaya, his hand just following through from a massive slap. Kaya hit the wall like a rag doll, and I just knew she was dead. Hyer, on the other hand, was alive, well, at least for a minute longer.

"Fucking inhuman bastard!" I growled, but as much as I wanted to beat him to death, I knew rage was for novices. I fired a bolt that slammed home between his shoulders, then advanced as he screamed and tried to pull it out, even though he couldn't reach it.

Turning, he faced me, but what I saw didn't mesh with what I knew. One side of his face was scratched, the skin weeping yellow fluid. Black flies buzzed around his face, biting and stinging him like hornets whose nest had been kicked.

"NO!" he bellowed, as he batted at the flies and turned wildly in circles. "They're in my ears! I can hear them!"

A mumbled word pulled my attention to the wall that Kaya had bounced off. She was up, holding her doll out in front of her like she was showing it off. I couldn't help but notice small gnats flying around its head in parody of Hyer's current state.

"What the–"

Kaya got to her feet and ran to grab my elbow and pull me to the stairs, "They are saying we should go," she said as if she hadn't just done...Whatever she just did.

Nodding, I turned, then remembered Hyer, and cocked the AR 6, before firing another bolt into his chest. "Burn in hell," I muttered, then grabbed Kaya's hand, urged her forward, "run, run!"

Kaya moved like a gazelle, leaping over the fallen and giggling like the whole thing was a game. Thankfully, the dining room was clear, and we got outside in mere moments, but outside it was chaos. Fire trucks roared down the street, and a pair of large Orcs used halberds and spears to force people on truck beds and buses.

"Quick, back to the alley!" I ordered and pulled Kaya with me around the side of the building, but not before being spotted.

"YOU!" a deep rolling voice I recognized called just as he slipped around the corner. It was the Orc from the Blockade, and he looked pissed.

"That's going to be a problem!" I complained and I

ushered Kaya ahead of me, motioning for her to stay low and hurry toward the canal I'd followed in. With a glance over my shoulder, I was relieved to see no one behind us, but I could hear the Orc as it ran, grunting with each step and growing angrier as it pursued.

"Get down in the canal, then head back toward the mill! If we can get out of sight, we might be able to lose it," I said just loud enough for her to hear.

"It won't do any good, they can track us." Kaya's face was suddenly contemplative, her eyes narrow, and for a moment it was like looking at someone else. Even her voice was deeper, solemn, and speaking with a certainty that was beyond her years. For a passing moment, she even looked old, wrinkles around her mouth and eyes, but then the moment passed, and it was just the girl, frail and looking scared.

"Track us how?" I asked, but she glanced down at my hand and knew what she meant. The damn Orc could likely smell my blood.

"Fine, run toward the mill, I'll go the opposite direction. Maybe we can throw him off long enough for—"

"Too late," Kaya sighed like she was a hundred years old. The Orc, his face twisted with anger, barreled over the edge of the canal, screaming a war cry that shook me to my bones.

A tangle of limbs bowled me over, and it wasn't just the Orc. Someone was on top of the creature, his blade sinking again and again into the back of the beast.

With a sudden move, it slammed Howl into the ground, then stood straight and tried to roar. The sound that came out was a pathetic high exhale as it breathed its last breath.

I spun ready to fight, but to my surprise Howl stood up, looking like an Apache god holding his bloody K bar and drenched in Orc blood. His eyes were fixed on the dead Orc, and as he reached down to wipe the blade on the Orc's clothes he said in his lazy Texas twang, "Looked like you could use some help, Sarnt."

"You came for us," Kaya nodded like an approving father.

"Howl, you crazy SOB, I'd drop you for twenty for abandoning your post if I weren't so glad to see you."

"I was relieved. Shank said it is a travesty to have an Army man hold a Marine's girl, so he took the TAC-50 and–"

A loud meaty thwack followed a pissed-off hornet sound of a large caliber round passing nearby, then the unmistakable sound of a body hitting the ground. Behind us, the Orc Howl had stabbed, had climbed back to his feet, only to present an excellent long-range target for Shank.

"That'd be him there," Howl said with a grin just as the far-off sound of the large rifle echoed in the valley. "Come on now, Doc is waiting, and we shouldn't hang around."

"It's your turn to drive, you up for it?" I said, feeling like Howl had earned it.

"Nah, it's better if I shoot." Howl surprised me with a slow grin, "I've got other surprises in store for 'em."

True to his word, the Bajah-style 'trophy' truck was parked a block down, tucked into an empty lot off the alley. Kate sat irritably in the back seat, her eyes darting around at every shadow and corner till they landed on us.

"Oh, thank God," she breathed. Then reached for

Kaya with a relieved look on her face. "Come here, Kaya."

For the first time since I'd known the kid, a genuine smile came to her lips and she rushed over, arms out for her mother. A wave of warmth flooded through me. I even felt a spring in my step as I bounded into the driver's seat and slipped behind the wheel.

Kaya's childlike voice turned rough and low, a man's voice from the throat of a child, and the man was pissed. "Get off me, woman! We don't want medication! She can't hear us…"

"Well, that ruined the Hallmark moment, Sarnt," Howl said as he looked over his shoulder, then scowled.

Kate was wiping the hair out of Kaya's eyes as the girl struggled against her. "Baby, you have to take the medication. You can't let them control you."

In the rearview, I could see her looking intently into Kaya's eyes, something akin to fear shadowing her face. "What the hell are you talking about, woman?"

"When they came, the El Dori, something changed in her. Like something came unstuck, and now Kaya can't always control it."

In the mirror I could see Howl looked down at them both in confusion. "Did you take some of Shanks pills or something?"

Behind me, Kaya fought and screamed, her voice seeming to change from that of a child to an old woman, then an old man. Each voice was distinct, and it sounded like she was speaking in several languages.

With my attention diverted I almost missed the massive shadow, and two luminance eyes that peered at me from the darkness.

"Warg!" I shouted and grabbed another gear,

flooring it to get up some speed.

Dark gray fur and teeth glowed under the LED lamps that flashed by us. I'd seen one of the massive wolf-like creatures run before and all out they could catch some cars, but not a truck with a Long Block engine and 495 Horsepower.

"Hold still! Kaya, damn it you have to take this!" Kate was wrestling with Kaya, while Howl pulled a MK 17 SCAR-H from between the seats and turned to fire out the sunroof.

"Keep it steady Sarnt, I'm about to have a conversation with this Warg."

"It is a thirty-caliber conversation!" I yelled.

Firing a three to five-round burst caused the Warg to jag left and pockmarked the road near its feet. It was gaining on us, but there weren't any open spaces for me to hammer the throttle on the small main strip in Podunk Idaho.

"Hold on!" Howl warned and from the driver's side rear a massive impact made the rear wheels scream, and the smell of cooked rubber flooded the compartment.

From Kaya a scream went up, but it was like three voices speaking at once.

"Let us speak!

Let Us Speak!

LET US SPEAK!"

"Unless she has directions to the safe back road, please shut her the hell up!" I bellowed.

Cracking the wheel to the right I cut in front of the beast. Howl let loose a long blast of 7.62 rounds that caused the Warg to yelp and duck away, but as we passed, it turned and raced after us.

Jerking to a sitting position, Kaya's head slammed

into Kate's with a hollow thump that made her scream in pain and protest. As she slumped holding her head, Kaya turned her head toward the beast behind us, and I could see the edges of her eyes bunch as she narrowed her gaze at the Warg.

"She isn't for you!" Kaya's old man's voice said.

"Sarnt, something is happening out there," Howl called between bursts of his rifle.

Glancing back once more I could see the Warg charging after us. Now there were small glowing lights that illuminated the beast's head, and the black flies were swarming its eyes.

The Warg snapped and twisted its head away. It was clearly in pain, its massive eyes blinking and weeping, and the distraction was making him an easy target for Howl.

"Hit it!" he yelled, and I could nearly feel his fist pump in victory. The Warg suddenly lost its footing, and like a horse that stepped in a hole. It went down in a cloud of dust, but I was already running through the gears and heading for the highway out of town.

"Let us out." Kaya boomed, and I felt a compulsion to do as she commanded but pushed it away.

"We need to get clear. That Warg won't be the only one in pursuit." I said, then heard a light buzzing in my ears.

"Sarnt, that Warg is still back there," Howl warned.

At first it was like a mosquito, then a fly buzzing near my right ear.

"Let us out
Let us out
LET US OUT!"

My vision narrowed, a creeping darkness from the

sides, and I could feel a fear growing in my heart. It was something primal, ancient, and dark that was pressing against me, and I felt my foot lifting from the gas.

"Don't listen Sergeant! You have to keep driving." Kate said between pain filled breaths.

"LET ME OUT!" Kaya screamed, and I suddenly realized she wasn't talking about getting out of the car. Whatever that was, that voice, that elder voice wanted control.

Howl grunted, a deep painful grunt and his weight slammed against the door, making the truck rock and buck.

"Kaya," Kate exclaimed, as she tried to wrap the wildly flailing girl in her arms.

The pressure was suddenly off me, and I smashed a gas pedal all the way to the floor. "Get that kid under control!"

Kate yelped then, and before I could look back small hands were clamped around my neck. Her grip was like Iron, and once more blackness crept around the edges of my vision.

"OUT!" Kaya screeched, then like magic she fell back into Kaya's arms.

"Easy Sergeant, the Midazolam has taken effect. She will be out while her normal medication takes effect. Just keep driving. Just get us there." Kate said as if none of that had just happened, and this was a normal medical patient.

For a while we drove in silence, the road ahead was empty, but I didn't feel like we were in the clear. Whatever I'd just witnessed had to be what all of this was about. Kate's research wasn't some think tank exercise, it was this girl.

"What do we do now?" Howl's voice was thoughtful and unsettled.

In the mirror, I could see Kate stroking Kaya's hair. It was oddly maternal for a woman who could seem so cold, but I think everyone was traumatized.

"We are just here to do a mission, Specialist. Now that we are back on track, we complete the job and move on to the next."

For another few minutes, the only sound was the road under our tires. Then I felt Howl shift and I didn't need to look at him to know he was shaking his head. "I don't think I'm doing the next mission, Sarnt."

I turned my head then. "What do you mean?"

"If Kaya really is blessed by the wéeyekin, that means she has a lot to teach us. To teach the tribes." Howl explained.

"You're just going to stay with them? You've done nothing but complain about them since we started," I scoffed.

"My tribe isn't what it used to be. With everything that's going on, maybe it's time we return to the old ways if we are going to stand a chance."

"Stand a chance with what? Making fireflies that bite and sting with some kind of native throat talking trick?"

"The spirits speak through her. We can only guess what it will bring, but I'm going to learn what I can."

Once more, we lapsed into silence. There was nothing I could do if Howl stayed with them, higher would likely be thrilled at the idea.

"Yeah, you might be on to something. I've been thinking about Shank. I think I'll go back after things cool off, maybe lend a hand helping him build that resistance cell."

Howl turned to look out the window. "Do you think we'll win this war, Sarnt?"

"No, not anytime soon," I admitted. "I don't think we get to go back to things as they were. Not them," I motioned to the woman, "And not for us. But if we keep fighting, who knows? Maybe someday."

"Then we'll keep fighting." Howl said without looking up.

"Yep. We will keep fighting," I agreed. As I looked at Kaya in the mirror, I wondered for just a moment who we'd end up fighting by the time it was all said and done.

A Wing and a Prayer

by John M. Olsen

The small town was like many, filled with locals who either loved the lifestyle or hated crowded cities. Nestled into the center of a broad valley, the town was surrounded by farms, apple orchards, and ranches that spread out for miles in every direction. A green and gold checkerboard of crops reached all the way to the mountains anchored in the distance.

Clarence Butler took in the view from his bungalow's front porch swing, but he grimaced as he saw an elf astride a bear, riding into town flanked by his marching private guard. There was little question that the elf, a Company Commander by the name of Dasan, was coming to see him. A hand-written letter of demands for tribute had arrived by courier the day before. The fancy piece of parchment sat on a wicker side table within easy reach. As mayor of Washburn, it was left to Clarence to deal with the invaders, to be a buffer between the elves and his citizens.

A shotgun sat propped just inside the closed front door, but he'd be a fool to try anything. Sitting just north of the border between Utah and Idaho, there was no backup, no military support, and no underground resistance. He'd seen the results of the invasion on the news, despite being so far away from the big cities. He and everyone else in town were on edge, and things were about to get worse.

The elf rode onto the lawn, dismounted, and tossed the reins to his front guard. "I see you received my letter." He nodded to the parchment.

"I have." The less he said, the better it would be. Don't speak except to answer. Some of the boys in town had learned that lesson the hard way.

"We will claim our quota as you harvest your fruit and grain and will take our share from the ranches as specified in the document."

This was where things would get difficult to follow his usual quiet protocol. "Your letter mentioned sacks of wheat. We don't do it that way. No sacks. We harvest it, then move it by the ton in wagons. We deliver it to a mill two counties away. We used to use our big trucks or train cars to make it efficient, but we don't have the fuel for the big equipment now."

The elf seemed momentarily perplexed, but then he smiled. "Ah, yes. Using the roads and rails. Yet another stinking blight on the face of the land, just like this dung-pile village."

"It's fine by me if you don't want us to move the grain for you, but that's the only way we're set up to move it. Would you like to come and claim it yourself from the town? We don't have the manpower to get the grain harvested and moved as it is." That was the thing about machinery and automation. It took fewer people to farm huge tracts of land so long as the equipment kept running, but that meant every person was critical even before fuel and maintenance became impossible to find. Harvesting by hand was a nightmare.

The elf toyed with a dagger, tapping the flat of the blade on his lips as he thought. "Very well. Use whatever method is available to deliver your quota to my camp to the north."

It was a great option, except for his people needing that grain harvest. Same with the cattle and the apple orchards. "We'll do what we can to meet the quotas you have demanded, but it's been a dry year, and the cattle have suffered. They're a little slow to grow this year, so the deliveries will be after the grain is all harvested and processed."

"I expect compliance, not excuses. Personally, I'd rather just let the orcs march in and pillage, but that's not a sustainable position."

Clarence smiled inside, sure that the elf was unaware of the information he'd given away. He wasn't in control, and he had superiors to deal with. Superiors who insisted on a long-term arrangement where the people served and provided.

"As I said, we will do our best to meet your demands, while maintaining our ability to keep working."

The elf's face darkened, but he soon covered it with a passive expression. "You would do well to remember our relationship here. I give orders, and you do what you're told. The first delivery will be due soon."

The elf also received orders from someone farther up the chain, and then he did what he was told. Clarence tucked the nugget of information away for later, sure there was some leverage there if only he could find it. If there were orders to maximize food production, if the elf had been told to work with the towns to maintain production, that meant there were resource and supply-chain issues.

If there was one thing he remembered from his years in the Navy over a dozen years ago, it was that nobody fought on an empty stomach. It was time for a town meeting.

***

There was no town hall to speak of; just a little office space with filing cabinets to hold official town paperwork, and a place on the street to park a police car back when the county sheriff still drove it. That parking spot had been vacant for weeks.

The wood-framed post office next door had been idle as well, with nothing arriving from Pocatello by horseback for weeks.

The town meeting was the biggest they'd had in years, so with Bishop Taylor's permission, they moved the meeting to the church. The old stone building from the early 1900s had seen the town grow from nothing. It still wasn't much, but it was home.

Everyone had arrived in high dudgeon, ready to protest the demands placed on them.

Clarence stood at the pulpit looking out at twenty residents in the front pews, with Bishop Taylor seated behind and to one side. "They're demanding tons of wheat, and more when other crops are harvested. I've broken it down by farm."

His brother-in-law, Peter Robinson, leaned back in and repositioned a pistol strapped to his ample waist. "And if we don't like it? What if we hunker down and defend ourselves?" It would have been a breach of etiquette to open carry at church if not for the recent collapse of, well, everything.

"We can't," said Clarence. "With only thirty, who could answer that call? We already know what happens if we organize and fight against them. Our wives all become widows. If one of us takes a shot at them, everyone will suffer for it."

Peter stood, waving his arms. "But you saw what

they're asking for. It's too much. We might get it harvested, but food deliveries out here have all but stopped. Everyone's been living off their gardens and emergency food storage. Even if we make it this year, there's not enough left to plant next year with their demands."

Bishop Taylor stood and motioned for Clarence to step aside. "I know things are on edge. I have a better feel than most of you on that because I talk with those who need the most help. I know what hardships people face here, down to a list of those with nothing to share. We have plans. I know who can share and who can't. We can make it through the winter, and that gives us time to plan. What that plan is will be up to Mayor Butler and the rest of you to work out, but getting all hot under the collar won't do any of us favors."

He returned to his seat but continued to give Peter a raised eyebrow.

After a few moments, Peter sat, noticing nobody else was riled up for a fight.

"Now then," Clarence said. "They know we've got an iffy harvest this year, and I played up the challenges we face. Our best bet for now is a work slowdown that ends up shorting our delivery. We need to look like we're busy working for them, but we can use that to skim whatever we can off the top. That might buy us a few months, long enough for someone a lot higher up the chain than our little town to figure something out."

Peter rolled his eyes. "So, we ease off, hope they don't notice, and hope for someone else to save us. That's too much hope and too little plan for me."

"I'm all ears if you have an idea that won't get us all killed and fed to monsters." Clarence glared at Peter, knowing he'd back down. He could barely plan a trip to the grocery store, let alone lead a rebellion. Still, it would be important to keep an eye on Peter and give him something to do.

After several tense seconds, Peter shook his head.

It took another hour to work out the details of how to hide as much as they could from the elves. It would be hard, but there wasn't a lot of choice.

"Then we have a plan. Teams go out at night to bulk up your basement storage. Just don't be seen, or you might be turned into an object lesson. Others will be out working where it's most visible, to keep their eyes where we want them. Peter, your farm is up north toward the elf camp. Can you do us all a favor and watch to see if they're watching or visiting our fields at night? I don't want anyone to be seen. Everyone else, let's pool our horse-powered equipment and make sure we get everything where it needs to be. I don't want any surprises."

Bishop Taylor closed the meeting with a prayer, pleading for guidance and inspiration in caring for their families, and for good to triumph over evil.

Clarence worked to hide his glum mood from the men leaving the chapel. They were down, and now the elves had come in with an extra kick to the gut. He stood at the door, patting shoulders and giving encouraging small-talk as they filed past on the way back to tell their families about their part of the plan. It wasn't much, and he hated the thought of a plan that did nothing but buy time. Sooner or later, that extra time would run out, and if anyone abandoned their farm to head somewhere safer, it would get worse for everyone that stayed.

***

The summer sun baked the ripe wheat in the field. It was dry enough to harvest, and the weather had cooperated for a change. If they waited too long, the wheat would drop and scatter in the field. It was a horrible way to reseed the field, so they would have to be careful with their timing. Clarence had been burning the candle at both ends, working by day, and sneaking out to skim from the fields at night. It was slow, grueling work without the loud tractors and other heavy machinery.

Dasan, the elf commander, hadn't even bothered to show up in person for this visit, opting instead to send a subcommander to clarify the commander's instructions. Clarence stood beside a useless combine beside his half-harvested field waiting for the elf to stop yelling about the shortfalls.

"This is a disgrace! Your lazy villagers have delayed and shrunk your delivery, and now you must make up for it."

"We're doing what we can." The statement was true, but it said nothing of the goal Clarence and his people had in front of them. "Look at this. I could harvest this field in a day if my combine worked. There's no fuel, and nobody to call for service to fix it if it breaks. Used to be, I could call someone in Pocatello or Brigham City, and have a tech here within a few hours. Now? We're cut off. How can you blame us for that?"

Dasan glared. "Failure is unacceptable. I can't let this go unpunished, no matter the cause. You have forced my hand."

That didn't sound good. He hadn't come to

complain, he'd come to act. "Let's not be hasty. With a little time, we can make up some of the shortfall."

"It's too late for that. I drew lots, and a home has been chosen. The family's garden and all the food found at the chosen house will be taken as a tribute. If there is still a shortfall, another home will be selected tomorrow."

"Don't hurt the people. We need every hand we've got. You need us to make this work."

"You don't need to explain to me the trials involved in losing slaves. You were warned. Your deliveries were short, and this is now your problem to fix if you don't want to see more homes targeted. Or you could give me a list of who to visit first. It is a perfect opportunity to make your personal enemies within the town suffer."

There it was. Another bit of information he could use. Even among those who worked together, there was division within the ranks of the elves. Jealousy, ambition, and all that went with it. But how could he use it?

Clarence removed his cowboy hat to wipe sweat from his brow, then looked across the valley to the seagulls circling in the distance above the dump. He pointed. "You know, there's a story about those birds. Over a hundred and fifty years ago, our ancestors arrived south of here and planted crops. A swarm of crickets invaded and began to eat the wheat crop down to the ground."

Dasan folded his arms, listening. "You're not suffering from a plague of locusts. You're suffering from lazy workers and dry weather."

"Right. But it's both a true story and a parable. The people prayed and fasted for relief, and seagulls arrived by the thousands. At first, they thought it was another plague, but the birds ate those crickets until they got too full to eat any more, then they barfed them up and ate another load. It happened over and over until the crickets were gone. The crops were saved."

"And what do you pray for, Mayor? Relief from oppression? Divine retribution? I have no boon to give, and the God you worship has not come down from heaven to save you."

"Not yet, He hasn't. Well, as Bishop Taylor tells it, the story is one of doing what you can with what you've got. If we do our best, God steps in to handle the rest."

Dasan shook his head as he turned to leave. "If birds come to your rescue, then you should gather them. They'll soon be all you have left to eat. A platoon left for town when I came to see you and has already evicted the family. Their garden and home will be stripped bare before the family will be allowed to return. If you don't want more of the same, increase your deliveries to what you promised."

There was no promise. Only demands. Clarence clenched his teeth and nodded. If everyone kept their cool, nobody would die. Bishop Taylor could take care of the family, but everything would be harder now. If one of the prepper families got hit, it could mean the loss of more than a year of supplies for a family.

Tempers were going to get hot, and he'd have his hands full keeping Peter or some other idiot from taking a shot that would trigger a brutal crackdown.

"If you've delivered your message, I have some people to check on."

"As Company Commander Dasan already told you, we demand compliance, not excuses. Good day, Mayor Butler." He stepped to the edge of the field where more armed and armored elves waited. He mounted a horse he'd confiscated from a ranch soon after the arrival of the elvish company. At least the subcommander didn't rank high enough to ride a war beast like the bear he'd seen the company commander ride, or the flying monstrosities he'd seen on the news during the fighting in the big cities.

The slowdowns were costing more than they were worth, especially if they had no warning about which house was next to be pillaged. He needed a better plan. He glanced back at the seagulls in thought as they scavenged for food scraps at the dump.

***

The Anderson's home was a wreck. The walls still stood, but the doors had been busted out along with half the windows. The family huddled across the street, embraced by their neighbors as the last elf-led wagon rolled away. They'd taken food, furniture, bedding, everything. This wasn't just to make up for food deliveries. It was meant to send a message, and the message was clear.

The only bright side was that the Andersons hadn't stockpiled a lot of food. The retired couple lived on their own, and they were already being fed by neighbors often. The lack of food had contributed to the elves going overboard with taking everything that wasn't nailed down. Clarence hated himself for thinking of the raid on the Andersons as a tactical advantage in preserving their supplies, but he'd take everything he could get.

Bishop Taylor was there, consoling the couple. They didn't attend church, but that didn't mean much as the community pulled together to care for their own.

Sniffles from the distraught couple became more apparent as Clarence stepped up behind them and the bishop. "Mind loaning me the keys to the church? We need to hold another meeting."

Less than thirty minutes later, most of the families in the town were represented by a mix of men and women able to step away from their jobs or homes for the emergency meeting. Clarence stood at the pulpit as before, the seats behind him empty. "The elves say this sort of raid will continue if we don't meet the deliveries they demanded. That idiot subcommander even offered for me to rat out the people I don't like in town to put them at the top of the list. Now we have to figure out how to deal with it. Make up the quotas or lose more homes."

A woman in the back row stood. "We can't make it all up. There's no way."

The residents fidgeted in the pews, looking back and forth at each other as if deciding who ought to be next. If the people were put under too much pressure, they would turn on each other like the elf had assumed they would.

He had to use whatever control he had over the situation. If they couldn't make the full delivery, raids would continue. But that meant he finally had something under his direct control...

"So, what if we give them a list?" he asked. "That means we know which house will be raided next. We can prepare. They won't find anyone's stash of guns and ammunition and freak out. We got lucky this time. Bishop Taylor will arrange things for the Andersons. But next time? We need them to be predictable. Who has the least stuff to move? We can start there."

The same woman said, "And what about food? We can move that, too. Preserve what we can."

Clarence shook his head. "That's why they came down so hard on the Andersons. They had next to nothing in the house, and they never planted a garden this year. We have to make it worth their while, but we have to control what we give them."

This was the absolute worst situation for a democratic process. They couldn't do it by vote, and nobody in their right mind would volunteer. Like it or not, he had to build the list and tell people where they fit into it. As mayor, he'd used the idea of eminent domain before to take a few feet from some front yards to put in a sewer line. This was the same, but on a larger scale.

He cleared his throat, then spoke. "I'll build a list. I can put myself on the top, so it's as fair as I can make it."

Peter piped up from the middle of the group. "That's stupid. You said it's supposed to be your enemy list. You can't put yourself on the top of the list, or they'll know what you're up to. Put me on top. I can get my guns moved tonight in case they come back tomorrow, like they said. I'll need help moving the nicer half of our food storage out, too. We can see how those elves like my stockpile of MREs."

That sort of response from Peter was the last thing Clarence had expected. The hothead was always in trouble, annoying his neighbors, and being a general nuisance. This was a side of him that Clarence hadn't seen in years. Maybe he'd misjudged his brother-in-law.

"Done. Thank you, Peter. Who can help him move stuff tonight?"

Several hands shot up, and Peter made note of them

before sitting down. With the list started, Clarence decided it was time to put more trust in his people to do the right thing in the face of a common enemy.

"I hate to ask this, but can anyone else volunteer? We're buying time and trying to give them as little as we can, but if we give them nothing, it will get bad."

Soon, he had a list of three "enemies" to turn in, assuring the safety of the rest of the town for several days as they plotted.

"Now, to make that sacrifice worth the effort. We need something new. Something besides just slowing down and shorting them. What can we do to look like we're delivering what they asked, but without giving the enemy all the food they need?" Wars were won and lost over logistics. A strong army required good supply chains, and that didn't change just because they had magic and dragons.

Voices rose from the crowd. "Poison?" Another said, "An ammonium nitrate bomb?"

Clarence shook his head. "No! Do you want them to kill us all? They would know it was us, and they would show no mercy. We already know that."

Peter gave a sly grin. "Vermin. What if we give them grain, but it's riddled with rat droppings?"

They'd spent decades controlling the rat population of the town. The idea had merit, but Peter had approached it from the wrong direction. A memory from earlier came to the fore. "Our garbage dump has a lot of seagulls. What would it take to lure them out to make a mess of the grain in an open-topped trailer?"

One of the men barked a laugh. "Leave the cover off the grain. I can carry some offcuts from the butcher shop in the back of a wagon to lure those winged rats from the dump to your trailer. Just take the road out closer to the dump when you drive north."

"Good. I want you to gather all the covers we use for grain transportation. Store them at Peter's house. And Peter, if you don't mind, let's hide those MREs, along with the rest of your food. I want those elves angry enough to take everything in your house, including those tarps. Are you okay with that? They'll do a lot of damage if it's like what they did to the Andersons."

"It beats what they'd do to me if I popped a couple of them with a deer rifle, and that was looking like my best option until now."

***

The elves raided Peter's home the next day, not giving the town a chance to gather enough food to cover demands. It hadn't taken much to convince the elves that Clarence hated Peter enough to put him through a raid, despite being related to him. The elves didn't understand everything about the local social dynamics, but they'd seen enough to know Clarence didn't care much for Peter. They came away from the raid with two cases of MREs and whatever had been growing in his garden behind the house.

Peter and his family had narrowly missed being there when the elves arrived, but they'd hidden at the neighbor's house. It had all gone according to plan until they lit up the farmhouse. down. It took three people to hold Peter down and keep him from shooting the elves when they started the fire. They were escalating, and Clarence was ready to raise the pressure as well. It would take extra care to keep everyone out of harm's way.

The gull-baiting trailer arrived at the rendezvous point with over a hundred seagulls hovering, diving, and squawking for a chance at the scraps stashed in the bed. The food was easy pickings compared to the garbage dump. Once the load pulled up near the uncovered grain container on a trailer, the driver flung the scraps into the container of wheat. The birds took to the air, but immediately descended on the relocated feast. They ate their fill over the next hour, then took up residency.

The next day, the wheat was a mess, with feathers and bird droppings everywhere. The driver delivered the load, dropping the container to the ground outside the invader's camp, then left as quickly as he could. With the food gone, the gulls winged their way back to the dump.

It didn't take long for a bear to appear on the horizon carrying Dasan, the company commander. Soldiers, both orc and elf, followed him. Clarence waited on his porch with a large Bible borrowed from the bishop on his lap while everyone else in town made themselves scarce.

The elf leaped from his mount at the edge of the yard and stormed forward to stand in front of Clarence with his hand on the pommel of a sword. "Explain yourself, or I'll behead you in front of your whole village."

The mayor set the book aside the wicker side table, noting how the elf's eyes followed his every move. "We increased the grain shipment from last time. We're working to avoid more raids, even though you didn't give us any time before the second raid."

"The grain was ruined! Polluted by animals."

This would take a careful balance of emotions. Too much finger pointing, and he'd end up losing his head. Too much sorrow or groveling, and the elf would know he was being played. With elves and their magic, Clarence didn't know if they could detect lies, so he kept to the facts. "Ah. Maybe it's because we were unable to cover the load. The covers were stored in Peter's house. Do you know who burned his house down instead of just taking all his food?"

Any commander worth the title would accept responsibility for the actions of his soldiers, but Clarence had a feeling that wasn't the same with the elves. Many of them would be happy to take a step up the chain of command at the first sign of weakness in a leader, or to punish an underling for a failure. Sure, they might not all be that way, but he'd seen it enough that he counted on it. He was glad to throw an elf subcommander under the bus.

"That is no concern of yours." Dasan turned, staring at the horizon like he wanted to burn a hole through the air. "If you can't cover the loads, you will use a container that has a solid top. I've seen you have access to them, and the extra labor to load such a container is your problem to solve. If you fail to deliver a full quota, two homes of my choice will burn."

The elf turned in a circle, his eyes lingering on Clarence's home to drive his meaning home.

Clarence was a great judge of character among humans, and he believed his skill translated to the elves he'd met. What would it take for Dasan to be so angry, yet not take it out on the human right in front of him? He'd made threats but hadn't acted on them yet. The anger was easy enough to figure out since one of his subcommanders had burned a home without approval.

Who would the commander fear, and what held him back from handling the situation with his typical brutality? There was only one explanation. He would have to report a failure to someone above him. This verified that the food wasn't all destined for local use, and the quotas had come down from elsewhere. He had his own assigned long-term quota to meet, and Clarence was making him look bad.

The townsfolk were the means of production, which gave them a measure of protection as a group, but Clarence couldn't rely on that to keep any individual safe. Someone could be turned into an example on a moment's notice, but they had to keep production going, or Dasan would continue to look weak.

The elf and most of his guard left at a quick pace, headed back to their camp to the north. Four soldiers remained a half-mile outside town, where they set up a temporary camp. The message was anything but subtle. They would watch the next load to avoid problems, human-caused or not. It was out of the question to hold another town meeting under the watchful gaze of the elves. This had to be handled one-on-one.

***

Bishop Taylor's kitchen looked like it came from a magazine ad with everything in its place. The showroom state of the kitchen was even more surprising to Clarence when considering that the bishop and his wife Evelyn cooked meals there to feed two dozen residents at a shot with nothing but a couple of camp stoves and an antique wood-burning stove. The scent of cinnamon lingered in the air from their latest efforts and a pan of frosting-drizzled rolls cooled on the counter.

Seated beside Evelyn, the bishop examined the wood grain on the walnut dining table. "I can't join you on your crusade, Clarence. I've done as much as I can, but I have a responsibility to be here for the people."

"Oh, I don't need you as a soldier. I need you as a cook."

Evelyn smiled. "Now you're speaking our language. Who do we need to feed?"

"Four elves camped outside of town."

Bishop Taylor raised an eyebrow. "They've never responded well to acts of kindness. We tried when they first showed up, remember?" He tugged up his short sleeve to show a healing scar on his left biceps from a close call with a blade-wielding elf.

The scar brought back memories of how the two of them had approached the camp when the elves had first arrived. After the Fae learned they'd come unarmed, they were beaten and sent home as a warning to remind them who was in control.

"I remember. I'll head out to talk to them on my own. They know I represent the town. What I need from you is a full meal for four, with dessert. The fancier, the better. We've got a two-pronged approach—"

"No details. We bake for you, you take them. If they ask, all we know is that they were baked for the elves as a gift. It sounds to me like you're trying to appease them, and I'll tell them that if I'm asked. Still, I remember some stories from the scriptures that have me concerned."

Clarence bared his teeth in what might charitably be called a smile. "I know the stories. No drugs, no poisons. Not even alcohol. Have the meal ready at six tomorrow evening, and I'll organize everything else."

It was time to act on the rest of his plan. He hated plans with so many moving parts, and the timing was critical.

Peter and the usual group of troublemakers gathered nets to catch as many gulls as possible at the dump, and took off from the far side of town, out of view of the observers. Next up, he prepared to load a twenty-foot ISO container onto the back of his old flatbed trailer and tow it with a team of horses. He'd drive it himself.

It would have been easier if he had access to a Rough Terrain Cargo Handler to move containers around, but his military days were long past. Once the trailer was hitched, he winched an empty twenty-foot container onto the bed of the trailer by hand. Things were taking too long with all the manual steps they were forced into with the enclosed container, but there was no choice.

With the container loaded, he drove to where a team of farmers had been harvesting wheat, loading grain into handcarts instead of the old, motorized cart they used to load trucks.

If the elves hadn't forced them to use a solid-topped container, things would have been easy. With a ramp, they could dump grain into the open top container. Now, they had to hand-wheel loads to the back of the container in stifling heat.

"We need this container as full as we can get it, and still be able to shut the doors."

\It took a lot of manpower to keep the grain flowing, but they loaded it one wheelbarrow at a time. After a long day with a full team, they couldn't add more without spilling half to the ground through the open door of the container.

"That's it. Thanks for your help, everyone."

One farmer from the team said, "This better be worth it. We won't last the winter if we give everything away."

"Pray for a miracle, just like Bishop said," said Clarence.

The four elves left behind as watchers stood in the distance at the far end of the field, observing as the container doors closed. After a few moments, they turned toward their camp.

The meal for the four guards would be waiting for them at their camp to keep them from wandering too far during the next hour.

Clarence drove the loaded trailer to meet Peter at their arranged rendezvous on the road near the dump, well beyond where the scouts could see.

Peter stood at the meeting point with his team, and gulls circled above. He limped over and scowled as Clarence climbed from his truck.

Clarence winced, imagining what they'd been through with the birds. "What happened?"

"We had to...improvise. We couldn't catch them, so we lured them along with us again. But this time, we're almost out of scraps, and they're getting angry. One of the boys had to run home and scrounge a loaf of bread when we ran low on bait. Open the container."

The man with the bread pulled some slices of bread out and tore them into small pieces, then flung them onto the ground near the container.

Clarence couldn't help but consider the last time he'd seen broken bread. It had been at church as part of the sacrament, representing the body of Christ. The bishop's talk about praying for a miracle dominated his thoughts. Maybe this was it. It didn't look like a miracle. The birds weren't here to eat a cricket infestation.

All he saw was a bunch of guys teasing seagulls into a raging frenzy.

There were a lot more birds than bits of bread, so the gulls squawked and batted their wings at each other as they fought over the bread.

Another handful of bread scattered near the open container door, drawing the birds closer.

As the last bits of tossed bread vanished, the man with the bread gathered up the rest of the shredded loaf and tossed double handfuls into the back of the container.

The angry birds swarmed in after the bread, and Clarence slammed the door shut. The metal walls of the container were not thick enough to muffle the rage of the birds as they fought for scraps in the dark.

It was time. "Everyone, scatter. Get to your farms, your homes, anywhere but here. Go around the long way so the elf scouts don't see you."

Peter waved everyone on their way to walk or ride horses home, but then climbed and sat beside Clarence on his wagon.

"I said, go."

Peter grimaced, then smiled. "I wouldn't miss this for anything. I'll even go unarmed if I have to."

"Fine. Leave your Hi-Point with someone, and you can ride along."

Peter dropped off his pistol and its worn holster with a straggler from his seagull team, then climbed back up beside Clarence. "You don't like my gun?"

"The Yugo of the gun world? Nah, you're fine. It suits you."

"Got that straight. I've put a thousand rounds

through it over the years. I think you're jealous."

They argued the pros and cons of different pistols as they made their way to the elf camp with the container. It kept their minds off all the ways they could die before the day was out.

Clarence prayed the wind would cool the container enough to make up for the sunshine's warmth. Too many things could go wrong with this. If he failed, he wouldn't be coming home. Maybe he should have let Peter keep his pistol to take an extra elf or two with them.

It was too late to change anything now. He was running on faith. He'd done what he could to look like he was meeting the demands of Dasan while putting up whatever obstacles he could. He'd done as much as he could to keep his people safe and supplied.

He wasn't naïve enough to think that's all it would take for plans to work. Being right didn't guarantee him success. Miracles didn't appear on demand, either. He and Peter were on their own, and his plan still had holes big enough to swallow him and his whole town.

"Well, Peter, I know we haven't seen eye to eye ever since you married my sister. I just wanted to tell you it's been a pleasure knowing you. At least occasionally."

"Giving up, are you? Screw that. You wanted my help. You asked me to help with sacrificing my house, your sister's house, without even asking her. Then you asked me to gather the birds. You know, that's the first time it sounded like you trusted me to do more than tie my shoes. Just get me there. I've got an idea. We either get our wheat back a little worse for wear, or we put the fear of God into them. Bird poop won't keep us from using it as seed grain in the spring."

The drop-off point, normally empty as far as the eye could see, held a delegation of elves.

Peter said, "Good. Now we won't have to wait for them to show up."

Most of the delegation looked familiar, but there was one elf Clarence was sure he'd never seen. His immaculate gold and green clothing set him apart, and the other elves deferred to him, even Dasan and his subordinate commander, Telles.

Clarence whispered to Peter, "I don't know what you planned, but this isn't the place for heroics. You didn't sneak your gun along, did you?"

"I'd love nothing more than to plug them all, but no. Just get me close enough for them to hear me." Peter's voice dropped until Clarence could barely hear him.

"If this is some noble sacrifice, we can rebuild your house. Don't go getting yourself killed. We can work things out."

Clarence pulled the horse team to a halt.

"I don't plan to die today, but if I do, it's up to you to make this pay off. Don't get down." Peter stepped onto the packed dirt of the drop-off area with an exaggerated limp as he made his way toward the elves with his scratched hands spread out and his head bowed.

"I beg you. Don't open the container. Let us take it back. It was the birds! They attacked."

The new elf gave a curious look to the company commander. "What is this about? You were commanded to deliver grain, and now this human is warning us. Explain."

Dasan looked to the sky for a moment with his jaw clenched, a look of fury growing by the moment. "They've been sabotaging us at every turn. Spoiled grain. Short deliveries. Now they're making up a new story. They must have shorted us again, and they're looking for a way out. The threat of losing more of their homes must not have been a sufficient motivator. Allow me to kill them as an example, and we will take full control of their deliveries."

"And have elves do the work of slaves? Are you able to meet my demands, or not, Dasan?"

Clarence couldn't tell if leaving off the rank was an insult or not, but Dasan's rage grew as he stormed over to the container, released the door clasps and swung them both open wide.

Grain spilled out at his feet after having settled in transit. But Clarence had only a moment to notice before pandemonium erupted.

Gulls screeched and flew past Dasan, with some slamming into him on their way to freedom. The angry gulls had been chased with nets, escaped capture, and had then been lured into a dark container and hauled for several bumpy miles. Reason fled as they erupted through the doors.

Peter screeched and covered his head as he collapsed onto the ground. "They're back! Don't let them near you. It's divine justice!"

The new elf twitched, but remained standing as he watched the birds. "Dasan, explain yourself."

Dasan fell back from the container, landing in a heap before scrambling backwards. He stood and ran back to kneel before his commander. "They told me of a local legend where the gulls saved their ancestors after they performed a ritual of some sort involving prayer and sacrifices. They weren't supposed to have magic here."

"Silence, fool!" The visiting commander waved a

hand, and both Dasan and Telles howled in pain for a moment then turned to stone. He eyed the seagulls as if preparing to destroy them or drive them away, but they had already fled as fast as their wings would carry them. His clenched fist dropped to his side.

With a brief disdainful glance at Peter, he turned to the guard. "If you value your lives, you will take this delivery and bring it with you when you break camp. We can feed slaves with it if nothing else. You're returning with me. Your commander failed to control the situation. Don't fail me again."

Peter must have grown a lot of common sense since he remained motionless, prostrated on the ground until the visiting elvish commander stormed out of sight.

With nobody but a handful of jittery guards about, Clarence closed the container, tilted the trailer, and dropped the container to the ground. Peter climbed back up to sit with Clarence, and they were on their way with hearts racing.

Peter's breath slowed, and he said, "Not what I was expecting. Who was that?"

"No idea. I suspected Dasan had his orders, and was collecting supplies for his commander. I don't know how far up the chain this goes, or when they'll be back to lean on us again. My bet is that they're not leaving for good. They're just regrouping. We have to take whatever we can from the harvest and leave for somewhere even farther off the beaten path before they figure out they've been had. I hear the valleys north of Bear Lake are still a neutral area. Not worth their effort to spread out that far."

"Right. You'll still have some who refuse to move. I've got nothing to pack, but I'm coming back up here after the elves move out."

"That sounds like the old Peter that did a lot of stupid things."

Peter shook his head. "Nah. All I want is to pick up two elf statues for target practice. It's the only time I'll be able to shoot one and live to tell the tale. Think they'll leave them behind?"

On the way home, the straight road once again gave Clarence plenty of time to think. Nothing had worked out as planned. Had it been a miracle, or had they stumbled their way into a solution that saved the lives of everyone in town through sheer luck? He knew which side of that argument Bishop Taylor would come down on. It all depended on if you believed in winged justice and the power of prayer.

John M. Olsen edits and writes speculative fiction across multiple genres and he loves stories about ordinary people stepping up to do extraordinary things. He loves to create and fix things, whether editing or writing novels or short stories or working in his secret lair equipped with dangerous power tools. In all cases, he applies engineering principles and processes to the task at hand, often in unpredictable ways.

He lives in Utah with his lovely wife and a variable number of grown children and a constantly changing subset of extended family. Check out his ramblings on his blog. Safety goggles are optional but recommended.

The North Way

By Cedar Sanderson

If you drive into Alaska, when you could drive in, before the Invasion, the first stop for lodging and civilization is Tok, sixty miles in from the border. There is a gas station before you get that far, where the Forty-Mile Highway splits off and heads over a lot of remote and lonely muskeg to wind up in Dawson, Yukon Territory, Canada. And there is a small trading post before you reach that. They don't stock groceries, and you can't get gas for your vehicle. It's a low building once full of military surplus and furs. When the military surplus market dried up due to Uncle Sam's changes in supply policy, the store stocks shrank, but there was always a trade in goods. Up there, far away from the supply chain, there's always a need for things, and you make do, do without, or build what you need.

That's Northway. And it's the way of the North.

"Will a rocket launcher take one out?"

Mike looked up from the catalog he was reading. It was older than the young man standing on the other side of the glass display case that doubled as a counter. He wasn't reading it with an eye to order, any more than the kid was asking with a thought of buying a rocket launcher.

"Hell if I know." Mike satisfied himself with this for an answer. "We can't take cards."

The kid had laid down a flimsy folding knife, and a beat-up Vietnam War era canteen, on the counter.

"I know that. The Internet's down, phones are down, life sucks and then you die."

Mike took the bill the kid pulled from a wad from his

pocket.

"Could be worse."

"What?" For the first time, he had the full attention of the customer. The kid's eyes were hazel.

"Could be a fairy slave. Worse than a good clean death." Mike slid the change back across the counter. "Want a bag for that?"

The young man shivered, then focused again. "Nah. Thanks."

Mike waited until the hurried footsteps left the porch, then settled back into his stool, and turned the page. They'd come, eventually. Busy mopping up the cities. Would be a different experience when they got out this far if they ever bothered. Magic or no magic, they could be killed.

The bell hung over the door frame jangled, and he looked up.

"Mike." The heavily bearded man pulled off his knit cap.

"George." Mike nodded. "You heard?"

"Ayuh. We figure one run, dead of night, might get past the patrols. But after that..." He waggled a hand. "Starts to get real squirrely for any big shipments."

"Dad said the same thing." Mike reached under the counter. "He said to hand you this."

The rifle wasn't new. The boxes of ammo Mike put next to it weren't either. They were reloads. New ammo wasn't a thing, not in Alaska post-invasion. Even gunpowder was in shorter and shorter supply.

What was next, Mike had wondered aloud during a long planning session in his parent's basement, the walls lined with his Dad's gun collection, sword fighting and hand to hand combat? The elves seemed to prefer that, but it was all advantage to them when a human had to stoop to that level.

"I'll make every shot count." George promised, checking to make sure the shotgun was loaded. "Strange to be getting help from Russia."

"Not Russia anymore," Mike pointed out, sitting back down. His hip was crumbling, but he'd put off surgery and now he regretted that procrastination. There was a doc in town, hiding out, but no OR. Just one of many reasons to make sure the elves didn't get a foothold here. They took and took and wanted more. "Siberia, or more correctly, warlords loosely allied and willing to trade over the Bering Strait. Does feel... wrong."

He was too young to have been in the military during the Cold War, but Alaskan memories ran long, and winter nights were made for storytelling.

"I'll collect Chris and head out as soon as it gets dark. Ice was creaking on the Tanana."

"Ice out in three days, Alyce says. She's got the sight, that woman." Mike shook his head. "I swear she has called it for the last twenty years if not more."

"Means they'll come soon." George opened the door, setting the bell off again. "See ya 'round."

Mike gave him a sardonic good wish for the mission. "Try not to use up all the ammo."

After the door closed, Mike stared into space for a while. First time in his life, he wasn't looking forward to the warmth of summer.

***

"When life hands you lemons," Chris grunted under

the effort of lifting his end of the wooden crate. It smelled faintly of petroleum products and was so roughly finished he was grateful for the protection of the leather gloves he was wearing. Once the crate was up and they had it moving, he finished. "Build a lemonade stand."

"And then the local council shows up to demand sales taxes and shuts you down for lack of proper permits." George grinned, white teeth flashing through his full beard.

"Well, yeah, but..." Chris had a little beard envy. He'd never been able to manage more than a few scraggly hairs on his chin. He'd have settled for a Fu Manchu, but no joy. He was doomed to be a baby face. "Not out here, man."

"Problem with out here." They reached the stack of crates they'd been making all morning, "Is finding customers."

"No shit?" George stretched and looked around. They were in a tiny clearing of the dense forest, and where they hadn't put down pallets, stacked two deep in staggered layers, the mud was ankle-deep. The road they'd carefully brought the big truck up in the predawn darkness, backing it all the way, was deeply rutted. There had been more than one close call where Chris thought it'd be more stuck than they could dig out. Getting it back out would be easier. He hoped.

More to George's point, there was no one else anywhere around. Just the two of them, the nearly empty truck, and the impressive stack of crates with their Cyrillic stenciling.

"Build it and they will come?" Chris laughed. "Let's get a move on with the last crates and then we can scoot.

Chances of overflight are low but not impossible."

"Ayuh." George walked with him back to the truck, his boots squelching in the muck. "This is where the contact said to make the drop. And when life gives you a shipment of arms out of Siberia, you do what the anonymous voice on the other end of the phone says."

At least they didn't have to worry about government spy satellites now. No, just big damn dragons... Chris shot a wary glance at the clear blue sky.

"We're lucky to still have cell service at all." He pointed out. "Mike said the Lower 48 is plunging back into the dark ages."

"That's an exaggeration." George bent his knees and waited for Chris to grab his end of the crate. "Pretty sure there's still electricity. In places."

"Well, I know there hasn't been a ferry from Seattle in a while."

The Alaskan boreal forest is an interesting place. Dwarfed by the permafrost mere feet from the surface, and at times when the ice lay only inches below the open water of the muskeg, non-existent, the spruce trees grew columnar with spiky branches reaching out in all directions, never heavy enough to shear and fall when dead due to lack of sun and stress. Other parts of it were more open, with thick layers of moss spangled in aethereal pink blooms of twinflower. Moose and bear pass through it near soundlessly. Rare is the human that can manage that. Most men chose to tackle the interior of Alaska from roads, or at least tracks hewn through the wilderness by long-ago bulldozers that left a mark kept open by those moose grazing on the willows that sprang up in succession.

It's a merciless place. The cold in the winter would

kill you. The mosquitoes in the summer will drive you mad. And yet, humans have inhabited it for as long as stories have been told. Adapting to their surroundings and stripping away the unnecessary trappings of refined civilization, because such things took time and energy they could not spare. Here, somewhere just north of the Tanana River, they planned to hunker down and wait, until the invaders got tired of the many ways Alaska can kill you. But they also planned to become like the mosquitoes, and madden the invaders...

"Right. Ready, George?" Chris looked around. Still, no movement in the woods.

"Ah, I'm gonna look."

"But that's not..."

George wasn't listening. He levered open one of the crates with a big screwdriver he'd grabbed out of the truck. Now, they both peered into the box.

"Well." Chris let out a low whistle. "Wonder if that'll take down a warg?"

"I don't think they are wargs, you know. More like gigantic wolves."

Chris, not to be deterred from his original question, reached into the crate to touch the round metal tube they could see. "Oh, this would totally take down a wolf."

"Not when it's protected by magic." George lowered the screwdriver, and Chris yanked his hand back before it was caught by the heavy wood. "It's not that easy."

"Nothing ever is."

They looked around one more time, but other than the chickadees and red squirrels there were no signs of life.

"Let's get the truck back." George shrugged his shoulders. There was an itchy spot on his back, and he kept telling himself that it wasn't someone watching, just needed a scratch.

"Ok." Chris ambled towards the passenger door. He, at least, didn't seem to be concerned.

It was a lot faster to get the truck out than it had been to back it in. George still drove slowly, aware that the mud in the ruts might be a lot deeper than it looked, and knowing there was no real hurry at this stage. That came later. After they washed the mud off the truck before returning it to the business it belonged to. No point in leaving stupid easy clues.

***

The watcher, understanding this, stayed where he had been the entire time. It hadn't been any trouble to conceal himself when the truck's engine rumbled earlier, and now he lay there, chin propped on folded hands, and leaned into the cold seeping through his heavy clothing. He lay on a folded oilcloth so stained and faded it blended well with the moss, and he was back far enough from the crude clearing to be out of sight under the thick spruce growth.

He could afford to be patient. He had all the time in the world.

***

Mike looked up when the bell tinkled, as though he hadn't heard the engine laboring up the driveway.

"Mornin' Walter," he greeted the old man who stepped through the door, sliding off his stool at the same time. He straightened, stiffly.

"Sit down, boy, I know you hurt."

"Sir." Mike did as he was told. Walter Northway walked closer, his dark eyes scanning the younger man's body shrewdly.

"What can I do for you, Walter?" Mike asked after an awkward pause.

"Need to set up a meeting." Walter was never one for a preamble. He'd been heard to explain it, once, and that had been passed down for generations. He only had so much time, he'd said, no point in wasting it.

"Yes, sir?" Mike knew there would be more, but it was impossible to hurry Walter, paradoxically. He might not want to waste words, but he spent much more time thinking them through than almost anyone Mike had ever met.

"Your Dad, Steve, and you better come." Walter named Mike's older brother.

"Where?"

"Here. Going to be someone needs to meet on neutral ground, but also somewhere shows we trust them."

Mike took a breath. The store's role in the community here in the Bush, tenuous as it was, meant this could jeopardize...

"Don't worry. Won't be soon and you'll have notice to make the place look half-empty and no-one around."

"We can do that."

They had already done most of it, moving the stock around to different buildings or even off the property, so a casual check would make it look like there was little of value there at the shop.

"Good. I'll send word."

Walter paused, and Mike held his tongue. Something about the old man always made him feel like he needed a trim and a haircut, and he felt the urge to babble. He sat straight and ignored the warning twinge in his hip.

"You are serving the human race, Mike. Never doubt that. Those are coming who would eradicate it, end our stories, and wield all power for themselves. Even so, we fight. And you fight with us, from your stool. Eh?"

Mike felt his cheeks flush and hoped the beard would hide it. "I do what I can, sir."

Walter nodded and left with as little ceremony as he had come. Mike, in the empty store, slipped off the tall stool and rubbed down the muscles that were threatening to spasm above the stump of his leg. The heavy prosthetic helped him to stand and walk, but it took a toll. Like everything did these days, it seemed. He'd ordered a new leg, before... and it hadn't shown up. A lot of stuff hadn't. Stuck a couple thousand miles away, he guessed. Or it could be as close as Anchorage, but with the portal opened there so the elves, fairies, whatever they were could take the military bases, it might as well be on the surface of Mars.

The muscles relented under the strength of his hands, and he tried a few steps, walking around the counter and over to the door. He hadn't heard Walter's truck leave, but he'd been a little distracted at the time. Risking looking foolish, he opened the heavy door and looked out.

The lot was empty. Across the graded gravel was the main house, and down the drive a bit was the bunkhouse where he slept alone now. He'd shared with his brothers for many years, and like them had moved away until just recently. Dan hadn't been heard from since the portal opened in Anchorage. Steve was in Tok. Mike watched the lights go on in the main house. Mom would be making supper, and riding herd on the grandchildren, who'd been moved out here for the duration. Further away from towns, they'd all decided, the better. That wasn't a problem for Miriam, who adored her grandchildren and promptly put them all to work around the place. Even two-year old Chuck had a chore, even if his was just making sure any pins his twelve-year-old cousin Nellie dropped while learning to sew didn't stay on the floor.

With six children in it, plus his parents, the main house was full to the bursting. And now, Walter wanted to bring some kind of special meeting here. Mike's stomach twisted. They'd have to move the kids, again. It was too much of a risk to have them here. He didn't know where they'd go... moose camp. He'd send everyone but Dad to moose camp.

***

The Alaska Highway passes through Tok, Alaska, on its way to Fairbanks, where it comes to an end. At Tok, there is a fork in the road, with the locals referring to the long, 700-some mile highway stretching to Anchorage as the Cutoff. This makes Tok, otherwise an unassuming small town deep in the interior, somewhat important if you want to move something overland from the lower part of the North American continent. In addition to this, there is the Tok International Airport, a small airstrip a short hop (in air travel terms) from the Canadian border.

It seemed likely, the residents thought, that at some point the Fae War would come to them, along the roads. The long bitter Alaskan winter had kept them sheltered, but now, with Breakup coming, that respite would end.

Some had already left, abandoning their home with as much as they could take, going anywhere they thought would be safer. Others hunkered down, hoping that staying out of sight would save them. And still others grimly prepared for a fight they knew they could not win, but to die without fighting seemed a waste. At least, they hoped, they could take one of the bastards with them.

When the squad of orcs trotted up the highway from the general direction of Anchorage, then, they found a half-deserted town. It wasn't until they had gotten as far into town as the Tok Lodge that they finally encountered a human.

Deila Samson, who'd cursed her mother for her name more than once, and she knew it was Ma's fault, since neither of them had a clue who Deila's father had been, looked up from behind the registration desk when the doors swung open. It was unusual for both to open at once, but not unheard of, so she wasn't overly concerned. Not that it was in Deila's nature to be concerned. That's why she was still here, still doing her job, even if she was only being paid in a place to sleep and food from the Lodge's kitchens. That, and IOUs both she and her boss knew were worth the paper they were written on. Still. It was better than nothing. Better than moving back in with Ma.

"Can I help..." The words died in her throat.

The three orcs looked down at her. They had to duck to fit through the doors, and that was something, since the Lodge had been built at some point in the misty past when there was money in Tok. The ceilings were tall, which meant the floors were cold in winter, and the doors were made to scale. The two shoulder-to-shoulder in front were squeezed together to fit through the double doors. They ignored her squeak of fright and surprise, then peeled off in opposite directions, swords drawn, eyes restless. The third orc, taller than the others by a full head crowned with grizzled hair, locked eyes with her and stalked towards Deila, who felt a wave of terror and then everything went all gray and sparkly before fading to black.

She woke up to the orc and the cook standing over her.

"Take me to the leader." The orc said, in guttural but clear English.

The cook made a high gibbering sound, and Deila could smell urine and see the stain on his pants. She sat up. "Can't you see he's 'bout scared to death?"

The orc looked way, way down at her. "I thought you were dead."

"Well," she sniffed, "I ain't. You want a leader?"

"Yes."

"What kinda leader?" Deila folded her arms over her chest. "Cause I'm 'Murican, and Christian, and Tok don't really have a leader, it's gotta council."

"Ah." He seemed to understand that. "A spiritual and symbolic leader will do."

"Walter Northway." Delia nodded. "You want Walter. Unless you're gonna kill him?"

He blinked. "Would it not have been better to ask that first?"

"I'm under a little pressure here!" Delia threw her hands up. "Y'can't 'spect me to think clearly!"

The orc shook his head. "Where can I find Walter Northway?"

"Are you gonna kill him?" Deila squinted up at him.

"No."

"How do I know I can trust you?"

"You don't." The orc now folded his arms over his chest, muscles bulging under his greenish chest. "Perhaps ask yourself how I can speak your language, and why I would have bothered learning such a tongue?"

She brightened. "You want to make a deal."

The orc just tipped his head slightly, and she took that as assent. "He's in Northway."

The orc scowled, his lips revealing even more of the long tusks that protruded from his mouth. "Do you make a jest at me?"

"What's that mean?"

"I will not be made a fool." He put a hand on the hilt of his big sword. Thing. She'd seen the other two orcs shifting behind him, and those steel whatsits didn't look like any sword she'd ever seen. Not even on TV.

"No, the village elder is named for the village. Er. Sort of. Anyway, Northway's down towards Canada 'bout an hour. Uh, that's in a car. You drive cars?"

"We do not." He turned and barked something in a strange language to his minions, who shoved their sword-things back into scabbards and then left through the big double doors again. "We may take you with us."

"Me?" Delia squeaked again.

Their conversation was interrupted as the cook, who had been quietly whimpering, collapsed to the floor like a dropped bag of potatoes, his eyes rolled back in his head.

"I can hardly expect him to give me directions. Or." The orc looked back into her eyes. "Drive a truck for us."

***

Delia refused to drive the box truck that was used for deliveries from the grocery store across the road. Chris and George would have recognized it.

"Look," she explained patiently to the orc-in-charge, who also seemed to be the only one who spoke English. "You won't all fit. Even standing up. Let's go get the school bus, and that will work."

"What is...?"

"Huh, you sound so educated. Well, it's bigger than the truck. And it has seats, so all your..." She gestured loosely. They were standing outside in the parking lot, now. The cook had been left to his own devices, although Delia had taken a moment to put a rolled-up towel under his neck to make sure he was comfortable. She'd figured out the orcs needed her, and her natural equilibrium had been restored. "Um, orcs can ride comfortably."

"We do not need comfort." He retorted stiffly. "We are warriors."

"I'm sure you are. I'm grateful I'm not fightin' you. But still, wouldn't it be nicer than shoving them all in so they are poking one another?" She pointed at the hilt of a sword-thing, which she had no word for, jutting out from the belt of the nearest fighting orc to her.

"How far is this school bus?"

"'Bout a mile thataway." She gestured to the north and east. "Reckon you walked this far, that's no trouble."

"Where do you think we walked from?" The big orc was doing that deadpan stare again. He'd never smiled, but there had been a certain release of tension in his face that had reassured Delia.

"Well, they said the elves had opened one a'them portals in Anchorage. That's about eight hours drive from here."

"Hm." He didn't give her another answer, but turned to face the group of orcs and barked an order.

"Hey, I can't walk that far." Delia protested when they formed into a loose square and started to trot away. "And how do they know where to go?"

"I shall go with you in your conveyance." The orc turned back to her. "They will follow."

"Oh, guess we'd better hurry." She pulled her keys out of her pocket. "I dunno how you're going to fit in my car."

Even with the seat pushed all the way back, the orc was nearly folded into thirds, plus overlapping into her space. He smelled of leather and woodsmoke and something she couldn't name. She drove carefully, guessing it was his first time in a car, and once she'd caught up with the squad, she drove around them on the deserted road and then pulled in front of them, trying to keep a reasonable speed to let them stay close behind her. Feeling a bit like the whole thing was a parade and she was driving the clown car, Delia crawled down the road. No one took a potshot at them.

That was the biggest surprise. There was no other human in sight. Like it had been planned, only if it had, no one had told her. Was she the scapegoat? She clenched the wheel tighter and tried not to push down on the accelerator. These orcs seemed to be uninterested in pillage and murder and other things. She hadn't even thought about those sorts of things until now. She stole a sideways glance at the huge orc in her passenger seat. He was looking out the side window, his face back to the relaxed mode. No, that didn't seem to be his intent.

She pulled into the maintenance road for the school, rather than the main parking lot.

"You'll have to break into the bus yard." She informed him when she'd pulled up alongside the gate to that. It was surrounded by an eight-foot chain link fence. It served to keep people out, and bears. Mostly.

"Yes." He took a moment to extricate himself from the car, and grimaced as he stretched back up to his full height. "That is a school bus?"

She didn't correct his pronunciation. There had to be a limit to his patience, after all. "Yes."

"Better size for orc." He trotted back down the road towards his orcs. Delia stood by her car, wondering if he'd just made a joke.

***

Mike twitched. He was standing on the stoop of the shop, looking down the driveway. A car had just turned up from the highway. On any given day this would have been no big deal. Today, he turned his head towards the main house, glaring. They hadn't gotten the kids packed up and off to camp yet. Steve was on his way, bringing antibiotics with him, since the 4-year-old Chase had an ear infection. They would leave once Steve was here. Would have left...

The car came around the corner and Mike relaxed. He knew that beat-up truck.

"Darrin." He greeted the young man with the thick black hair.

Darrin shut off the engine and talked through the open window. "They are coming. Marched into Tok about two hours ago."

"Shit." Mike did the mental math. Steve should be up within minutes, but... "How long until they get here?"

"They march about six miles an hour. Stop every two hours. Stop two hours before dark to camp and eat." Darrin shrugged. "Tomorrow. Midday, maybe."

Mike looked over the top of the truck, at the sky to the north, where Tok was, and thought about it. "All right. We will be ready. Thanks, Darrin."

"Don't mention it. I was never here." The young man flashed a big grin which revealed he was missing at least one tooth. "I'll let Walter know."

"Know what?" Mike shook his head, smiling in spite of himself.

The pickup started and Darrin made the turn in the gravel lot without hitting Mom's flowers. He knew better than to incur her wrath with that. They might be facing orcs, but Mom could really hurt you.

Once the truck's engine was out of hearing, the main house door opened and Dad stepped out, a shotgun on his shoulder, and a bandolier of shells slung over one shoulder.

"They coming?"

Mike nodded, limping towards the old man. Dad's cheeks looked more sunk in than they had, and his steel-gray hair stood on end.

"Tomorrow, Walter thinks. They are marching from Tok."

"We'll send your mother and the kids to camp now."

"What about the meds?"

"Steve can send them with one of the boys."

They heard another engine coming off the highway, and both turned to look. Before the vehicle even came into view, they had both recognized it and relaxed.

"Won't have to wait, then." Mike commented as his brother's truck rounded the corner.

"I'll tell the boys to bring the Argos 'round." Dad shouldered the shotgun again.

The six-wheeled off-road vehicles would hold four each, leaving little room for supplies when fully loaded, and requiring two of the kids to ride in the back cargo area. Six kids, Mom, and Aunty Gus from the village, in three of the vehicles. It was going to be tight.

"Mom will get a moose." He said to himself, as Steve shut off the truck and rummaged on the passenger side. They wouldn't starve. Hunting season was now whenever they were hungry, at least.

"Need a hand?" Mike moved slowly around to the passenger side.

"As much as you need a leg." His older brother slid out of the truck. "Grab a box of that ammo, won't you?"

Mike looked into the footwell, which was packed tightly with vintage olive-drab ammo cans. He pursed his lips into a whistle. "Where did all of this come from?"

"We evacuated Tok." Steve sounded tired now that he wasn't trying to make a joke. "Sent as many as we could up toward Moon Lake, some to Tetlin. Hoping that as it's off the highway, they won't notice it."

Tetlin didn't have any roads to it. The Tanana River cut it off from the Alaska Highway, and boggy muskeg made a road from Tok financially idiotic. The supplies flew in, in summer, and over the river by snowmachine in winter. Or dog sleds.

"Quite likely, unless they really do have eyes in the sky."

"I think someone would notice a dragon. Not like

some far-off government satellite."

"Unless they are running those, now." Mike shrugged. He grabbed a can with both hands. "So, what goodies have we got here?"

"Five."

Steve was interrupted by a flood of excited children pouring out of the front door. They were followed by their mother, the dog, and finally his father.

"Dad!" One of them shrieked, and suddenly Steve had his arms full of four offspring.

"Josh." their grandfather barked. "Go get the Argos. Gus, go with him and Carla."

Steve ruffled his oldest son's hair and said something quietly, then the boy took off for the garage.

"I have Chase's meds, Mom." He held out a bag. "The clinic is shut for the duration, they sent some other stuff along. And Mike, there's a box to be kept here in the shop."

Mike nodded. He'd put the ammo box down to help with the kids, so he'd have to move all those things. But not until the kids were safely off on their way.

Mom gave Steve a hug, then handed him back the bag. "Help Gus load, please. Mike, can you tie the beast up?"

Mike whistled, and Stash wiggled his way over, his tail going a mile a minute.

"Come on, boy. You're going to get stepped on."

Stash knew the drill, and relented in his attempt to jump on Mike, or get back to the mass of children - there were only four at the moment, but it seemed to be double that number. They certainly made enough noise for several times their number. That, and the three Argos come up from the big garage down behind the house, buried the sound of the approaching vehicle.

The yellow bus came around the corner before any of them knew it was there. Only Stash, who had just been clipped to his run, pricked up his ears. Even he didn't make a fuss... because he knew that engine.

"Schoo'!" Little Chase greeted it with outstretched arms. He was too young to go, but he'd been there every morning to see his siblings off on their long rides.

Delia popped out of the doors, her arms raised.

"Nobody panic!" She shouted.

They all stared at her. The orc that stepped off the bus made its springs bounce a little.

"I have come for peace." He announced.

The orc's sudden arrival generated a chorus of shrieks and squeals from the children, who fled as a body towards the house. Stash went crazy barking and lunging at the end of his lead. The off-road vehicles breasted the rise behind the house with a roar. Dad shouldered his shotgun and was moving his finger to the trigger when Steve batted the barrel upwards.

"Dad! We were supposed to have a meeting here, remember?"

"A meeting isn't those... those..." His father ran out of words.

"Mom, go inside and call Walter." They still had a landline, had never had anything else, since there were no cell towers anywhere near enough to have a reliable signal. Steve turned away and started towards the bus, keeping his hands out away from his sides, but not raising them. He wasn't going to give the impression of surrender. Behind him, his father let the barrel of the shotgun track downward again, until it was pointed at the orc. He kept his finger off the trigger, though.

Mike came around Steve's truck and fell in beside him as they walked silently towards the two people outside the bus. He could see, now, there were a lot more in the bus. Very big, hulking shapes were visible through dusty windows.

"You said you came in peace." Steve spoke when they had reached a close enough distance for easy speech.

"I said 'for peace' as we came in war, to your plane." The orc corrected in a very precise English accent. "We came with those who had enslaved us. Who would use us to fight for them once they had broken our spirits through defeat in battle."

"You want to join forces with us."

"We would like to find a way to drive them back where they came from." The orc inclined his head. "To whom am I speaking?"

"Steve." The human male put his hand out. "Just Steve. And you are?"

The orc looked at the hand, then at Steve.

"You shake his hand." Delia had been standing there with her hands on her hips, head moving back and forth as they spoke. "Like this." She stepped around the orc and took Steve's hand in a handshake, then stepped away. "It's a greeting, but also to show you're not meanin' to hurt the other guy."

Mike opened his mouth to correct her, then closed it again, with a shake of his head. She wasn't far enough wrong that he was going to complicate this already surreal situation.

"We came to meet Walter Northway."

Steve kept holding out his hand. "If we say you're ok, he'll come here to meet you."

Mike blinked. That hadn't been part of the plan. Then again, neither had the orcs showing up in a Tok school bus driven by a receptionist.

"There were small humans when we arrived." The orc was looking over Steve's shoulder.

"My children." Steve bared his teeth in something not even a creature from another world would think was a smile. "We meant to have them well away."

"You are wise. We will do them no harm. Our own children are... unreachable. As our wives and families are. Hostages."

The orc lifted his hand, abruptly, and clasped Steve's forearm. "We have no choices. We must abandon our inclinations and duty, to reclaim our honor."

Mike tensed. His brother and the orc speaker locked eyes for long enough to make Delia shift nervously off to the side.

"I'll call for Walter." Steve released the orc's forearm. "You never gave me your name."

"When your leader has arrived, then I shall reveal it."

The orc folded his arms over his chest and looked off into the distance.

Steve turned to Mike. "Go talk to Mom. I'll stay here." He looked at Delia. "I need to talk to you."

Delia flicked a nervous glance up at the orc, who had stilled enough to be a statue, and was paying no attention to the conversation happening literally under his nose.

"Uh, ok?"

"Did you willingly bring them here?" Steve took a step toward her.

"They said they needed a driver, and I was the only person left in town, it looked like."

"You didn't hear the evacuation order?"

She shook her head. "I figured if I did as they said, they might not kill me. Or... other things."

"Uh." Steve looked up at the orc, who was still ignoring them. "So, you brought them here to kill us?"

"No! They said they wanted the leader. I figure they wanted to talk."

"Why here, though?"

"I don't know how to find Walter. I know how to find your family, and that you could tell me how to get there."

Steve closed his eyes for a moment. Then he took a deep breath. "Stay here, Delia. Don't come toward the house."

"Why? I gotta pee!" She did a little dance to emphasize this.

"There are trees. Over there." Steve gestured. "If you come toward the house, someone will shoot you."

She whimpered. Steve took a step back and looked at the windshield of the bus. The other orcs were very quiet there. None of them moved at all, which was remarkably good discipline. Better than human troops, he admitted to himself.

There was a quiet scuff of a footstep behind him, and his oldest son walked up next to him.

"James, please go inside."

"I want to meet the orc, Dad." His son crossed his arms over his chest and stared up at the impassive orc, who was gazing off into the distance. "Someday I'll be fighting alongside them, and I want to know what kinda people they are."

Something in that sentence got the orc war leader's full attention. He looked down at the teenager, who looked back up at him without flinching at the green-gray skin, pebbled and rough like it was covered in lichens, the twisted tusks stained yellow along their length where they projected out of his thin lips. He opened that mouth now.

"You are a child."

James elevated his chin in pride. "Not anymore. Now we are at war."

The orc shifted his gaze, glowing golden eyes intent, to Steve.

"You were sending the children away when we came."

"We were." Steve bit out, each word an effort. "And still going to."

"Wise. And you, young warrior, were riding out to keep them safe?"

They couldn't have missed the Argos as they had been visible for a moment before parking behind the house out of sight, not to mention the noise of the engines.

"I was."

"Good. Such a mission is good learning, and you can practice, until we fight elbow-to-elbow." The orc extended a huge hand, tipped in blacked talons. "I look forward to those battles, young James."

James put out his slender, tanned hand and shook, somewhat awkwardly with the size difference and unfamiliar custom to the orc.

"Now that your father will think less of me for digging below your discipline, you should ride, but I would be honored if you would take a small token of our agreement."

The orc shot a look, and what might have been a

wink, at Steve, before lifting a necklace over his head. One of many he wore, it was leather cording twisted and waxed, with a dull gray pebble knotted into it, and a pair of speckled feathers tied on a few inches away from the stone.

James looked at his father, and Steve took a deep breath, then let it out slowly before nodding.

James took the necklace from the orc and paused. He shoved a hand in his pocket.

"And I don't have anything fancy, but here." He pulled his fist out and shoved his hand towards the leader, opening his fingers to reveal his pocket knife, a mid-sized folder with a black plastic handle. He'd lost too many in his short life to have yet been trusted with a good knife.

"I accept." The knife looked like a toy on the orc's palm. "I have your name, James, son of Steve. Mine is Re'Druas, son of V'dic."

"Pleased to meet you, sir. I guess I'd better go now."

"Safe travels. Keep the young ones well, they are all of our future." The orc's mouth tipped down, his sorrow visible to both the humans. "Such we shall fight for. Endure." He pressed his fist to his chest.

"Uh... We will endure." James imitated him, then hurried away.

Steve looked up at the orc instead of watching his son. "You have no children of your own?"

The sound of an engine slowing, then turning off the highway onto the long driveway made the orc's long ears twitch slightly. Steve recognized it as familiar and relaxed slightly. Walter was coming to them.

"We had children when the defeat at the hands of the elves took my tribe. Now?" He spread his massive hands wide, palms up. "They are on the other side, slaves, subject to punishment for our misdoings. We cannot assume they yet live."

Walter's nephew pulled up beside the school bus. Steve saw him peering through the windshield, wide-eyed.

"I'm sorry for that." Steve said. "I reckon that's why we mean to put up a fight as much as we can. Can't do much 'gainst magic, though."

Walter got out of the car, leaning on his cane, and the orc turned to meet him.

"Walter Northway."

"I am he." Walter peered up to look at him.

"I come to swear fealty." The orc dropped to one knee, his head bent.

"Even if I knew what that meant." Walter's voice was testy, and his eyes narrowed. "We need men who can fight with us, not bend their knee. So, stand up, or better yet, let's go sit on the porch and have a talk."

"Would your men like a... do you drink coffee?" Steve asked, shrugging.

Walter cackled. "Even if you do, don't drink his dad's brew. Strong enough to float a mule shoe, with the mule still attached!"

"I thought I was fluent in your language. I was wrong, and I am humbled." The orc stood up again. "I am... this is not the custom."

"Maybe not for you, or the elves." Walter leaned on his crossed hands, draped over the cane top. "We do this our way." The 'or not at all' was left unspoken and very clear.

"We are familiar with tea." The orc turned and made a gesture. The bus's springs creaked as several thousand pounds of meat in the form of orcs made their move to disembark.

"We've got some of that." Steve sounded dubious.

"Better see if your mother will agree to setting up tables out here." Walter squinted as orcs started to file off the bus. "I don't think they'll all fit inside."

***

Mike looked up at the bell's jingle. The door opening surprised him. There hadn't been the sound of an engine coming up the drive to give him fair warning.

The... person who came through the door set off his internal alarm bells, and he slid off the stool, casually resting his hands on the shelf under the top of the counter.

"Can I help you?"

"Perhaps." The familiar accent was orcish, but the orc wasn't one of the friendly ones. At least, so far as Mike knew. "Are you Mike?"

Well, they said the elves could read a man's mind. They also said tinfoil didn't help.

"Ayuh." Mike remained wary. The shaggy green exterior turned out to be a coat. A sort of ghillie suit, as he unfastened something and straightened up, so it fell to his sides and showed him to be small, for an orc, wiry and gray-haired with long thin braids falling down alongside his face. Orcs didn't grow beards, but this one's tusks came out top and bottom from his mouth, where the others usually just jutted upwards.

"The time has come to rain fire on the city."

Mike felt his eyebrows trying to climb off his forehead.

"Even if I knew what that meant..."

"The message is not for you." The old orc raised a hand. "I have been watching. Here, where you have the weapon that will make a difference. And there, where they are harried from every side by the wild animals and humans alike. The time has come. The Red Arrows are called to strike swiftly and unerringly."

"I don't..."

Mike was interrupted again, this time with a dismissive gesture.

"I am going back to my watching. You need only convey the message."

There was another jingle of the bell, and he was gone again.

Mike reached for the phone. It had been a long summer. The evacuation of Tok had to be carried out twice more, after that first encounter with the orc war party defecting to their side. That had been an interesting, for values of the word, parlay over mugs full of hot black tea, sitting on his parent's porch. It hadn't been until much later that the humans realized the deal was sealed before Walter had even showed up, by the trust and confidence of a child. Re'Druas wore James's knife, somehow braided into cords, around his neck. The children had been recalled from the camp, after a time, then sent there again, only this time with an honor guard of the orcs, to keep all of them from being seen in the village. There were no children, and few women, left in the village or town, now.

The leaves were turning gold on the aspen, and snow would follow the fall of the leaves. The cold would grip the land, and then... then would be the time to strike. The elves were not well-adapted to the arctic conditions. The orc tribe and their human allies were. It might, possibly, turn the balance to their favor.

"There was a weird old guy." Mike said without preamble. "Yeah, just now. Sure, see you then."

He hung up the phone. Even if there was someone listening in, it wouldn't be clear that he expected another visitor in about a half hour.

He was back on the stool, balancing a book in front of him against the cash register, when he heard the engine on the driveway. There was a short silence, then the bell told him someone was coming in.

"Howdy." Greg looked tired, deep dark hollows under his eyes. He'd lost Chris, his right-hand man, a month earlier in an attempted supply run. They didn't know exactly what happened, but it had provoked a convoy of enemies arriving in Tok, then passing through after a precursory search of some buildings. If Chris had talked, it had been to lie. The elf in charge found nothing in the almost-deserted town and had left again.

"Got a message to pass on." Mike didn't get up. Greg leaned against the counter. "Ready for it?"

"Ayuh." Greg had a small notebook in his hand. There was no point in not writing stuff down if the elves could just pull crap out of your head, he'd pointed out at one point during the planning. If they could, of course, do that easily then their resistance would be futile. It seemed they couldn't do it, or at least not all the time.

Mike repeated what the old orc had told him. "Got it?"

"I do. I'll run it by Walter. Little hard to get it to Re'Druas right now."

The orcs were several hours travel from the village.

"Yeah. I know. Well, can't be helped."

"At least we get to fight back, eh?" Greg straightened up, a grimace like a smile on his face.

"You think that's what this means?"

"I sure as hell hope so. We've got the capability to rain fire on 'em, although I dunno how your old dude knows that."

"That we do. Getting it in range is going to be tricky."

"We don't need horsepower. We got orc power!" Greg grinned savagely.

***

In the end, they did use a truck. The big diesel engine rumbled, but the sound was muffled with the falling snow, and even the sharp-eared orcs reported it couldn't be heard from more than a few hundred yards away. Certainly not a mile away, where the target lay sleeping.

The multiple rocket launcher system had been around, in its most basic form since the time of Napoleon. The Russians doted on the idea and had developed multiple versions over its decades of use in their wars, including the modular one that had been crated, shipped, and carefully reassembled before mounting onto a construction dump truck and brought to this place. When the signal came, they would fire forty-eight missiles with thermobaric tips, and a square kilometer of city would be obliterated. Humans would die. So would orcs, elves, and other invasive species who had crossed over with them.

The cold was their friend, and the snow. The orcs, wrapped in hides newly tanned and smoky from the fires they had been tending in small groups while the entire force gathered, were moving through it with the confidence of creatures born to the North. The Alaskans were moving with them, wearing arctic boots and holding rifles with hunting scopes that would allow them to deal death from a distance in the chaos following their single strike. It was all they could do. It would have to be enough.

It was time, and the roar of the rockets overhead made their hearts pound. They might never go home again, but they would damn sure make certain there would be a home under the flicker of the aurora borealis. The North gets in your blood, and it calls to the men who have walked under the midnight sun. The arctic creaks with ice, and those who can endure it, they linger. There is no other like the man who has wintered where nature kills all who are weak. The way of the North is lined with death, and in the distance the aurora whispers.

Cedar Sanderson's long and checkered career started with being paid in plants. Since then, she's come to prefer money, and has tried many ways to earn it: balloon twister, face painter, children's librarian, scientist, cosmetic chemist, author, artist, and many more. Currently she writes for a living with facts, and on the side she writes fiction for fun.

Author of ten novels, countless short stories, and a children's book, she has also edited an anthology, and illustrated five coloring books. A born researcher, Cedar's passion for reading metamorphosed into writing, fueled by her long interest in history, infectious disease, food anthropology, and human behavior. After her four children had reached a suitable age, Cedar returned to higher education and obtained a Bachelor's of Science in Forensic Science and Investigation with minors in Chemistry and Molecular Biology, which enabled her to finally display the credentials to match her passion for scientific research.

Hopper Station

By James Copley

Fifteen months after the invasion

The ancient TA-312 battery operated field telephone clacked loudly. Despite the nearly twenty-mile loop, the electrical pulses still drove the cold-war technology with ease.

"Base." I answered as I held the handset up to my ear, pad and pencil ready, waiting for the rest of the observation posts on the field phone loop to check in.

"Oh-Pee two," -- "Oh-Pee three," -- "Oh-Pee four," the rest all chimed in. The fact that Observation Point One was skipped meant the call came from OP-1, located south and west of the farm at a well camouflaged hunting blind situated just outside the town of Willows. That spot also had line of sight to a long stretch of Interstate 5, and it was a good place to figure out if we had visitors of the unwelcome kind heading our way.

"This is Oh-Pee one, S.A.L.U.T.E. report as follows," came a scratchy voice.

"Size; Six orcs on foot, one elf and one orc on wargs, total of eight enemy combatants.

"Activity; In pursuit of a civilian vehicle. White

sedan.

"Location; Traveling north, Tehama Street, intersection at county road forty-eight.

"Uniform; House En'durel colors flying from the standard on the lead warg.

"Time; Now.

"Equipment; The elf has bright-armor and sword, probably wands, too. The mounted orc has a shotgun and sword, ground-pounders have spears or war axes.

"Additional Info; Unrecognized civilian vehicle, with no markings."

"Report ends." The voice paused for a moment. "You want us to help the car, Mr. Jones?"

"No," I replied. "You're too vulnerable there. We'll see what we can do if they take the turn onto Bluegum Road. Oh-Pee two, I want you to put up the 'Cheese' sign. If they know what it means, they'll make the turn, and we'll see if we can't scrape their barnacles for them. Oh-Pee three, the QRF will be forming up on your position, so AFTER they get there, I want you to wire up your claymore and get ready to paste that damned elf with it as soon as he reaches the ambush point, just like we trained, ok?"

"I'll get it done, Carson," the basso voice from OP Three replied.

"Right, anything else to report?"

"No, Sir." -- "Negative." -- "Nope."

"All right," I responded. "I'll call out the QRF. Charlie, if they don't turn, don't try to flag them down. We can't risk a false flag giving away our methods. The Underground Railroad is depending on us. Now let's get to it. Base, out." I ended the call and placed the handset back onto its weathered olive-green case. Life on my brother's farm had really changed over the last year or so.

Taking a few quick strides out to the porch, I reached up and grabbed the rope attached to the dinner bell's clapper. Four sharp clangs, then two, then four again signaled the Quick Reaction Force that it needed to head out to 'ambush site two'. The reaction team poured out of the barracks building's break room and into a pair of Jeep Wranglers dedicated to their use. They'd practiced for a couple months, but this was the first time they were trying an ambush for real. Both vehicles had roll bars and pintles mounted on top for heavy weapons, but I'd told them explicitly not to break out the machine guns unless they were about to be overrun. We weren't a combat unit, per se, even though there were about thirty people staying at the complex. We needed to hide in plain sight rather than let the elves know resistance fighters were in their midst. Revealing the big guns would severely limit future operations by focusing the elves' attention on our neck of the woods.

I jogged to my old pickup and drove to my battle station. I was overwatch, in case the enemy had something with more range than the shotguns and spears. I was no special forces sniper like the one in the movie, but I could hit a five-inch circle at four hundred yards with a scope, no problems. I wouldn't even be pulling out the Bushmaster BA50 .50 caliber bolt action for this. My Winchester .30-06 would probably do just fine, but I still missed having my brother around. He'd been caught up in Europe when the elves invaded, and I hadn't heard from him since. It would have been nice to have some company on overwatch that really knew how to shoot that big monster. It was his rifle, after all.

As I settled into the prepared sniper's nest, I chuckled at the setup. One of the kids had figured out that a children's slide from a park playground in Willow was the perfect mechanism for a fast getaway from the sniper's nest, so along with the ladder for going up and down, the old metal slide was installed. It led down to the parking spot which was surrounded by trees to hide the vehicle. I settled the rifle against the bench rest and clicked my handheld radio for the first time.

"Farmer Six, in position and set."

"Six, this is Base," came an immediate reply from Julie, who was manning the radios and field phones at the farm while I was gone. "Oh-Pee two says the sedan made the turn at the old cheese factory and is headed your way. It's not moving very fast, though, and there's lots of smoke coming from the engine. He's not sure it'll make it very far. The warg riders cut the corner, and are closing in."

"Understood, Base. Get the rest of the scouts out of bed; they might be fake-chasing the car and we're the real target. Set up a base of fire angled on the road just past the grange building."

"Already moving, boss."

I scanned along the road, but the wargs were still screened by the olive trees along both sides of the road. Even without leaves, the olive orchards provided significant concealment, which the ambush team was making good use of, but it worked both ways. Until the orcs were fully in the 'basket', there was a danger the ambushers could be flanked. I reminded myself that only three of us at the farm were prior military, and only myself and one other were combat arms.

Gerry Patterson, the guy at OP Two was a former

Army truck driver. In this day and age, that meant he had a lot of experience driving through ambush-prone areas, and he knew how to react to an ambush. Unfortunately, he had no experience performing an ambush. Old Joe Bedortha, on the other hand, was a former Marine Infantryman back in 'Nam, which was why he was in charge of training up the ambush team and assault squad. The old man was a walking encyclopedia of platoon and squad level infantry tactics. If he didn't know about it, it probably didn't exist. If he'd been younger and still able to run at all, I would have put him in charge of everything, and just handled all the logistics for him. As it was, he was observing from the driver's seat of one of the Jeeps. He ran the actual ambush, while I was stuck with overall command. Needs must, when the devil drives, I thought to myself. In some ways, this engagement was going to be Gerry's final exam before becoming the QRF squad leader.

"Farmer Six, this is Five, over." Old Joe's voice came over the radio.

Speak of the devil, and he shall appear, I chuckled to myself. "Go ahead."

"The elf and his bodyguard are going to miss the claymore mine and will be out of the basket by the time the main squad gets here. They're cutting through the orchard as well as the open field, and I won't have line of sight here in a minute. You'll have those two leakers, unless you want us to engage them now from long range and lure them back. But then we'll have lost the element of surprise and there's no telling if the elf will go past the mine or not coming from that direction," Joe reported. "Your call, Sir, either way."

Shit.

I tried to think of ways to still trap them all without exposing my troops to a flanking attack by the equivalent of mounted cavalry, but I was coming up blank. It looked like we'd have to allow the wargs to reach the sedan before we could nail the rest of the patrol. I hated to do it, but I couldn't sacrifice the mission for what might be an attempt to infiltrate us.

"Stay down, Five," I finally responded. "Stay in the engagement basket. I'll keep an eye on the warg riders and see how they respond when you open fire on their backup. If we can take them out first, we'll have a better chance against these two."

"Wilco, Five out."

Well, that decision was made, but it looked like I was going to need the .50 cal anyways. It was the only known way to pierce elf armor with just one shot without using explosives. I slid down the slide to my pickup, set the Winchester on the front seat, then grabbed the sniper rifle's Pelican case from the truck bed. Climbing back up was a pain while carrying the bulky box, but I'd figured out the trick of it a few rehearsals ago. With a few practiced movements, I laid the hard case at the back of the perch and unsnapped the latches. The enormous rifle was in two pieces. First out was the barrel and upper receiver assembly. I swung down the bipod legs and set it on the floor. Next was the stock, trigger group and lower receiver assembly. In some ways the rifle was just like a giant M-16. I quickly mated the upper and lower receiver assemblies together, pushing the locking pins in place. I lifted the fully assembled rifle onto the rifle rest, grabbing a full five-round magazine as I did. In a few smooth seconds, the rifle was welded to my cheek, loaded and ready to go. I popped the scope covers and sighted in on the road as it exited the olive orchards.

I was just in time. The white-ish car spewed dirty blue smoke from underneath and was maybe making fifty miles per hour. Gerry had said the wargs were cutting the corner, so I trained the scope to the left, trying to spot them when they cleared the trees.

There they are.

Now it was just a waiting game. As much as I detested it, I was going to have to let the damned elf and his orc bodyguard get to the civilian car before the fireworks started at the ambush. If I fired too early, I'd give my position away and I'd be dead since I had no one to back me up. The idea was to get both riders distracted by the ambush, so they wouldn't realize that the sniper fire wasn't coming from behind them. If I fired too late, the people in the car would probably die.

"Basket in five minutes," Old Joe's calm voice came over the radio. Damnit, they're here already!

I took a deep breath as the elf pulled alongside the far side of the car and unsheathed a wand, shouting something at the driver. It was almost as if he wanted the occupants alive, which raised the hair on the back of my neck. I'd heard horror stories of the kinds of torture that awaited members of the resistance who were captured. I let my breath out slowly, just like I'd been trained so many years ago, and focused on my sight picture, hoping against hope that Old Joe would start the fireworks just a little bit early. It was not to be.

The elf brought his wand up and pointed it towards the occupants of the car. I'd always been amazed at Joe's ability to stay calm, no matter what. In the end, I guess his tutelage helped me, because I never even thought about the shot. I just fired.

The bullet traveled at over twenty-eight hundred feet per second out of the BA50's thirty-inch barrel, crossing the four hundred and fifty meter distance in zero-point-five-three seconds. It smashed into the elf right in the middle of the sniper's triangle, dead center in the upper torso. The impact of a full ounce of copper jacketed lead traveling at over twice the speed of sound was significant. And yet, it still wasn't enough to fully pierce the enchanted bright-armor. Physics was still a thing though, and the impact caused the unprepared rider to flip ass over teakettle backwards off his mount, momentarily causing the second warg to skitter and hop to avoid his tumbling body. It also completely destroyed the enchantment on the silvered armor, the resulting thermal byproduct actually causing it to flash like a miniature sun as it struggled to dissipate the absorbed energy as heat. The car swerved out of control then skidded to a halt on the gravel shoulder. I cycled another round into the chamber and zeroed in on the tumbling elf, who was bouncing to his feet after barely a couple seconds on the ground. He pointed his wand at me and started to shout something when my second shot took him in the right shoulder, sending the wand flying into the dead grass on the side of the road.

 I didn't see any of that happen. I was already tracking the second rider, hoping against hope that the orc wasn't paying attention to where the elf had been pointing. I wasn't that lucky. This sucker was more experienced than I hoped. His head swiveled like a tank turret and zeroed in on the only building in sight. I could see his small black eyes lock onto me through the scope as he turned his warg and charged. I cursed as I frantically cycled the bolt action to get another round chambered.

Finally, the bolt seated forward on my third round. This is why snipers tend not to survive against patrols, I remembered grimly, unless they could shoot from a hidden or inaccessible position. The National Guard sergeant that handed over the two machine guns and pintle mounts three months ago said that lots of civilians had died trying to snipe the orcs and elves. If you didn't get a headshot on them, they tended to charge the attacker instead of seeking cover. With elves, even a headshot wasn't a guaranteed kill if they had time to raise their shields, unless it was either a very high caliber or very high velocity. The military was now using saboted light armor penetrator (SLAP) rounds, which were working out pretty well, but they were really hard to find. The sergeant had given me a couple wooden crates full of ammo for each caliber we had, which oddly enough was exactly all he'd carried in his SUV when he'd shown up. I'd really wondered if we'd had an information leak somehow.

The charging orc was already nearly halfway across the field. I hurried to regain my sight picture through the scope and squeezed the trigger. SHIT, too high! I jacked another round into the chamber and forced myself to slow down, even as the sprinting warg brought the orc within one hundred meters... eighty... seventy! Aim low! I fired my fourth round, again missing the orc entirely, but slamming into the warg and destroying its right shoulder. The warg plowed nose first into the loamy soil only thirty yards away, but the damned orc successfully jumped clear, aiming his sawed-off shotgun as he landed. I ducked away just in time as a blast raked my position with pellets. I abandoned my heavy rifle. It would survive or not, but it was too unwieldy to help me now. Diving down the slide for the second time that day, I drew my Beretta from its holster and swiveled to the right where I guessed the orc would come from when he made it around the two-story shed.

I guessed wrong.

With a paralyzing roar, the orc swept around the left side and barreled into me, flinging me sideways and pinning me against my truck. It hurt like a son-of-a-bitch, but I managed to pivot away enough that I didn't get the wind knocked out of me. Spinning from the impact, I jammed the pistol into his gut below the armor and started pulling the trigger. I got three rounds off before he flung me sideways into my truck, grabbing the pistol with his huge, taloned hand and tossing it behind him. I took the opportunity to bring up a knee in the small gap between us. I figured that hitting his armor would probably hurt me more than him, so I pounded my knee as hard as I could into the fresh wound. He roared in pain again and tried to backhand me. I ducked under the blow and clamped on to his outstretched arm with both of mine. Since I had lost the pistol, I had one chance to put this guy out of commission. There was no way I'd ever win a boxing match against a behemoth like this, but as they say in Brazilian Jiu Jitsu, 'Leverage is King'.

I swarmed up his torso, planting one boot in the mangled mess of the wound in the orc's guts and bracing the other against the side of the truck, which now sported a huge 'Carson shaped' dent in the door. The orc growled something really vicious sounding, but I had neither the time nor the inclination to figure it out. Shoving as hard as I could against the truck, I threw my weight into the thrust to bring the orc down on his back.

I wrestled both of my legs around his arm in a classic arm bar and started arching my back to apply as much leverage and pressure as I could, trying to dislocate his shoulder. If I could disable an arm, I might be able to get to the pistol, or failing that, the Winchester in the front seat of the truck before he figured out how to rack the slide on that shotgun of his with only one hand.

He was enormously stronger than any human I'd ever gone up against. I had his arm locked out straight and he could no longer reach me with his other hand, but, astonishingly, he was slowly pulling his fist back to his chest, dragging me closer and closer to his other hand, which now held a wicked looking iron knife. I was screwed. This guy was going to be able to break out of the arm bar by sheer strength alone. I screamed in frustration as my two-handed grip around his fist started to fail.

An arc of silver flashed out of nowhere, neatly taking off the orc's head, missing my straining legs by the thickness of my pants. The resistance against my arm bar vanished, and the orc's shoulder popped out of its socket before I even had a chance to react. The sudden silence was deafening as my body continued to shoot adrenaline into my circulatory system. The splash of hot blood on my face and hands was utterly revolting, but it was definitely better than being dead.

"God DAMN, that's disgusting!" I spluttered, trying to keep the blood from running into my mouth. Who knew what diseases or parasites these guys might have, I dreaded as I tried frantically to untangle myself from the corpse. There was still another orc nearby unless whoever had saved my ass had already taken them out. Considering the lack of roaring, I was guessing they had, but I wasn't taking that for granted. I needed to get out from under this dead asshole, but one of my legs was stuck under the orc's massive torso. The sheer dead weight, combined with the sharp edges of his mangled armor piercing my pant leg, was easily resisting my lack of leverage. I couldn't even sit up.

"A little help here?" I called out to my unknown benefactor.

"Hold on," an out-of-breath female voice answered. "I'm looking for something to use as a lever."

I know that voice! I suddenly realized. But from where?

"Do I know you?"

"I don't think so, but give me a second…"

I heard the smashing of wood, and I felt it as something was shoved under the orc's shoulder, levering it up a bit. I finally freed myself and tried wiping the blood and gore from my eyes, which just served to move it around a bit. I sat there, still blinded by the viscera. Okay, plan B, then.

"There should be a canteen in the door pocket of the truck, along with a roll of paper towels. Could you get that for me, please?" I requested. "I can't see shit for all the blood in my eyes."

"Oh, sure. Sorry about that." The roll of paper towels was placed in my hands. I could hear her opening up the canteen. "Tilt your head back and keep your eyes closed," the voice instructed. She then rinsed the quickly-clotting blood from my eyes.

"Don't apologize, I was about to get creamed before you ended his ass. I assume the elf is dead?"

"Yes, you can assume such since we're all still alive," she answered as she finished rinsing off my eyes. "You should be good to go now, but be careful," she advised. I unrolled a few sheets and used them to finally wipe everything away from my eyes and open them up.

"Holy shit," I exclaimed as I caught my first glimpse of my rescuer. She was longer wearing the distinctive Butte County Sheriff uniform, but I was never going to forget that face. No wonder the voice sounded familiar! "Deputy Samuels!"

"That's right," she offered. "But I'm sorry. I don't remember who you are."

"Oh, uh… yeah," I stuttered, suddenly tongue-tied. "Um… I'm Carson Jones. We ran into each other outside the hospital over in Gridley, back on Day One. I had a downed pilot with me…" I searched my memory for the name, as I hadn't seen the guy again since. "Puckett! That's right! Eric Puckett!"

"Well, I'll be damned," she grinned. "It is you! I can hardly recognize you under all that blood though." I slowly climbed to my feet with a little help from the Deputy. As I finally gained my feet, she handed me back my pistol, which funny enough was the same one she'd handed me back in the beginning of the war. The parallels to our last meeting were not lost on me.

"Still protecting me, after all these months," I smiled. "Did you need the pistol back? I have other ones now."

"Nah, keep it," she waved vaguely at the pistol. "Besides, I've got someone I want you to meet."

It was at that moment, the 'basket' erupted in gunfire, a mile away. Samuels spun around, suddenly brandishing a fancy-looking silver sword which seemed to appear out of nowhere. I patted at my shoulder where the handheld radio should have been, but unsurprisingly, it was gone.

"Hold up, Deputy," I quickly reassured her. "That's my guys taking out the infantry that was with this bastard. If I can find my damned radio, I can get a report." I searched around the truck with no luck but then heard a squawk coming from the weeds near the shed. A quick radio call reassured both Deputy Samuels and Old Joe, who'd had a few acerbic comments about leaders and snipers getting into wrestling matches with orcs when they were supposed to be keeping their heads down. The battle, such as it was, had already concluded with no casualties on our side, and no survivors on the other.

I retrieved the sniper rifle and policed up the spent brass to reduce the signs of our presence. Although, there's not a damned thing I'll be able to do about that orc without a crane. The two of us then headed out to where the smoking sedan was still idling on the side of the road. I walked up to the wounded warg which was still whimpering in pain where it had fallen and put it out of its misery with a carefully placed pistol shot. The other mount was nowhere to be seen. A man, dressed in an old woodland camouflage pattern military uniform was crouched over the elf, who was very obviously dead. It had a gaping hole in his neck, probably from the shotgun slung over the man's back, over and above the damage I'd done with the .50 cal. Damn, those guys are hard to put down!

As we approached the car, the man stood up and turned our way. I'd had my suspicions when the deputy had been eager to introduce her companion, but it was really nice to have those suspicions confirmed. Lieutenant, correction: Captain, from the subdued rank on his collar, Eric Puckett stepped forward to shake my hand.

"Well, I'll be damned!" he exclaimed with a huge grin that nearly split his face in two. "Carson Jones, as I live and breathe!"

"Heh," I chuckled. "I guess I'm double-damned, 'cause that's what she said, too."

Deputy Samuels shook her head in mild exasperation at the quip.

"Well, you did!"

"Quit messing with Bethany, Carson," Eric chuckled. "I just got my partner all trained up to trust me, and now you're messing it all up."

"You both know I can hear you, right?"

"Fine," I groused mockingly, then turned to Puckett. "I was actually kinda shocked you remembered my name! You weren't in great shape when I left you at the hospital in Chico."

"I've had a lot of time to think about it, and believe you me, I'm not going to forget an ugly mug like yours, especially after you pulled me down from that tree when my chute got snagged."

"Meh, I guess we're even now since you and your partner pulled my nuts out of the fire here. So, 'partner', eh? And 'Bethany'?" I gave her a suspicious looking squint. "How come he gets to know your first name, and I don't?"

Her face went slack, and I quickly retracted the question. "Sorry, not my place."

"No, it's okay," she replied soberly, the mirth gone from her demeanor. "Jacob died in the first week. I've had over six months to get over it. You had no way of knowing. And we're both really glad you showed up when you did. That car's engine has just about had it."

"Well," I said, trying to change the subject. "Now that my foot's out of my mouth, let's go see what kind of loot we can get off these sons-o-bitches. Oh, and we'll get one of the jeeps to tow you over to the farm, see if we can't get you fixed up. There's a couple mechanics on the QRF that have been helping us keep everything running. I'll have to send a crane for all the orc bodies and that damned warg. We'll dump them off in the coastal mountains to the west to cover our tracks."

Eric suddenly spoke up. "Hey, Carson. There's two people hidden in the trunk, and I'd rather not let them out until we're under cover. Let the people in the jeep know not to scare them, as they'll likely shoot first and ask questions later."

"How about I let you handle that, then, and Beth here can follow me to my truck."

"Sounds good."

"Now, little Miss Deputy Samuels, about that sword... do you realize how close you came to my knee?"

***

"So, how's your leg feeling these days?" I asked several hours and a long shower later.

Eric slumped down into the recliner with a sigh of contentment, a cold beer in one hand. He took a moment to savor a sip before answering. It had been a long day for everyone.

"Good as new, which was weird as hell to experience."

"How so?"

"Did you know that we humans can have magic,

too?"

"I've suspected it but haven't seen any evidence to prove it yet."

"Well, take it from me, we can and do," he explained. "An honest-to-God prayer-powered healer showed up a month after you got me to that hospital. He prayed over my leg, then went to sleep in the hospital chapel. Next thing I know, my leg healed itself almost completely. Even the pin the surgeons put into the bones to hold them together just dropped out through the cast and onto the bed. It was the creepiest thing I've ever felt, bar none."

"Who was he?"

"He wouldn't say his full name, or where he was from. He just said he was a Cleric of Christ, and we should call him, 'Steve'. He did that whole song and dance on a few others in the hospital, then just disappeared. No one knows where he went."

"Wow!" I shook my head. "And after that?"

"Well, you know how JKO crashed, right?"

I paused for a second, confused. "Not really. I remember what AKO is. It's 'Army Knowledge Online'. Can't say I've heard of the other, but I can probably guess."

"Yep, same thing, but the 'J' stands for 'Joint'. It serves the same purpose as AKO did, but it's for all branches. Anyways, their credential and email servers got hacked and destroyed a couple weeks after the invasion. Rumor had it the elves had already penetrated the data, so no one is sure if the hack was to prevent further intrusion or if it was some collaborator trying to hinder military communications." Eric paused to take a sip of his beer, the condensation dripping from the bottom of the bottle. He smacked his lips as he swallowed, sighing contentedly before continuing.

"Either way, we're severely limited in bandwidth for secure comms. We've got the ECaTS network that the elves don't seem to know about, but that's limited to dial-up data over actual telephone lines and really old legacy computers based in the sheriff and CHP offices across the state. There's no consistent communication with any federal organizations at all.

"We got sent south to hand carry a report to what was left of Joint Forces HQ and request confirmation of orders. Got met by some captain halfway there, who handed Bethany that sword she's got. Said she'd probably need it in the future."

I nodded in understanding. "I wondered where she'd gotten that thing. And I, for one, am really glad she had it, even if it took a few years off of my life in fright. Looks Elf-made."

Eric gestured vaguely in the direction of Bethany and her sword with his beer bottle. "The captain said it was actually Dwarf-wrought, meaning it's nearly impossible to break, then enchanted by elves. Looted off one of their knights, or something. Anyways, he told us to report in at a thrift store, of all things, just outside of Galt. That was my first contact with the Resistance. They aren't there anymore, or I wouldn't be mentioning it, of course. Not that I don't trust you, mind, but you know how it is."

I took a swig of my own beer before nodding again. "Makes sense to me. I got talked to by a clerk named James at the feed store in Willows," I admitted. "Same deal, not there anymore. So that's how you knew about the 'cheese' sign, then?"

"I knew to look for a handmade 'food next right' sign, yeah," he explained. "This is the first time we've had to use it though. Every other time, we weren't harassed at all."

"Every other time?"

"Yep, this is our third trip just this month. Which makes me think there's more teams out here than just mine and yours."

"That would follow, yes. You're the first rescue for our reaction team, but like you guys, mostly we don't exchange names or addresses," I confirmed. "You know, Eric, I never asked before, but how's your family? They're ok up in Fresno, right?"

"Nah," he answered. "My parents lived in the South Bay Area. They died when an airliner crashed on top of their house. Drakes took down everything in the air that day. Just unlucky, I guess."

"Crap, man! I'm sorry."

"Eh, I've had time to get over it. At least I wasn't married with kids. I'd have been going nuts in that hospital with that kind of dread hanging over me."

"So how did you meet up with Bethany?"

"She showed up at the hospital in a busload of wounded almost as soon as I got out of surgery the first time, when they put the pins in my legs. She was all cut up and burned pretty badly on top of that. I remembered her name from the stuff you told me, and when I saw 'Samuels' on the door of the patient room, I figured I'd look in on her. We kept each other company for a while there."

He paused, looking down at the floor for a moment as if remembering. "First, she was dealing with the loss of her husband. Then the burns got infected. The doctors were scared that we'd lose her, but that same cleric that fixed my leg also fixed her up. I thank God every day for having that man show up when he did."

"What happened to her husband?"

"He was killed just after the Battle for Yuba City. She took his death pretty hard. She kept fighting with the retreating Air Force security forces until a patrol car she was using for cover got hit with one of those incendiary spells. That's when they shipped her up to Chico, because by then the Oroville hospital was completely full."

"She's a tough lady, I think. Not many would be able to keep fighting like that after losing a spouse."

"More than you know," Eric replied with a haunted look. "She's saved me from the pit of despair a couple of times now." He coughed as if trying to change the subject. "It's been a long trip these last four months."

"Double wow!" I was amazed. "So, I take it you two're an item now?"

He just grinned shyly, and I had my answer.

Eric and I talked quite a bit over the next several hours while Beth set up their passengers in the guest suite. He said it wasn't just healers that were showing up in the human population, but also mages, witches and all manner of magical talents, almost all of them completely untrained. But one thing he showed me in particular that was of immediate use was shield piercing runes.

"These will only work on larger projectiles, right now." Eric carefully demonstrated with an electric engraver on a .50 caliber copper jacketed round held in a padded vise. "It's all about the amount of surface area available for engraving. Doing it by hand I can maybe fit three runes on the bullet here before I run out of space, but I'm just a beginner at it. And don't ask me how it works, I don't know."

"And this'll pierce that armor they wear?"

"It'll help. The effect stacks with each additional rune. I saw one with fifteen runes on it go right through an inch of steel. At the very least, one with three will crack any magic shields the orcs have, leaving the bullet to damage the actual armor. This doesn't mean it'll work on an elf. Those guys generally have better shields and better armor. It takes at least ten or more runes on a round to even reach the skin on an elven knight. Or an IED or artillery round to the face, I heard that works too. Bombs only work if they don't know they're coming."

"Well, shit," I grumbled. "I guess truck bombs and VBIED's are going to become a thing again."

"I don't know how effective they'd be at hitting their strongholds. Hell, the really powerful elven mages have shields that can withstand a MOAB just fine if they have enough warning. I don't think anyone's tried a thermobaric bomb yet, and before you ask about nukes, the positive action locks on them are all locked down with the fall of the White House. No codes means no nukes, until someone who knows how opens them up and redesigns the trigger mechanisms."

"Lastly," he finished. "You can catch them unawares. But good luck with that. They've learned not to drop shields any time they're even visible from the outdoors."

"Good to know!" I was impressed and disappointed at the same time. I wondered if there were ways to automate the running process, and asked Eric about that when he finished.

"They're working on ways to use CNC machines to

do what they're calling 'micro-runing', but it's still in development," he answered. "Eventually, they'll get it small and fast enough that we can even start putting them on small caliber rifle and pistol rounds."

He handed me the runed .50 cal round. "There are other runes you can use, too. It's all in that pamphlet I gave you. Cooling runes, which will actually work for refrigeration. Heat runes, which I don't recommend for cooking, as there's no easy way to turn them off and on. If we can figure out a switch for the heat runes, we might even be able to stack enough of them onto a bullet to make a magical incendiary round, though."

"Plus, and this is way far in the future," Eric emphasized. "There's apparently ways to enchant a magazine without runes that will affect the cartridges that are loaded into it, but no one has figured that part out yet."

"I look forward to seeing that!" I held the .50 cal round up, tracing the runes with my finger. Fascinating!

Eric finished cleaning up, putting the tools back into the bag he'd retrieved from the car. "I'll make sure they send a caseload of ammo out your way as soon as they start making them in bulk, which will have to wait until Bethany and I get to Redding."

"So now my question is, what next? Where do you need to get to right now? Redding, or somewhere else, first?"

As I asked that question, Bethany stepped into the living room from the kitchen, a glass of lemonade in one hand and a tray of cheese and crackers in the other.

"Julie said you two were in here, and said you'd probably be hungry," she said as she set the tray down on the coffee table. "Our passengers are set up in one of the guest rooms, and the only ones that saw them were me and Mr. Bedortha, who insisted on seeing what all the fuss was about."

"Yeah, security is kind of his job, besides training our squads in infantry tactics," I replied. "When you said, 'the less we know, the less we can tell', I figured he'd be our best bet, as he doesn't normally leave the farm anymore. Less chance of a leak, and he'll keep his mouths shut around my boys, no worries." I grabbed several pieces of cheese and popped one into my mouth. "They're downright terrified of him, you know."

"I can see why. Not much gets past him, I imagine," she agreed. "Okay, that works. We'll be out of your hair as soon as the car gets fixed, I guess."

"You're no trouble, Beth! And I don't have any hair for you to get into anymore, anyhow," I quipped, running my hand across my bald head. "We were just catching up and all, figuring out if I needed to help you get somewhere, or if it's all still secret-squirrel stuff."

"Oh, well, for that, it's Eric you need to talk to. This is his mission, not mine. I'm assigned to him more from inertia than anything else."

"Well, that and a personal preference, I hope." Eric chuckled as Bethany blushed. "Like I said, we're headed north to Redding. Someone else takes them on from there, through some other method, but 'need to know', ya' know? Everything is being headquartered out of the regional CHP offices, since there's still a line of secure communication between them."

Bethany chuckled. "Yeah and thank God for cheapskate phone companies."

I looked over questioningly.

"ECaTS is an old legacy system from before the

internet," Beth explained. "The phone company that provided the service was too cheap to upgrade them to standard network connection."

"Ah."

Eric grinned as well before continuing. "Bethany was the one I took with me when I went south the first time and she's stayed with me since."

The door opened abruptly. The young woman who'd been manning the field phones walked in with an urgent look on her face. "Carson, another truck is on its way in. Charlie out at OP two just called it in. It's a special delivery. ETA is five minutes." She ducked back out to let more people know.

"You expecting visitors, Carson?" Eric said with a hard look in his eyes.

"Honestly yes," I answered with a slight grin. "I never formally greeted you, but well; Welcome to Force Majeure Farm, also known as Hopper Station, of the Underground Railroad, '2016 edition'. We aren't a resistance cell here to sabotage things and ambush elves. Well, I should say, we aren't just a resistance cell, because I am certainly not above causing a little mayhem every once in a while, but we don't actually seek out encounters with the pointy-eared fuckers. We have a much higher calling."

Understanding finally dawned on Eric's face. "Oh shit, we almost burned your entire operation to the ground by turning in here!"

"Well, kinda, but that didn't happen, so it's water under the bridge for now," I assured him. "I will say this; you're damned lucky that the quick reaction force was in here for training, or we would not have been able to do an effing thing to stop them."

"As for the refugees, we get between two and three groups a week through here by car or truck. Some official, like you guys, some not so much. Some even on foot and crawling through the weeds to avoid notice. There's not usually combat involved. We give 'em a place to hide, sleep, eat and clean up, then move them on to the next station. The Resistance, as you know, has been exfiltrating people out of the cities as quickly as possible. We're also assisting with that."

Eric shook his head. "I'm aware of that, of course, because I'm one of the ones escorting critical personnel."

"Right," I replied, nodding to both of them. "You guys are handling the high-profile cases and such. The valuable people, with special skills?"

"Yeah."

"Well, not everyone gets an escort. And it's not just people from the Capitol either. Anywhere the elves have set up shop, we get refugees. I'll be honest though, things have begun to worry me."

"How so?"

I stood up to look out the window as I pondered how to express what I felt. I shook my head in disbelief. "I thought the elves said they were going to leave our local governments in place. I mean, Sheriff Honeah is still tooling around, I just talked to him last week. But then I hear the stories coming out of the Bay Area."

Seeing the approaching headlights, I turned around to my guests.

"Come on," I said, waving my hand in invitation. "Let's go see who's in the pipeline today. I think it will be enlightening for ya."

***

The man, who I knew only by his handle, 'Jonathan Walker', pulled up with his stepside farm truck and drove directly into the drying shed through the main rolling door. Eric and Beth followed me in through a side door. As all the doors finally closed and the all-clear was called out, the lights slowly began to come up, only dimly lighting the interior as we didn't want it to be seen through any cracks in the walls. The truck's cargo bed was filled with six rusty-looking fifty-five gallon drums. The lids were a little loose, and a foul-looking fluid leaked from the gaps.

"Hey Walker," I called out once everything was lit up.

"Hey there, Issac," he replied, calling me by my Rail Name. He walked to the back of the truck and opened up the tailgate, but instead of hopping up to unload the barrels, he reached in behind one of them. I heard a click and what looked like the bottom half of the barrels swung out to reveal a hidden compartment. Two women and a seven- or eight-year-old boy were huddling inside. He waved for them to get out, reassuring them.

"It's ok. We're safe at Hopper Station. This here is Issac Hopper, the Conductor at this station. He'll be taking you on to your next stop. For now, just rest up and eat something." He pointed at the small fridge and cupboard stood in a corner next to three camping cots set up next to them.

I nodded in greeting, signaling some of my people to come help out. Two older ladies came over and started pulling pre-made sandwiches and potato salad from the refrigerator, while Old Joe brought in some pillows and blankets and set them on the cots. I tended to keep the younger men out of the drying shed when we had visitors, as many of the people coming through tended to be a bit traumatized, especially the women.

These two looked like they'd been through some rough times. One had a black eye and defensive bruising all over her neck and arms, as if she'd been strangled. The other just had that 'lost' look I'd learned to recognize from countless refugees over the last year. At first, we thought it was PTSD, then we learned it was something much worse. Mind-rape, often combined with the regular type as well.

"Go get Julie," I said softly to Joe. "She's got another patient." He looked over at the women and nodded, anger burning in his eyes turned around and left the shed. The kid just looked scared, but at least he didn't look beaten or starving. I'd seen both before and it made me sick to my stomach with helpless fury. That moment, those people, they were what made all of the work and the danger worth it.

"Beth, could you sit with them for a bit? I don't think they want to talk to any men right now, and we need to get this truck out of here, and we're turning off the lights to do it. And, Beth," I whispered as I passed. "No names, theirs or yours."

"Sure," she replied in a subdued voice, unable to tear her eyes away from the new arrivals.

I waved for Eric to follow me. We turned down the lights again, then opened the rolling door. Walker started the truck back up and drove out of the shed, pulling to a stop at the house. I followed and approached the driver's window as he shut off the ignition.

I stopped next to his door and leaned on the side

mirror. "Anything special I need to know before you go?"

"Sisters," he replied, wiping the sweat from his bald pate with a dirty kerchief. "The boy belongs to the younger one with the bruises. We broke the geas on the older sister, but she's still got after-effects. Won't talk. Obeys instructions, but make sure you're careful of what you tell her to do, she doesn't understand nuance very well right now. The little sister says she got beat up for trying to keep her from getting raped. Didn't work. For either of them. Fucking elves..." he spat the last with seething hatred. "Just like my daughter."

"We'll get ours eventually, Walker."

He shot me a baleful stare. I didn't take it personally; I knew it was directed at the situation, not me. "See you next time."

"Yep." He started the truck again and drove off, spewing gravel underneath overly-bald tires of the old truck. I have to remember to get him some new tires. I knew he couldn't afford them with just his regular income.

"What's a geas?" Eric asked. He blanched at my expression, but after a moment I calmed down and explained.

"A geas is a magical mental compulsion, but it's usually pretty literal unless an actual mind mage is involved, which apparently House En'durel specializes in."

Eric thought for a moment. "I think I've run into that before, but I didn't know what it was back then."

"How fucking hard is it to be sure of that?" I snarled, pointing back at the shed.

"We caught one of our people down in Lodi with

some kind of compulsion that had been cast by an elven scout, but way more subtle. We figure when the scout got killed a couple months later it suddenly stopped, or at least that's our best guess. The poor guy was mentally destroyed afterwards. He couldn't handle the fact that he'd been used to kill several hundred soldiers by being forced to report their whereabouts when they called into their unit. He took his own life a few days later."

Goddamnit... I winced. I knew I should have kept my mouth shut.

"So, what's the plan to deal with it?" I asked, changing the subject and silently apologizing as loudly as I could. "Are we going to respond? We got this railroad set up, but I'm getting sick and tired of this passive shit."

"The Guard is doing what we can, but we took a major hit in the initial invasion, and then another one when the bastards somehow got into the military personnel files and started rounding up anyone on the rosters. Within the cities which got invaded directly, only the soldiers and veterans that weren't at their Home of Record those first two weeks seemed to avoid capture. That seemed to trickle to a halt after the JKO database got hacked and broken. I suppose we have some hacker out there to thank for that."

"Shit. I guess so." I looked south into the darkness, even though there was nothing to see. "Should we expect more groups like yours coming up from the Bay?"

"Well, you should always keep an eye out for trouble, but I think most everybody escaping after this will have to come out on foot. Human vehicles just aren't allowed to enter or exit the Bay Area control points unless it's one of their drivers, and I suspect they may have a version of this geas thing on them."

"Right," I replied as I stood up. "You an' Beth go do your thing. I'll have someone bring you up some clean clothes and a basket for the dirty stuff. At the very least we can get you cleaned up before you have to leave."

***

I took Beth with me when it was time to head to the next station. Instead of a farm truck, our station had a box truck, like a U-haul, with a hidden compartment in the floor. We put a pallet of produce on top of the door and headed north, passing a couple of elven checkpoints on the way. Beth was awfully quiet on the trip up. I figured she was still processing what she'd learned the night before.

We pulled into the feed store just after noon, pulling into their enclosed loading dock before stopping. The station's crew closed the door after us, and a forklift ran in to pull out the pallet before we could open up the compartment to let out our passengers. "It's ok, we're safe at Tubman Station. This is Harriet Tubman," I gestured at a young black woman who walked up as they climbed out, and I made introductions. Looking at Harriet and gesturing to Beth, "Harriet, this is Betsy Ross."

"Rail?"

I shook my head. "Bull."

Her eyebrows went up for a moment, but she quickly recovered. It was an unusual thing to add someone to the named roster that wasn't part of the Underground, but I wanted her and Eric to be able to use the stations if they had to for the rest of their trip. The name 'Betsy Ross' would be passed down the line to become her recognition password, along with a short description to other conductors and stationmasters. I also meant that I vouched for her. Calling her a 'Bull' meant she was a Guard or Police, in railroad slang. I gave 'Harriet' a quick briefing on the refugees, and we headed back to the farm.

It took a couple days and a parts delivery from Tubman Station before their car was ready to travel again. Not once did I catch a glimpse of the pair of hidden passengers. Bethany took them their food, and they never left the guest room, which was fine with me. If it were something that threatened the safety of the farm, I was sure Old Joe would have told me.

***

The dawn of the third day found the three of us gathered in front of the farmhouse. The passengers had slipped back into the trunk before daylight, the car's fuel and fluids were topped off, and its engine no longer spewed smoke everywhere as it ran.

"Well, Eric, Bethany," I said. "It's been really nice having you two here, regardless of the circumstances. I hope you and Beth get your passengers to where they need to go and know that you always have a place here. Consider this your home. Even if you're bringing trouble behind you, we'll always be here to scrape it off for you."

Eric shook my hand. "I promise we'll be out here more often, now that we know where you are." Bethany also came up and gave me a friendly hug. "And I'll remind him when he forgets."

"You'd better," I smiled gently.

"And I won't forget what you showed us, Carson," she finished. "I promise, we're working on a way to stop this, just give us a little more time."

Bethany took the driver's seat and closed the door. Eric was about to follow suit, but suddenly paused with a puzzled look on his face.

"Couple more things," he quietly murmured, so Beth couldn't hear. "If you ever run into a guy named Joe Buckley, you need to turn your hat around and wear it backwards while you're talking to him."

I looked back at him, confusion written on my face.

"Last thing. I promise. I have no idea what to make of it, but I think that captain down south had a message for you. He said, and I quote, 'Tell him Dale is fine', but I have no idea who or what that means. He didn't name you specifically, he just said I'd know."

My breath blew out in a huff and my eyes glistened with unshed tears. A great weight I'd not realized was there lifted from my heart. "Yeah, it's for me. Dale is my older brother. He and his family were in Europe on Day One. This is actually his farm, not mine. It's named 'Force Majeure' in honor of our mama, who always complained it would take an 'Act of God' to get him to move out of the house. She was right," I finished. "His wife, Jenny, was and continues to be his miracle. They met when her car, all on its own, slid into his in an ice-covered church parking lot."

Eric's smile was infectious. Nothing further needed to be said, and soon they were driving off into the rising sun.

***

As they disappeared around the first bend in the road headed towards Tubman Station, Old Joe came up beside me, the ever-present cigarette hanging from his old lips. "Intrestin' folks they got in that trunk."

"How so?" I asked, curious that he even mentioned it, given how strict he was about operational security. "Do I need to worry?"

"Nah, no threat to us at least," he replied as he turned back to the house. "But you wouldn't believe me if I told ya."

James Copley is a former Non-Commissioned Officer of the U.S. Army, having served over twenty-one years in both Active and Reserve/Guard units, variously trained as Infantry, Communications, and Ordnance specialties before finally retiring from the Army National Guard in 2016. During his service, he deployed four separate times, twice to Iraq and twice to Afghanistan.

He is currently working as a software engineer in Central California with his wife, two children, and two dogs. Reading was his number one passion from a very young age, and more recently he decided to try writing his own. Feel free to join him on his writing journey!

Where There's Smoke…

By R. Kyle Hannah

The steady pop of semi-automatic carbines, punctuated by the echo of high-caliber rifles, ripped through the sunny afternoon. Rounds ricocheted off the asphalt road, the trees, and farm buildings on the outskirts of town. A handful of men stopped working in a ditch, grabbed their rifles, and returned fire. The war months earlier put everyone on edge, even though it never reached the rural areas. The incoming bullets kicked up dirt and skipped off the asphalt. The defenders were outnumbered and outgunned.

The mid-afternoon April sun beat down on the small town east of Birmingham, Alabama. Farmland, punctuated by fence posts and mailboxes, lined the sides of the two-lane road that curved through the countryside. Heat waves radiated from the pavement and sunlight glinted off a nearby pond. Carrion birds circled high overhead, waiting for their meal. Dogs whimpered and hid from the incoming gunfire.

Buddy Johnson and four others moved across the pavement to a cluster of trees on the edge of a plowed field. A lone John Deere tractor sat in the center of the soon-to-be garden. Rounds punched holes in the tires and the twenty-year-old machine listed to its side.

"Bill," Buddy called, pointing to the edge of an apple grove, "see if you can take Chad and Eric and flank those bastards." He slid around the tree he hid behind, aimed, and fired three quick shots. Someone yelped in the distance, and he pulled back a half second before a handful of bullets blew the bark off the tree. "Tom and I will hold here."

Bill Brumbly, a middle-aged auto-mechanic, gripped

his AK-47, nodded, and took off at a run. He made it four steps before his body twitched and blossomed crimson. He danced like a puppet on strings before he fell face first into the dirt. Chad and Eric, one step behind, dove for the ground and crawled back to their place in the trees.

The fire increased and the four remaining men ducked.

"We need to get the hell out of here!" Tom Sizemore yelled. The mid-fifties retired postmaster wore dirty coveralls and a sweat stained straw hat. His wide eyes seconded the fear in his voice.

Buddy fired another trio of shots without looking. He glanced around the tree, saw more than a dozen figures moving through the trees, and nodded. "Go! I got your back!" The former Marine, still fit despite his beer gut and more than fifteen years past retirement, grinned through his gray beard. He spun around the tree and emptied the rest of his magazine as fast as he could pull the trigger. He hit nothing—didn't expect to—but he sent the bandits diving for cover.

His three charges ran.

Buddy calmly dropped his magazine and slapped in another in one smooth motion; his training driving his muscles without thought. He slapped the bolt release, edged around the tree, and let loose with another dozen rounds. He was rewarded with a scream and saw a man slide down an embankment. He ducked back as rounds pinged around him. He put his back to the tree, felt the rounds impact the trunk, and searched for his small, inexperienced fire team.

Chad and Eric Smith, teenage brothers, stood next to an outbuilding behind the barn at the edge of the farm.

The boys, both tan with long blond hair and scruffy half-beards, waved Buddy forward. Neither raised their guns to give him cover.

Tom hid his slim figure behind a water trough. A line of bullets punched holes in the wood and dirty liquid spilled onto the muddy ground. He ducked, waited for the incoming rounds to stop, then returned fire. The Smith brothers added to the outgoing barrage.

Buddy took his cue and left the trees. He spent a total of three years in the Middle East — Afghanistan, Iraq, Saudi Arabia, Yemen, and Djibouti — but never once had to dodge this amount of gunfire. He zig-zagged his way across the fifty yards of open ground. Bullets kicked up tuffs of dirt around him. He felt a tug on his right side and dove behind a partially disassembled bush-hogger. He lay flat on his back, panting, and stared up at the clear blue sky.

"I'm too old for this shit."

Another volley of fire tore at the ground and barn around him. Buddy grunted, rolled over on his stomach, and opened fire at the advancing bandits. He visualized each man as a black on white silhouette on the range during boot camp almost forty-years earlier. He released a breath, brought his sights onto an advancing target, and gently squeezed. The man fell face first into the plowed field. Buddy shifted his aim and repeated the process. That man fell and slid in the loose dirt.

The attackers, dressed in woodland camo, spread out along the edge of the open field. Several ran to the abandoned John Deere; a few others ran for an irrigation ditch. The leader — a maroon beret perked at an awkward angle on his head — waved them forward. Buddy sighted on the man, his finger whitening on the trigger.

A gust of wind stirred the dust in the field. Gigantic wings flapped and fire fell from the sky. The field exploded as a red and blue striped dragon streaked from the sky. A blast of heat roiled over Buddy and the others; it knocked the Smith Brothers flat.

The dragon rose into the air, hovered a moment, turned, and plummeted back toward the farm. Its wings fanned out behind him, and the beast zipped toward the earth. Fire streamed from its open mouth and lit the surrounding woods on fire. It pulled up at the last moment, arching back into the sky to come around again.

The bandits disappeared in the second sortie. Those not immediately incinerated ran around the field on fire, their screams echoing in the cool afternoon. Buddy Johnson blanched, forced the bile back down his throat, aimed, and put the bastards out of their misery.

The red and blue dragon flared its wings, creating a dust storm as it landed. The maelstrom of dirt and debris put out a few of the fires while fueling others. Buddy, Tom, and the Smith Brothers all turned away from the flying debris, eyes tightly closed. His ears rang from the firefight, and he wished he had packed earplugs with the rifles.

The air settled, the dust storm died down, and Buddy turned to look at the dragon. A tall, slender elf in glistening gold armor sat on the beast's back. Long blond hair trailed down the rider's back. He carried no weapons that Buddy could see, but knew the Fae had to be armed. Never heard of one that wasn't.

The ground vibrated, like a minor earthquake, and a dozen orcs lumbered across the scorched field. They averaged more than a foot taller than Buddy's six-foot-two frame, and their muddy green skin seemed to soak up the sunlight. They formed behind the dragon, clubs, maces, and swords in hand. The lead orc, a red-arrow tattooed on his left breast, looked at Buddy and licked his lips.

"Human," the elf spoke in perfect, non-accented English. "I am Lord Karo, the new Governor for this region. Who is in charge here?"

Buddy Johnson stared at the elf for a moment, gasping for air after the battle. Adrenaline slowly left his system, giving him the post-battle shakes. "This is my farm, or what's left of it." He hooked a thumb over his shoulder. "The mayor's house is a couple of miles that way. Large blue house, can't miss it."

Lord Karo stared at the four men, a smirk on his face. "Are you not going to thank me for saving your lives?"

Buddy stared at the devastation around him. The plowed land, almost ready for planting, lay scorched and burning in some areas. The nearby forest blazed; smoke roiled into the clear sky. The tractor was melted to slag, useless. He looked at the elf. "Thank you? THANK YOU? You just destroyed any chance we had of a harvest!" He glanced around again. "The only thing still standing is the damn apple orchard!" He pointed to a stand of perfectly spaced trees on the far side of the nearby road.

"That is by design," Karo replied. "I like apples. If you wish to stay in my good graces during my tenure here, then keep them coming." He leaned forward on the dragon's neck. "And you are welcome, human."

He turned and nodded to the orcs. They moved out as a unit, the ground reverberating as they ran. They rounded the corner of the farmhouse, hit the main road, and disappeared in the direction buddy indicated.

"Pass the word, human," Karo said in his even, unemotional tone. "There will be a meeting of all humans tomorrow in the town center. Everyone must be there. If they are not, their absence will be noted." He shook his head in a human-like manner. "You do not want to be on my list, human."

The dragon rose into the air, circled the farm twice, and headed after the orcs.

"What the hell?" Chad Smith asked.

Buddy rubbed his chin. "Kid, I got no idea. The war was months ago and a long way from here. I got no idea what's going on, but one thing's for sure. It's trouble." He rubbed his chin and nodded toward the road. "You and your brother better start telling folks about the meeting."

"What do we do?" Tom asked as the two brothers headed toward the asphalt, rifles in their hands. Neither had any tactical awareness; something Buddy vowed to remedy the first change he got. "We never thought the elves would take an interest in this little town."

"Yeah, well, apparently the war has finally come to us," Buddy said. "We'll do what we've always done, Tom. We'll fight."

"Fight? Against dragons and orcs?" Tom incredulously shook his head. "I can't believe I even said that!"

"Believe it. And yes, we'll fight. Not today, hell, probably not tomorrow. But believe me — we'll fight." Buddy looked around his smoldering farm. "But first, help me put out these damn fires."

***

They called the center of town The Mall; a three-hundred-yard expanse of flat earth used for concerts, heritage day celebrations, t-ball and pee-wee football practice. It was packed shoulder to shoulder with residents on a cool, overcast Thursday. Smoke from the nearby fires hung low, choking those gathered. Many coughed and wheezed. Hundreds of people, many with masks covering their faces, stood and stared at Lord Karo. The elf paced back and forth on a hastily constructed stage at the end of the giant, open field. He wore his golden armor and a short, sheathed sword on his left. Orcs—both white hand and red arrow factions—flanked the sides of the stage. The dragon lay curled on the nearby road.

Mayor Tim Florentine stood on the edge of the stage, his suit and tie neatly pressed and laundered. He wore his salt and pepper hair slicked back, combed-over his growing bald spot. He wore a red mask with the University of Alabama logo and carried a hand-carved cane with an onyx topper. Buddy Johnson, Tom Sizemore and three members of the city council, stood behind him.

"Fair citizens," Lord Karo began, his voice amplified by a pulsing amulet around his neck, "thank you for coming." He turned to Mayor Florentine. "This is everyone?"

"Everyone that could make it," the mayor replied. He nervously shifted from foot to foot. "We have a few sick and infirm, a few police and fire firefighters on duty, and about a dozen men fighting the fires out at the dump."

Karo frowned. "I said, everyone. I do not wish to

repeat myself for those not present."

"The fires out by the Johnson place are bad," Florentine explained, pointing to the smoke in the air. "It is a health hazard and—"

"I am not interested in excuses, human," Karo stated, his voice calm and even. "I simply wish my orders carried out."

"You started the damn fires," Buddy snarled.

"Buddy," Tom Sizemore grabbed his arm. "Don't."

Johnson jerked his arm away and stared at the elf. "You could at least put them out."

Karo slowly turned his emerald eyes to the farmer. He stared at the man in overalls, a rifle slung over his shoulder, and tilted his elven head to the left. "Ah, you are the man I rescued yesterday." A smile touched his lips. "You were saying something about a fire?"

"Yeah," Buddy Johnson smirked. "You and dumbo over there," he hooked a thumb at the sleeping dragon, "set my damn farm on fire. Remember that?"

"Buddy!" Tom hissed.

"No, he needs to hear it." Johnson took a step forward. "You remember?"

"I remember saving your life, yes," Karo responded, humor in his eyes.

"Well, you also set the local dump on fire." Johnson waved a hand toward the sky. "See the smoke? You destroyed my farm and set the garbage on fire. Listen to that?" He pointed toward the crowd. "All that coughing? You did that!"

"I saved your life," Lord Karo stated. The humor left his face and his voice turned serious. "Be careful with your tone. I can just as easily end it."

The orcs grunted their agreement and licked their

lips.

The dragon raised its head, yawned without opening its eyes, and lay back down on the asphalt.

"What are you going to do about the fire?" Johnson persisted. "You claim to be the new governor, then fucking govern! Show us that you—"

Karo moved in a blur, drew his sword from its scabbard on his left hip, and slashed Buddy's throat. The elven steel blade sliced through the farmer's neck like tissue paper. Johnson stared at the crimson-stained steel a moment, a confused look on his face, before his head rolled back off his neck. His body stood for two more seconds before collapsing in on itself and crumbling to the grass.

The crowd gasped and took a step back. A few women screamed. Angry shouts pierced the hazy afternoon, punctuated by the distinctive click-clack of bolts and slides. A dozen men stepped forward, weapons in hand.

The orcs stomped forward, glee in their eyes. Screamed punctuated the early afternoon and the rear of the crowd turned to flee. Another squad of orcs blocked their path. One of the new arrivals grabbed a man by the head, picked him up, and flicked his wrist. The man's neck snapped. Two other orcs grabbed the man's legs and the three began a ghastly game of tug-o-war. The man's body split, and each orc stuffed their portion in their mouths.

"Silence!" Karo called, the amulet projecting his voice across The Mall. His words floated over the crowd and every human turned to look at him. The Orcs snarled their disappointment but did not eat anyone else.

"The fire is a human concern, not mine," Karo stated, an edge in his tone. "I will not tolerate insults or belligerence. Nor will I tolerate disrespect. I called you here today to tell you that I will rule you with a firm, but fair, hand." He pointed to Johnson's body. "This human has given me pause. Perhaps I should reconsider my approach."

"Lord Karo," Mayor Florentine began, a quiver in his voice, "Buddy Johnson does not speak for the community. I do. And I can assure you that we will abide by your directives."

The crowd murmured, a mixture of acceptance and disobedience. Not everyone in the town agreed with the mayor.

Lord Karo turned and scanned the humans. He saw wide, fearful eyes, snarls, and hatred. His eyes fell on a man near the stage. The man wore jeans, black leather boots, and a black polo covered by a dark jacket. He stood, relaxed and observing, with his arms crossed. The rest of the crowd appeared to give him a wide berth. "You." Karo pointed. "What is your name, human?" The townsfolk nearest the man took a step back.

"Holloway. Mark, Holloway."

"You do not share in my promise of fair governance?"

"Not my place to say."

A thin smile touched Karo's lips. "And why is that, Holloway, Mark Holloway?"

"I'm not from around here. I'm just passing through."

The crowd took another step away from the man.

"He's a spy for the bandits!" someone yelled. Murmurs of bandits and spies flitted through the gathering. Lord Karo let the rumors fly and pondered the accusations. His brows furrowed. "Where are you from, human?"

"Georgia; heading for Louisiana. Heard they needed help on the shrimp boats."

"A traveler? How interesting. Tell me, Holloway, Mark Holloway, are you not concerned about bandits? Or the Fae?"

Holloway shrugged. "I figured I won't mess with nobody. Nobody gonna mess with me."

"How very human."

"Thanks."

"So, tell me," Karo prompted, the humor returned to his tone, "what do you think?"

"About what?"

"The fire and smoke."

"I'd rather not."

"Why is that, human?"

"I don't want to end up like that feller," Holloway said, pointing at Buddy Johnson's corpse.

The townsfolk grumbled, cried, and snarled. Karo ignored it. "Speak freely, human."

Holloway scrunched his nose in thought, looked down, and dug the dirt with his boot. "Well," he said in a slow drawl, "the way I see it, you want to run this place without too much hassle. Right?"

An amused smile touched Karo's lips. "Go on."

The traveler raised his head and waved his hand toward the crowd. "And they just want to live their lives without getting killed."

"So?"

"So, why don't you work together?"

Karo and the orcs laughed. Karo's sound was light

and comical; the orc's grunted and stomped. Screams echoed from the crowd as pine needles rained down from the trees and nearby houses shifted on their foundations. Birds, spooked from the orc grunts, took to the sky. Murmurs and jeers replaced the screams. No one liked that idea. Whispers of running Holloway out of town rose to conversation levels, then shouts.

"Silence!" The crowd quieted and Karo turned his attention back to the traveler. "You expect me to work with humans?"

"Well, that's the way I see it," Holloway said. He hooked his thumbs in his belt loops and spit a stream of tobacco juice on the ground. "We both have laid claim to the planet. We can go on fightin' and hatin', or we can learn to live together." He shrugged again. "Either way, it's your call. I'm just passing through."

"We—we could really use your help, Lord Karo," Mayor Florentine stammered. "The smoke is creating health problems and the stench is awful. It would go a long way toward goodwill if you…"

Karo turned and stared at the mayor until his voice trailed off, the sentence unfinished. "I set the rules here," he stated. "The concerns of humans are irrelevant."

The smoke grew thicker as the afternoon wind shifted to the west. Karo wrinkled his nose at the new smell. His eyes watered. "What is that stench?" The orcs grunted in pleasure and licked their lips. The dragon buried its snout within the folds of its wings.

"That is the dump," Mayor Florentine stated.

Tom Sizemore touched his arm, leaned forward, and whispered something in his ear. The mayor suspiciously eyed him, and Tom nodded his head. He waved toward Karo, encouraging the mayor.

"The, uh, the smoke may also be b—bad for the apple orchard," the mayor stammered, confused.

The elven Lord looked to the east. Smoke filled the horizon, blocking out the sun. "I do like apples," he muttered. He turned back to Holloway and received a non-committal shrug. "So be it," Karo stated, never taking his eyes off the stranger. "In the name of goodwill, the Fae will assist the humans to put out the fire."

***

"What is it you wish, human?"

Mayor Florentine nervously shifted from one foot to the other, and leaned on his cane while he stared at the floor in what had been his office. Now it belonged to Lord Karo. The elf sat behind his desk, towering over the mayor like an adult to a child. "We, uh, we request to use explosives to open the pit," his voice cracked, and he cleared his throat. "And then bring in the fire trucks to, uh, douse the flames." He looked at the elf to judge his reaction.

A thin smile touched Karo's lips. "And if I refuse?"

"I'm told this is the best option. We—"

"Told by who?"

"The fire chief, Captain Bill."

"Ahh," Karo said. He sat back in the plush leather chair, the seat groaning under the elf's weight. "And you wouldn't think of using the explosives against the Fae?"

The mayor blanched. "I, uh—we, uh—no—no, sir! We only want the fire out. Our elderly population is having a hard time with all of the, uh, smoke in the air."

"Hmm," Karo rubbed his chin in thought. Florentine

thought it made it appear more human, and he slightly relaxed. "I will agree to your terms, Mayor. But, a squad of orcs will be present, to ensure you adhere to the terms of our deal."

"Yes, sir."

"And Mayor?"

"Yes, Lord Karo."

"Any action toward the orcs, the dragon, or myself," he paused, and shook his head, "well, let's just say that I will have one less town in my governorship. Understood?"

"Y—yes, sir."

"Very well." Karo rose from the chair, and it almost sighed in relief. "Shall we go?"

The two left the municipal building, a two-story block building painted a ghastly dull green, and headed back toward The Mall. A squad of orcs—white hand faction—took position behind them as they walked the two blocks. Mayor Florentine nearly jogged to keep up with the longer-legged elf.

A few hundred townspeople remained, clustered in small groups along the edges of the city center. The rest had already left to tend to livestock or prepare to fight the fire. The blue and red dragon had moved from the asphalt into the middle of the field and lay basking in the afternoon sun. It kicked its legs like a dreaming puppy and snorted; a wisp of smoke drifted from its nostrils. The crowd backed away.

Karo walked to his pet and fondly rubbed its jowls. A soft growl—almost a purr—filled the air. The elf Lord touched his amulet and his voice projected across the gathering. "Good citizens. The mayor has explained the merits of your plan. I have told him the consequences of betrayal. We have reached an understanding." Murmurs slid through the crowd like a wave; quickly silenced by a hiss from the orcs.

"Where is the fire chief?"

A man in overalls stepped forward. He wore a windbreaker with Engine Two embroidered on the back. Wrinkles stretched from his eyes and creased his forehead in parallel lines. Bloodshot eyes showed his fatigue. "I'm Captain Bill Nelson, fire chief."

Lord Karo stared at him for a moment. "You have what you need to save the apple orchard?"

"Yes, sir," Captain Bill replied. "We got explosives from a construction site in Birmingham, and I have six fire trucks filled with water from the Coosa."

"The Coosa?"

"The Coosa River," Bill pointed over his shoulder.

"Then proceed, human."

Bill nodded, turned, and waved a group of men to follow. "Let's go. This has to be synchronized precisely or…" His voice trailed off as he moved out of earshot.

"He appears capable," Lord Karo stated, nodding to the remaining crowd. "You choose your leaders well." He turned to the mayor. "Come. Let us observe." Karo moved to the dragon, rubbed its flank, then climbed onto the beast's back.

"You—want me—on the back of that?" Florentine stammered. His eyes widened and his cheeks flushed.

Karo laughed, a light, whimsical sound. "Of course not, human. You will stay on the ground. I will observe from the air. And remember, any aggressive move by your people will result in the destruction of the entire town."

The crowd gasped at the comment amplified by the

amulet. The dragon rose on all four feet and spread its wings wide. It flapped once, stirring dust, dirt, and grass in the air. The citizens ran away, as did the mayor. An elderly couple fell and lay in the grass, covering their heads. A cluster of children, around ten years old, ran through the maelstrom, arms wide and laughing. The dragon crouched and, with a ground shaking flap of its massive wings, took to the air. The kids fell, rolling in the grass, propelled by the blast. Their laughter filled the town. The dragon belched a roar that shook the city's windows—cracked a few—and circled the center of town twice. It headed east toward the smoke rising on the horizon.

Mayor Florentine waved the dust and grass particles from his face and watched the dragon fly away. He told the parents to mind their children and moved to help the elderly couple. They rose, uninjured, and waved away the questions and concerns.

The army of orcs rushed past, their heavy footfalls shaking the earth. Part of a building collapsed under the vibration. The human population moved to get out of the way as the red arrow orcs raced down the road after Lord Karo. A handful of white-hand orcs remained in the city center, eyeing the nervous humans.

Florentine leaned on his cane and wiped the sweat from his brow. He motioned to a group of men nearby. "Do you still have comms with the fire station?"

"Yes, sir," one of the men said. He wore ratty jeans and a light blue jacket over a Van Halen t-shirt. His red baseball cap sported the Alabama UA. "Captain Bill just arrived on site. They are getting ready to blow the charges."

The mayor nervously glanced over his shoulder at

the white orcs milling around the open park. One leaned down, sniffed a little girl, and licked its lips. The girl's mother grabbed her and ran away. The orcs laughed. "Tell them to stick with the plan," the mayor ordered. "No shenanigans."

"Yes, sir."

"Not yet," the mayor muttered. "Not yet."

***

Lord Karo smiled at the breeze flowing through his lightweight outfit. The pale blue robe denoting his governorship, as well as his blond hair, streamed behind him as the dragon soared through the smoky sky. The ground flashed below him in a blur.

He tugged the reins, and the dragon circled the smoldering trash dump. The mile-long patch of earth stretched beneath him. A simple gate blocked a single dirt road leading to the landfill. A trio of buildings occupied the center. The majority of the refuge pit had been ground and covered over. A quarter mile section on the western side lay open and smoldering.

Smoke drifted from several dozen crevices and holes in that corner of the landfill. Piles of dirt and bulldozers sat to the south of the pit while a dozen red fire trucks, lights flashing, sat positioned to the east. Long hoses stretched out like beige veins from the trucks. Nearly a hundred men moved between the trucks and the bulldozers.

Karo nudged his mount higher, and the smoke thinned. He did not know the power of the pumps of the fire trucks, but he did know what that much water would do to his dragon. A beast that breathed and lived in fire did not do well in a wet environment. A hard lesson learned in the early days of the war in New York; and the jungles of Central and South America during the rainy season. He patted the beast's neck.

The sharp crack of gunfire punctuated the steady hum of engines below. A scream echoed across the landfill. The humans below froze in shock. Everyone turned to the wooded north. Karo followed their gaze and counted thirty men moving through the trees, firing on the run as they attacked the fire brigade.

"Let us watch these humans, little one," Karo mused. "They are indeed fascinating creatures." He circled the dawning battle with a bird's-eye view.

The gunman, wearing woodland camouflage, moved with military precision. They darted from tree to tree, providing covering fire as they closed the distance. Well-aimed volleys found their marks. The local firemen fell. Bullets pinged off the fire trucks; ricochets careened into the trees, the dirt, and other firefighters. The fire was forgotten; the survivors scurried behind the trucks.

The bulldozer crew returned fire. Untrained country boys filled the air with lead and hit nothing but did stall the advance. The military trained bandits dove for cover behind trees, rocks, and an errant hunting stand on the edge of the forest. They regrouped and peppered the armed townsfolk.

Karo circled, watching.

The firefight between the two groups intensified. The citizens outnumbered the bandits but lacked the skill of the attackers. The sheer volume of fire from both sides found their targets; bodies fell and littered the landfill. A grenade arched across the battlefield and exploded, sending debris in every direction and opening a hole in the smoldering refuse. Smoke billowed from the explosion. The bandits used the smoke screen to advance.

The ground shook. Leaves and branches fell from the trees. Rock and dirt tumbled into crevices. The bandits paused their advance and turned toward a distant rumble. The squad of red-arrow orcs stormed across the field, axes and clubs ready for combat. Their feet dug into the soft dirt, slowing their advance. Their battle cries morphed into grunts of exertion. The bandits turned their firepower on the advancing behemoths. The bullets bounced off their armor or dug into the orc's flesh but did little to stop their advance. Another grenade exploded and an orc disappeared in the fiery blast. The lead element found firmer ground and the Fae surged forward. The bandits turned to retreat.

Captain Bill shouted an order, dropped his arm, and hit the deck.

Lord Karo opened his mouth to shout a warning.

The landfill exploded.

Debris, dirt, garbage, and bits of orcs and humans filled the air and rained down on the firetrucks in a green and crimson mist. Wet thuds reverberated through the afternoon as the remains smacked the earth. Fire raged in the open crater of the landfill and the stench of cooking meat overcame the smell of the smoke. The firemen grabbed the hoses and moved toward the dump. Water flowed.

Karo silently circled.

The sun slowly sank to the west as the firefighters poured thousands of gallons into the open landfill. Each truck left twice and refilled from the Coosa River. Crews rotated through the night and the battle raged on. A cave-in cost them a fire engine and six men. When the first fingers of dawn touched the sky, the exhausted firefighters dropped their hoses and helmets. The fire was out.

Daylight added color to the monochromatic night and the citizens got their first look at their handy-work. A one-hundred-yard crater, filled with water and sludge, identified the site of the explosion. Thick black smoke no longer filled the sky. A cloudless morning greeted the exhausted workers.

An echelon of white hand orcs occupied the road leading to the dump. Lord Karo stood at the head of his warrior element. His dragon, blue and red scales glistening in the morning light, lay sleeping behind the orcs. Off to the side, standing in the mud and debris, stood the last of the red orcs. Only four remained. They growled and kicked at the dirt but said nothing. They had lost nearly their entire contingent in the explosion.

Captain Bill, covered in sweat and soot, ordered the bulldozers forward. The massive machines roared to life; diesel engines belching smoke. The yellow earth-movers pushed forward and filled the crater with dirt. The engines died and the humans moved forward to critique the job. They shook hands, clapped each other on the backs, and congratulated each other.

Lord Karo laughed, climbed on his dragon, and flew away. The orcs followed. The white orcs moved with purpose, their lines straight and heads held high. The red orcs, battered, beaten, and dismissed, slowly trudged behind.

***

Mark Holloway watched the dragon disappear into the distance, lowered his binoculars, and shook his head. He lay prone under a hastily constructed hide-site and rubbed his tired eyes. He slugged back half a canteen of water and reached for an energy bar in his satchel. A wave of dust attracted his attention, and he raised his binoculars.

Two doorless Jeeps traveled the bumpy road leading to the dump. Mayor Florentine sat in the passenger seat of the lead vehicle. He held onto the overhead bar with white knuckles, the color drained from his face. The Jeep stopped and he quickly exited the vehicle. He paused to compose himself before heading directly toward Captain Bill. The two shook hands and began a circular route through the landfill.

Holloway scanned the skies for the dragon or other threats, found none, and slowly packed his things. He donned an olive-green pack and quietly slipped into the woods. He traveled slow and light, his footfalls nearly silent among the evergreens and cedars of Alabama. He had grown up not far from his location and had hoped to someday retire to the nearby lake.

The war delayed those plans.

Two hours later, he stopped beneath a water tower in the next small town. He dropped to his knees near a dead, hollow oak, and listened. Only the sounds of birds, insects, and small scurrying creatures greeted him. He finished his canteen, pulled a small shovel from his pack, and set to work. Twenty minutes later, he pulled a long nylon case and a hard-sided box from the base of the tree.

Sergeant First Class Mark Holloway pulled his weapons from the nylon case, checked them, and donned his gear. The weight of his body armor, the .45 on his thigh, and the M-4 across his chest made him feel whole. He had missed the comforting weight of the firearms while undercover. The gear in place, he folded the nylon case and stuffed it into his ALICE pack.

He turned his attention to the hard-side case about the size of a large computer carrying case. He opened it and slowly took out the equipment he needed. He unfolded an antenna, set it facing south, and then connected it to a small SAT-COM radio. He set the proper crypto for the day and checked his watch. He nodded, flipped on the power, dialed in the frequency, and slowly adjusted a dial until he heard the proper tone.

"White Wizard, this is Hobbit, do you copy? Over."

A garbled reply filtered through his headset. He slightly adjusted the dial and tried again. "White Wizard, this is Hobbit, do you copy? Over."

"Hobbit, this is White Wizard," a metallic voice called. "Identify. Over."

"Mike-Seven-Hotel, ODA 2032," he replied, using his initials and rank as his personal call sign. "Intel report for Operation Destroy the Ring, over."

"Proceed, Seven-Hotel."

"New Governor in central province of Alabama. Appears capable, demanding, and deadly. Advise against direct action at this time. Break." He released the transmit key, took a breath, and gathered his thoughts. "Local bandit issue resolved. Anticipate no further incursions from the group designated Alpha-Four-Three. Break.

"Rift between Red and White contingents growing. Advise implementing Lazarus at first available opportunity. We can exploit that relationship. Break." He took another breath. "Will rendezvous with the remainder of the team in four days at the designated location. Over."

"Roger Seven-Hotel. Any other news from your area, over."

"Affirmative," Holloway said, a smirk of disgust on his face. "Local politicians are not, repeat not, an ally. Local mayor in the pocket of the new governor. Any further operations in this area must be done without local knowledge. How copy, over."

"Roger that. Proceed to rendezvous. Will alert the rest of your team. Over."

Holloway nodded. "Roger. Seven-Hotel, out." He slowly packed his equipment and slid the Sat-Com box inside the already overstuffed ALICE pack. He leaned against a tree, ate an MRE, and contemplated the future of the small town. *They might make it if they get rid of that suck up of a politician.* He smirked, remembering Buddy Johnson. *And don't do anything stupid.*

He finished his meal, packed his belongings, and slowly slid the ALICE pack on his shoulders. The bulging carrier weighed more than sixty-pounds, but Holloway shrugged it off. He had carried far heavier for far longer. He checked his compass, faced north, and began walking.

He had a long way to go and a lot more fighting to do before he could retire to the lake.

Award Winning Author R. Kyle Hannah is a self-professed geek and lover of all things sci-fi. He began writing in high school as an outlet for an overactive imagination. Those humble beginnings, combined with real life experiences from a 29-year career in the Army, have spawned a half-dozen full-length adventures and a handful of short stories.

"Reminiscent of Arthur C. Clark" is how Writer's Digest describes his first novel, To Aid and Protect. His TIME ASSASSINS Trilogy (Time Assassins, Assassin's Gambit, & Assassin's End) has met great praise from authors and readers alike. The series is a time travel adventure that chronicles futuristic assassins who travel back in time and rewrite alternate timelines into our history. The trilogy features a Pinnacle Book Achievement Award Winner and an amazon Best Seller.

Tukor and The Iron Maiden

By Brian Gifford

Tukor didn't like Texas, but he did like "biker bars". Those particular human ale houses, such as the Roadkillers MC roadhouse in which he sat, came closest to the warrior halls from home despite the lack of honor in the humans themselves. The tribes of human fighters called "motorcycle clubs" reminded him of the sietchless nomads of the plains where he had whelped. They were touchy and violent and loyal to their own, and they valued freedom above almost all else. As for Texas, the people here made him… uneasy. They did not seem to be easily cowed, and he grew less confident of his tribe's future the longer the humans took to be pacified. This town, Wichita Falls, seemed to seethe with resentment and foreboding. It occurred to him that the elves infesting his tribe's ancestral lands might feel the same of his people there.

The bar in which the kezneg leader sat was typical of the sort, the smell of blood and sawdust almost overpowering the stink of human machines and the watered-down swill they called beer. At least the music booming from the wood and cloth boxes over the bar was worthy of the Uruk-ki. Tukor thought the "death metal" was the reason he returned to the bar each week. That, and battle, though most of the bar's regulars wouldn't make eye contact with him anymore. He sighed and turned back to his beer. He thought idly that Death Metal Clan had a nice ring to it, if he were ever free again. The elven ring on his little finger, earned as a war leader, felt slightly warm as he listened to the conversations around him.

"I'm telling you, the Bishops are on their way here, right now!" Bishops? Why did the human sound concerned? Tukor hadn't realized the humans took their religion so seriously.

"Stitch told me Hummer's biz fell through, and they're pissed." Tukor's ears perked up a little; there might be battle tonight after all. He decided to piss before combat and stood from his stool at the back of the bar. All the humans at his end of the room went silent and looked at him warily. He snorted. It had been weeks since he'd smashed one of the regulars; their fear verged on cowardice.

"What about him? If the Bishops tune him up, that big-assed platoon of his'll come in here and level the place, and none of the pointy-eared fuckers'll bat an eye."

Tukor paused at that, turning his head slightly to hear the response.

"Well, best make sure that don't happen. You know how he is; he loves a good brawl. If he gets into it, we make sure he comes out clean. He's a scary fucker, but he's kinda our scary fucker." Tukor had learned over his months in Wichita Falls that this word, "fucker", was something of an all-purpose placeholder. While not polite, it was not meant to be taken with offense. He felt a small glow at their inclusion of him; they were puny and poor opponents, but they came back each week and didn't appear to hold a grudge. That was worthy of some respect.

He resumed his walk to the back door, passing the "restroom" by. The characters were gibberish to him, but he had heard the bikers refer to the room before, and the translation made no sense. There were no hides or straw pallets for resting inside the tiny room, and he didn't think he would ever become used to relieving himself indoors. It seemed... unclean, so he passed by the undersized door and headed for the exit.

He ducked his head as he pushed through the back door and into the cool night air, the stink of garbage from the overflowing "dumpster" assaulting his senses. The large metal box smelled so pungent he didn't feel wrong adding to the miasma. He opened his trousers and grunted softly as he relieved himself. He finished and was tying himself back up when he heard a hissed word behind him, too soft to make out but angry nonetheless.

He turned and located the sound; it came from around the corner of the building, and he stepped around an old motorcycle frame to see who had spoken.

As he approached the end of the wall, he heard a meaty thud and a muffled cry of pain. He turned the corner and saw a large human biker, his fist pulled back to strike a partially disrobed woman, almost as tall as the man, with her face being held against the shadowed brick wall. The male's pants were around his ankles, and the woman's arm was twisted up behind her back.

Pure molten hate erupted in Tukor's chest as he realized that the male had struck the female in the course of attempting to violate her. This man would suffer before he died. If this had happened in his clan, the warrior who dared so would be struck down before he could speak; his own mother would spit upon his mangled corpse and his name would be struck from the songs, never to be spoken of again. Murder was a word that couldn't apply to vermin such as this.

The man spotted the orc and tried to get his pants up with one hand while keeping the female subdued with the other. He failed to do either, and Tukor was astonished when the female erupted back from the wall with a violence and purpose he could not have bettered. She ignored her torn garments and swung with all her might, connecting with the man's head at the same time he stumbled over his tangled trousers. The man went down in a cursing heap and the woman landed atop screaming like an enraged hassen-löwe. Her freed hands were a blur as she struck and scratched and tore at her would-be violator, and his curses turned to screams as she found his exposed manhood and proceeded to ensure he could never violate another female ever again. Finally, her chest heaving and her movements nearly exhausted, she sat back on her haunches and found a large brick with her hands.

"Consider this a divorce, you raping sonofabitch!" Her arms stretched over her head, and she brought the brick down with a terminal thud.

Tukor found himself at a loss. He had never seen a human woman act in such an orcish manner. He wanted to offer assistance, but she was fierce and strong, and his assistance was no longer necessary. He wanted to congratulate her on her victory, but he intuited that this impressive female would not appreciate his condescension. His need to kill replaced with a dawning respect, he settled for removing his tunic and holding it out to the woman silently. She stared at him, and for just a moment he wondered if he would be forced to defend himself or flee. He couldn't decide which was worse.

Luckily, she spared him the choice and accepted his tunic, slipping it on over her pale skin. The garment was much wider than she was and came to the middle of her bare thighs. She looked at her torn blouse and skirt and started scrubbing at her face and hands with the shredded fabric. Suddenly she sank to her knees with a keen like a wounded animal, almost tipping over in her distress.

"I killed him! Holy shit," another baffling human turn of phrase, "after five years of his bullshit, he…" She trailed off and looked up at the orc. Tukor stood as still as possible, trying not to frighten the fascinating creature away. The night air was pleasantly crisp on his bare chest, and the female stared at the crisscrossed scars displayed there in the moonlight. She swallowed and stood up, facing the orc squarely.

"He deserved it," she glared without flinching, only the shaking of her hands revealing the overwhelming terror that surged beneath the surface. "If that means I'm next, so be it. You guys like the death penalty for any crime, right?" Her fear visibly transformed back into savage defiance. "Bring it on!" she growled.

Tukor growled in return, exulting at this woman's strength and spirit. Intense admiration for her ferocity filled the warrior, replacing his surprise at finding such an orcish soul in a human female. The woman jumped a little at the sound, then, mistaking his growl for challenge, spread her arms with a grim expression, prepared to face impossible odds on her feet and with her eyes open.

When Tukor spoke, his voice shocked him almost as much as it startled the battered woman. "Be at ease, fierce maiden, justice has been done. I intend to honor you above all others. While my mother is not present in this plane, I will send to the west for a senior matron of standing to speak to your mother on my behalf. May I know the name of your honored mother, that I might direct the good matron to her?"

At first he thought the elven ring had not worked and the female did not understand him. Then he wondered at the combination of laughter and tears that cut through the dirt and blood on her face. "I'm not sure I understood all that. But if I heard you right, I'm gonna need a little while to figure out how to respond. I just got out of a relationship, see." Her laughter redoubled, sounding more than a little hysterical at the edges.

Tukor brought his fist slowly to his chest in salute, wonder and confusion warring in his core. His sire had told him that sometimes it was like this, like lightning striking out of a cloudless sky. He wasn't sure it was ever meant to apply to a human female, however.

"Honored maiden, perhaps we should go inside. I

will get my kezneg to dispose of this filth." He gestured toward the back door, remembering as they walked side by side what he had just done next to the door. He was certain she would not notice his stink beside the stench of the dumpster; he was also certain he'd never wished he'd used a latrine more in his life.

***

When Tukor stepped back into the bar, the normally raucous space was deadly silent. The maiden had preceded him, and when he stepped around her to see what was happening every male in the bar had stood from their tables and were staring at them with lethal judgment in their eyes. Tukor fought to keep his temper, but if any of these men believed the maiden to have been at fault, he would kill every male in the room before he allowed one of them to touch her.

One of the older men stepped forward, his hand on a large knife sheathed at his side. "What happened, Misty? Did this big fella hurt you? Where's Hummer?"

Tukor's mind refused to accept the words for a moment, then his rage came flooding back. These conquered people believed him to be so lost to honor that he would hurt a maiden? Shame blossomed beside his anger as he remembered the things he had done during the invasion outside of Fort Hood, the humans he had casually slaughtered in the fighting and the looting after. He didn't realize he was growling until the maiden put her hand on his chest.

"Lowell, if he was the one who hurt me, you think he'd give me his shirt? It was Hummer did this," she gestured at her dress. "An' he ain't coming out from behind this bar ever again." She paused as if to let her words sink into her husband's tribe, allowing the question of who killed Hummer to fester a moment. "And Lowell, I'm the one that kilt 'im. I won't be a victim anymore, and 'Big Fella' here saw the whole thing. Called it a matter of honor and said justice had been done."

Tukor wanted to tell the maiden his name, but he refused to be so forward. His honored matron-in-place would give his name to the maiden's – her name is Misty! – mother. For the moment, he couldn't fault the moniker they had chosen for him. A distant rumble nagged at his ears, growing louder by the second. Some of the bikers near the door went to see what it meant. They returned immediately, agitated. "Lowell, that's the Bishops, man. They're almost here, and it looks like the whole chapter's coming."

The man called Lowell looked at Misty and Tukor again, then visibly set the problem aside for the moment. "Alright, get ready boys. They're not coming here to make nice. Everybody out front, we don't want to get stuck in here if they decide to light us up." Tukor followed the bikers, his blood singing from the possibility of a fight. So many strange feelings in the last few minutes had left him strangely tired and irritable; a straightforward battle sounded wonderful. Misty made to follow and Tukor put his hand out to stop her.

"You are hurt and need to tend your wounds. You should stay here." Tukor thought the words entirely reasonable. Misty, however, did not.

She stepped right up to him, her pointed finger almost touching his nose. "You don't have any say about what I do, Big Fella. Hummer didn't own me and see what trying got him. The Roadkillers are my people, I'm not staying here alone." Without another word, she turned and walked toward the front door.

Tukor smiled. "Maiden. Before you go, I would suggest finding trousers. Many great warriors have battled without covering themselves, but it does not seem to be your people's way."

It turned out Misty colored an interesting shade of purple when she became embarrassed.

***

Misty must have had some latent magic in her blood, for she joined Tukor amongst the bikers mere moments later clothed in loose leather trousers and a black collared shirt several sizes too large for her. She silently handed Tukor his tunic, and for a moment he wondered to himself why he wished she had kept it. The leather tunic was his favorite, after all. He pulled the tough but supple enchanted warg-hide over his shoulders just as the rival tribe arrived. Misty had taken the time to wipe her face clean, but cuts and bruises from her beating were obvious despite her efforts. Tukor wished this Hummer were still alive so that he could be made to suffer still, but Misty looked tense and ready.

An unending stream of "choppers" roared off the Old Henrietta Highway into the roadhouse's enormous dirt parking-lot, coming to rest in an impressively organized double row of dark paint and gleaming chrome. The newcomers sat atop their metal mounts, presenting themselves with a mighty roar of their engines that went on for some time. At last, a large man at the beginning of the first row raised his fist and the host went silent at once. His arm came down and all the riders dismounted as one. The demonstration of discipline was sobering to Tukor, who reminded himself not to underestimate his opponents. These humans had defeated the elves once upon a time, and with far less martial ability than they had now. Despite this reminder, anticipation sang in his veins.

The Bishops gathered behind five men of their ranks, clearly the leaders of the nomads. Lowell and three of his men stepped forward, and Misty elbowed her way through the Killers to hear what was being said. The men parted for Tukor without prompting, and he arrived behind Lowell just as the senior Bishop began to speak. The gray bearded biker looked over Lowell's shoulder as Tukor arrived and his eyes narrowed in anger.

"Well, that's one question answered. You're not in the shit with the pointy-eared bastards because you're working for them. So, my guns are gone and here you sit, pretty as a fuckin' princess without a care in the world. I lost six guys on that run, Lowell. Where's Hummer?" The man acted like a war leader but looked like a fat money-counter.

Lowell snorted. "You picked a hell of a day to show up, John. This ain't the best time to talk business, you know what I mean?" Lowell hitched an eyebrow meaningfully in Tukor's direction.

The Bishop leader looked at the orc. "Where's your people, big-boy? Ain't you worried about all us nasty humans all by yourself?" He giggled a little to himself, then returned his gaze to Lowell without waiting for an answer. "No, I think we deal with this right now, alien backup or not. You owe me for that shipment. Two hundred gees. And you owe me for the six guys I lost to your friends here, twenty kay each. So why don't we round that up to an even three-fifty for my trouble, and we'll be on our way." A nasty chuckle shivered through the crowd of Bishops.

Lowell sighed. "You really want to do it this way? A lot of boys're gonna get hurt; weakens us both at a time when we can't afford that kinda thing."

John smiled. "We can afford it, even if you can't. So, what, you're telling me you don't have my cheese?"

"You know goddamn well we don't have that kinda cash, even if I was willing to fork it over on your say-so."

John's smile grew nastier. "You know what, that's fine. I'll do you a solid and take this firetrap off your hands." He put his hands on his hips and looked over the crowd of Roadkillers at the MC's roadhouse. "It's not worth what you owe me, but I'll call it even-Steven. Just leave your bikes and walk away." The Killers started shouting angrily, and Tukor felt the battle rushing toward him. Misty would be right in the center of it; he contemplated dishonor.

"Lowell-human, move. I would speak with the Bishop war-leader." Tukor picked Lowell up by his arms and gently set the human down to the side. "You are called John of the Bishops. I am Tukor of the Blood Water Horde, Third Son of Glortho Drake-Stalker. I claim the right of challenge and offer contest, five of your champions against me." Tukor hoped the human wasn't familiar with the ways of the Uruk-ki; if asked he would have to explain why he claimed challenge-right, and his claim was tenuous at best. "If I win, your supposed debt will be forgotten, and your tribe will go on its way. If your champions slay me, Roadkillers will become as one with the Bishops, and you will remain as their chief." He saw Lowell pale at his words, but the human said nothing. He was smarter than he looked.

John of the Bishops looked shrewd as he frankly sized Tukor up. "Lowell, you're right that a fight right now would weaken us both. Our chapter would be stronger if you joined us, but we'll survive either way. You're independents, and you know your days are numbered. You really want this freak to speak for you?"

Lowell looked at Tukor, an odd expression on his flat human face. "Yeah, I think I do."

John giggled a little, then shouted over his shoulder, "Bring up the Brute Squad!" The crowd behind him parted and five of the largest humans Tukor had ever seen stepped forward. He felt a relieved grin tugging at his tusks and schooled his face to stillness.

The Uruk leaned down to Misty, speaking quietly. She looked at him warily but nodded once and pushed out through the crowd. A moment later, the rumble of a chopper engine sped off to the west. John watched the lights of her bike speed away, the furrow in his brow deepening.

Tukor had to spend some sand in the glass if he were to make his scheme work, so he decided with an internal smile to further play to the humans' ignorance. "Lowell-human, a drink before battle, it is custom. A large mug of your finest ale for each of the honored challengers."

Lowell looked at him, skepticism plain on his face. "What, now?"

"Yes, Lowell-human, now." He willed the human to understand him.

Lowell shrugged, "It's your show. Stitch, six beers for the 'honored challengers.' The finest, he said, so make it the Natty-Ice." He glanced back at Tukor and winked.

***

Tukor took a few minutes with his beer, enjoying the mounting frustration in John of the Bishops' face. At last he was done, and he judged the moment to be right. He gave his empty mug to Stitch, the last to do so.

He faced the Bishop leader and spoke briskly, "The challenge is ours, so the choice of weapon is yours." Tukor struggled not to smile as John's eyebrows rose at the sudden change in tempo. He guessed that the man would choose thundersticks, believing the orc ignorant in their use; he was not disappointed.

John recovered his composure and smirked. "I think we'll go with shotguns, then." Tukor was glad; his hands did not fit human "pistols" and "rifles" as well. Besides, the boom of a shotgun was a fitting warrior's call. He heard Lowell call for Bertha, a name he'd not heard at the bar before. Moments later a mighty weapon was laid in his hands.

"She's a Remington Model 10 with a custom extended magazine; holds ten shells. She's a ten gauge and kicks like a pissed off mule, but I imagine you'll be able to handle her." Lowell ran his hand along the stock lovingly, and Tukor understood the human to be the weapon's keeper. He failed to understand most of the words the man said, except to know that the weapon was mighty indeed. "You know how to work one of these?" Tukor racked the pump action, caught the ejected round with his right hand and loaded the free round back into the magazine in one fluid motion. He had traded much loot for a smaller but similar thunderstick and had spent the appropriate time for a seasoned warrior to become one with his weapon. Lowell grinned, and John's mouth fell open in surprise. "Make us proud, boy."

Tukor understood the human to mean no offense, and his sense of bond with the Roadkillers grew as he prepared to fight for them. His head spun at the events of the night.

"What do you say, John? The train tracks across the road? I have a feeling we're not gonna want to have the rest of our boys in the line of fire for this one." The Brute Squad looked at the massive shotgun in the orc's hands nervously, second thoughts plain on their faces. Tukor knew of the tracks Lowell spoke of and marched across the street toward the open space without pause. The Brutes were left to follow or show their cowardice.

He stopped in between the metal rails, and the crowd of Bishops and Killers lined the banks of the berm above. His opponents stopped twenty paces away, grouped like thugs rather than spread out like warriors. He raised his voice again, "Lowell-human, raise your pistol and fire when you are ready. The challenge will begin upon the sound of your weapon." He was taking many liberties with the nature of a challenge, but these untrained weaklings knew nothing of the ways of the Uruk-ki. He would not confuse them with a ceremony they did not understand and would not honor if they did.

Lowell stood straight-backed and confident at the lip of the berm over the tracks, John slouched two paces further along. He pulled a shiny pistol from the back of his belt and held it in the air. He looked at the Brutes. "Are you ready?" The Brutes held their shotguns boldly, trying to mask their unease. Their weapons were a mix of the long and the short versions of the human shotguns, and they nodded one by one.

Lowell looked at Tukor. "Ready, son?" Tukor almost lost his focus at the surprise invitation to the human tribe and brought himself back to the battle at hand with difficulty. Something else to be unraveled after. He nodded as well.

"Fight!" The pistol shot was loud in the night air, and the crowd behind the two war-leaders erupted in excitement as the combatants raised their weapons and fired almost as one.

Tukor fired the first shell at the right-most warrior and saw blood from the heavy pellets sprout in a hand-wide group at the top of the man's chest. At the same time, he felt the sting of pellets in his arms and face, but his tough skin reduced the damage done even by the human's "buck shot." The pellets that struck his tunic and trousers sparked off the lightly enchanted garments as if striking metal. He felt the force and heat of the blows, but they did not penetrate the toughened warg-hide leather. With a roar, he reached down and scooped a huge handful of gravel from the railroad's ballast bed and hurled the stones with all of his considerable might at the Brutes remaining. The men flinched and cursed as they were struck, and the shot man crumpled backward at his mortal blow.

Tukor's blood sang as he charged toward the men, using their distraction to close the distance. He howled as the four remaining experienced warriors worked the pumps on their weapons and attempted to get them lined up on the sprinting orc. Tukor racked his own weapon and pointed it one-handed at the left-most warrior. The man had a panicked expression on his face as the orc's weapon strobed the night with vengeful fire, and the man's face violently disappeared into the night.

The three remaining warriors managed to get a second panicked shot off as Tukor, and death, approached, one of them striking him in his left arm and making his hand go numb. If either of the other two hit the maddened orc, he did not feel their shots connect. Then he was among them, and their time was over.

The orc stood, his chest heaving and his heart singing in victory, his foes sprawled in death around him. In the distance he heard a motorcycle approaching, and he hoped he had timed his victory well enough. He looked at Bertha, impressed that it was still in working condition after he had beaten two men to death with it, then down at his final opponent, a giant of a man who stared at him even after his soul had fled. Poorly trained opponents all, except the last. He, at least, had had the sense to employ his useless boomstick as a makeshift club rather than trying again to fire at a moving opponent so close. Tukor reached down and closed the warrior's eyes, then turned the man's head so that his neck didn't look quite so broken.

His arm and face throbbed and he could feel blood trickling down from his wounds, but the feeling was quickly returning to his hand. Whatever had been hit apparently wasn't important. That was good, as he was likely to need that hand in the next few minutes.

He turned and faced the crowd above him, only then registering the cheering of the Killers over the sound of his blood pounding like war-drums. He howled his victory back at them. The engine sounded closer, but the Bishops did not look resigned to his victory. John the

Bishop looked as if he were choking on a bone, and Tukor added anger to the things that could make a pink human's face purple.

John turned to Lowell and behaved exactly as Tukor expected, without honor. "This was a bullshit contest. He didn't say nothin' about magic pants and shit. You cheated, just like the elves." Tukor approached, and when he was close enough, he racked the pump on the wonderful weapon Lowell had given him. He would need to change the opening around the "trigger", but he was able to easily fire the weapon with the tips of his thick, sharpened nails. His skin began to swell around the pellets buried in it, and the bleeding slowed and stopped. Digging them out later would hurt, but the scars would be a welcome addition to the tales of his exploits.

At the sound of his weapon chambering, John jumped a little and looked down at the orc. Tukor casually shifted to speak to Lowell, just happening to bring the weapon in line with the enemy leader. "What say you, Lowell of the Roadkillers? Was the challenge bullshit?"

Lowell grinned and shook his head. "No way, my friend. That was all on the level. I've never seen anyone do something like that, but we need to talk when our friends hit the road." Lowell needed to decide what he intended; was his earlier offer of adoption true, or did he intend to be an ally only? Friend, or son? Tukor believed more questions would be required to solve the mystery of these people. He hated mysteries.

Lowell turned back to John, smiling with his teeth. "Well, it seems like you've overstayed your welcome. As agreed, get the fuck out of my town."

John looked at the orc, then at the crowd of armed and ready men behind him. The noise of the chopper grew closer, and with it came another sound. It was the sound that Tukor had been waiting for, hobnail boots on the run. He grinned and faced the Bishop leader directly.

"My troop approaches; they will be angry that they missed my challenge. We should have waited for them. However, if you wish to break your word, I believe we could expand the challenge to a more general contest. My people are always up for a good fight." He grinned at the visibly pale human, showing his teeth much as Lowell had done before him.

John stared at him for a few long moments. Finally, he raised a hand over his head and circled it in the air three times. His men cursed and spat as they went but go they did. They roared away leaving behind an expanding cloud of dust and a triumphant nomad tribe. Tukor looked for Misty and saw her staring at him from astride her bike. He started toward her, and she shook her head once, then revved her engine and sped off to the east, away from the Bishops. Lowell cleared his throat behind him.

"Boy, we need to talk." Never had truer words been spoken.

***

Tukor woke as the first horn sounded, rising from his pallet in the barracks located in the former Boys and Girls Club of Wichita Falls. The brick building had made an ideal camp for the orc contingent, with space for several keznegs to bed down at once. The furniture of the former tenants had made excellent materials for fortifying the structure's entrances, and the rubble wall the local humans had erected under the orc's whips provided a strong camp from which to pacify the city.

Digging out the pellets from the human shotguns had been just as painful as expected, and his wounded muscles had stiffened overnight. He stretched widely and stood, admiring the pattern of wounds on his arms and anticipating the excellent scars they would create. He picked Bertha up and examined his new weapon in the dawn light, reminding himself to trade his smaller boomstick for the craftsmanship Bertha needed to become truly fearsome. The gnomes would surely accept such as his old weapon in trade for the work, and then some. The leather scabbard he had made for his old weapon fit Bertha poorly, but it was enough to carry it for now. He had never owned a named weapon before; the prospect warmed his chest.

He kicked the lazy amongst his warriors awake and walked to the cook pots in the parking lot inside the rubble wall to break his fast. His stomach rumbled at the smell of porridge and roasting meat. The "cow" the locals raised was tasteless, but filling. It lacked the musk of a proper cut of voog, or better, a human thigh. He glared at the dawning sun in spite, trying not to count the number of glasses of sleep he'd been allowed after the events of the night last. As he dipped his fingers into his meal, a call sounded from a youngling sentry on the wall.

"War leader, there is a human female here asking to speak with you. Should I show her my boot?" The youngling's bravado rang false, trying too hard to be fierce and confident. Tukor was reminded of his time as a youngling. He also had tried so hard to be like the warriors around him. It was that memory that gentled his hand as he cuffed the insolent brat on his way over the wall, barely drawing blood from the soft-tusked youth in passing. There could be only one human female that would speak to him by name, and the youth's manners left his mind as he spied the familiar motorcycle in the street beyond the makeshift walls.

"Back to your duties, infant," he muttered absently. "See the line leader after your watch and ask him to discipline your tongue." He remembered too late that he was still wearing his ring. Discipline should not be heard by the conquered; it gave them ideas.

"Fair maiden, you look well this morning. How fares the Roadkiller tribe after last night?" He stopped a respectful two paces from her, his fist on his chest. He didn't care if the watch saw him showing respect to a human; she had earned it. Besides, his orcs had celebrated his victory with the Killers late into the night; any rumors would already have been spread.

"We need to talk. Will my bike be safe if I leave it here?" Misty looked uncomfortable at her proximity to the fortified orc camp. Her glances at the former City Hall across the street, where the elves and their White Hand orc bootlickers had ensconced themselves, were understandably nervous.

Tukor nodded. "There is a green space two crossroads from here, called Bellevue. A… park? Your people seem to like those places almost as much as the elves. Would that be acceptable?"

Misty nodded in return and began walking toward the park, waiting tentatively for Tukor to follow. When he did, she tried several times to walk at his side, but he refused to be so forward and remained a respectful two paces behind. It was a position of honor, guarding her back. To the elves and the humans, it would look like a guarding escort. Their inability to understand the difference was not his problem, so he and Misty walked in burdened silence until they reached the park.

Highway 287 swept by overhead as they stepped in amongst the grass and trees. There was little noise. Few vehicles were allowed to operate inside the city without a strict geas against causing harm. Motorcycles had been deemed no threat, but still drew attention. The high ground above and behind him made Tukor's back itch, and the trees and stone walls and benches reduced his sightlines. The whole place was a warrior's nightmare. Misty, on the other hand, seemed calmer in the green oasis, and she walked to a low dressed-stone wall and sat. She looked at him as he stood away from her and patted the wall next to her. "Will you sit?"

Tukor felt an unaccustomed panic at the demand, both desiring to sit close to this fascinating human maiden and knowing that it would be far too familiar to do so. She was no pleasure slave or chattel to do with as he pleased. She watched his face and smiled a little at what she saw there. "I won't bite, I promise." He tried not to flush at the images that provoked.

Tukor compromised by sitting two paces away and facing forward, watching Misty carefully from the side of his vision. He couldn't understand why he was sweating. Her smile made his chest feel strange, and seemed right somehow, despite her lack of tusks. Homely as her hawkish pink face was, she seemed more fierce and lovely as the morning wore on. The bruises and scrapes on her cheeks and brow were badges of honor and strength.

"Good maiden, this is not proper. I should not be here alone with you; my matron-in-place has not even been found yet. I would ask again for your fair mother's name, that I might send the matron to her in honor." He ground to a stop, unsure how to proceed. He was unused to such indecision, and he did not like it at all. Not one bit.

"Yeah, that's what we need to talk about. Am I getting from all that old-school stuff that you're interested in me? Because I'm not ready to date yet. And I like tough guys, but you're… different from other guys I've seen. The whole situation is different; you know? Even if I hadn't just killed my husband last night, this would be a little weird." Misty's words tumbled over each other, and she stopped abruptly at the last.

Tukor felt a fist squeeze his chest. "Fair maiden, are you saying you would not accept a bid from a matron on my behalf? That I am unworthy of you?" His vision narrowed and he distantly wondered what sort of sorcery was happening to him.

Misty was silent for an eternity, or several moments; Tukor wasn't sure. "I don't know. I'm guessing a bid is like a proposal. You seem like you could be a good guy, but our worlds are so different, you know? I know Lowell offered you both rockers last night, full membership in the Em-Cee, so I think you're gonna be around. Why don't we see what happens? I'm not saying no; I really like the way you respect me, I need more of that in my life. And I appreciate what you did last night, but that's not the basis of a relationship." She seemed to mean what she said, but he didn't understand what she meant by "relationship." He only heard that she was willing to consider him, and his heart soared in hope.

"I don't understand your ways, but I understand patience. I will accept Lowell's offer, and I will honor the Roadkillers ways so long as they do not ask me to break my oaths. A warrior is nothing without honor, and I would not be worthy of you if I were honorless. We will…"

"What do we have here?" said a musical voice behind them.

Tukor cursed himself for a fool. The voice belonged to one of the elven lordlings, and he was a cruel one. He turned slowly, keeping his hands away from his weapons. Four elves stalked across the grass, spreading out to surround the low wall on which they sat. "Do you not kneel for your betters, beast?"

Tukor knelt off the bench, slowly placing his weapon-hand over his heart and his heart-hand to his brow. The elves' laughter tinkled in the air. "Not you, slave. I was talking to the other beast. Kneel, human." One of the elves took Misty roughly by the hair and forced her to her knees. Tukor began beating down the killer that erupted within him as soon as the elves touched the maiden, repeating the fact that he would die before he could reach her if he were to raise a hand against the elves. Their trespass had earned them death; he needed to be disciplined if he were to live long enough to mete it out.

"Now, now, she isn't so bad. She's almost as big as one of the orcs, and just as ugly, but she moves with a certain ponderous grace. I can't help but wonder if she might provide a welcome change from the emaciated waifs you seem to prefer, Lyridas." Their laughter was beyond cruel, for behind it lay the certainty of their actions. Nothing Tukor could do could stop them in this moment, and that was a battle he was unprepared to fight. He knew then why so many of his people had died during their conquest; Uruk-ki weren't built for servitude, they were built for battle and freedom. The elves required one without the other, and his people languished in dishonor.

"No, even you wouldn't do something so foul. At least put her out of my misery, she's been damaged by someone else already." The ringing sound of a blade being drawn turned Tukor's every muscle to stone. If they harmed her, he would fall soon after for he would not be able to live having done nothing. He would die on his feet trying to sink his tusks into one of the hateful elves' throats. He managed to shift enough to see Misty's face and knew himself for the coward he was.

Her face held no fear, not so much as a line creased her brow. The shame at his impotence melted away in the light of the maiden's rock-steady fortitude. Her eyes met his, and he knew she understood. His muscles relaxed and he felt strength return.

The elf moved his hand from her neck and grabbed a great lock of hair, smoothly severing the dark tresses with his razor-sharp blade. "With the way she stinks, imagine Yrpadian's face when he smells this in his sleeping pallet. It will take him hours to figure out where the stench is coming from. Let's go, I want to get there before he returns from the western patrol." With that, the four deadly magic-users drifted toward the 'High School', where the elves had made their quarters. Tukor waited until long after they must have gone, then waited longer still. After an eternity, he stood, and gestured to Misty to do the same.

"This place, the elves, they're too dangerous. You

must not return here without good reason. You humble me with your strength; I would not have believed anyone could face their death with such calm had I not seen you do it with my own eyes." He saluted her and gestured back the way they came. "Please, I need to get you safely back to your machine. If you are harmed by our masters, I would die soon after."

She stopped short and turned suddenly. "You don't get it, and you need to stop treating me like I'm going to shatter at any little thing. I've been dealing with shit like this for years, this was every day with Hummer. He used to play with his .45 just to see how nervous he could make me. Those elves have no one to stop them; neither did he. I've had lots of practice staying calm in these situations. This was just another Tuesday. Goddammit, I thought I was done with that shit!" He looked down, but her hands shook not at all. An amazing female, indeed.

At her motorcycle, he sent her off with a quiet promise. "One day, soon, those elves will die at my hand. I swear it to you, Misty of the Roadkillers." Using her name for the first time felt right, and it felt like another promise besides.

***

Tukor's kezneg was assigned to patrol north. The humans were being uncharacteristically quiet, and the elves' new northern neighbors were taking the opportunity to press on the equally new borders. Their route would take the orcs two days to run. Their simple orders were a welcome relief from the confusing feelings of the last days, and the two minor clashes with opposing patrols were excellent distractions.

He and his orcs were approaching Wichita Falls once more when Tukor heard the rumble of an approaching motorcycle. His heart lifted and his unease returned in force; he still didn't know what would happen with the human maiden, and two days of thinking hadn't cleared his mind. His eyebrows raised in surprise as the rider approached and he realized it wasn't Misty's bike. Lowell idled to a stop next to him on the road, and he called his gaggle of warriors to a halt.

"Son, they took her," Lowell stated without preamble. For a moment, the words didn't register, then Tukor's world crashed in on him.

"Where, and how long ago?" His warriors picked up on his tension and hefted their weapons in anticipation, shifting in place and looking for a threat.

"We heard from some folks in town that she rode in a few hours ago to see you, and you weren't there. One of the elven fuckers saw her trying to talk to the little orcs on the wall, and took her 'on suspicion of sedition,' like they needed an excuse. Her bike is still at the barracks with the keys in it, but I didn't go close enough to pick it up, I just came to find you." Lowell's face was pinched in helpless fury.

Tukor didn't make a conscious choice, the decision had been made the moment they took her. He turned to Panchok, his second. "Take the shataz back to the barracks; they are yours now. I will see you in the next life, or the one after that."

Panchok stood in his way, stopping him from running for the center of the human city. "What is it you intend, war-leader?"

Tukor considered cutting his friend down where he

stood; Panchok saw his death in his war-leader's face but stood his ground. Tukor felt a sting in his eyes; his friend would be a good leader. "I will go to the City Hall and cut down every elf and White Hand in my path until she is free, or until I fall in the attempt."

Panchok nodded as if it was what he expected to hear. "Your maiden, she is worthy of your life?"

Tukor simply nodded in return, not trusting himself to speak.

"Then we will go with you, war-leader. You carry our honor with you, and we would not miss such a fight as this. Fall we may, but songs will be sung about us. Besides, it will be good to kill some of those White-Hand traitors. A reminder that we are not yet tame might give them some humility." Panchok's fist slammed into his leather armor, and his battle brothers followed suit, the sound like that of the war-drums his people had followed into battle on the plains of his birth.

Lowell cleared his throat. "I didn't understand, but I think I got the gist; you and your boys are gonna fight the elves in the middle of the city? With what you have on you right now?" Tukor nodded again, his chin high against the expected protest from the human tribe-leader. The consequences to Wichita Falls in the likely event that they failed could be catastrophic.

Lowell smiled. "Well, we might be able to do just a bit better than that."

***

It seemed Lowell was something of a trickster. The weapons deal the Bishops had been so angry about losing to an elven patrol, it turned out that Lowell had been involved from the beginning. He had expected the elves to annihilate the Bishops when they found out what was being traded, and they had. But the weapons had never been at the trade to begin with. He hadn't expected the Bishops to blame the Killers for the deal going sideways, but that was the nature of business in the new world. Hummer had set up the trade, but Lowell hadn't liked the deal from the beginning. Sabotaging the deal let his people keep the guns and took the Bishops down a notch. And Tukor had helped his Killers come out unscathed.

Better still, Lowell had managed to get his hands on a limited number of special bullets from the resistance further west; runed ammunition supposedly capable of punching through elven armor. All Lowell asked in return for weapons and support was information on the enemy in the city. Tukor betrayed the elves with barely a pang in passing; a small dishonor here was the only way to give his people a chance at freedom. More, it was the only way to free his... to free Misty. Lowell listened without comment as Tukor's words made the picture in the city clear.

When the column of orcs arrived at the roadhouse behind Lowell's bike, the structure was a wasp-hive of activity. Apparently Lowell had planned to go in after Misty with or without Tukor's help; the orcs were simply added force. There were maps of the center of the city on a table in the middle of the packed bar when Tukor arrived, shaking the dust of the road from his feet.

Tukor's second came inside with his war-leader while the rest of the orcs waited outside. Tukor translated for Panchok as they went.

Lowell began as soon as Tukor arrived. "There are

three targets: City Hall, the Hill school, and the Boys and Girls Club. Misty's in City Hall, we don't know where, but we're assuming she's either in the basement dungeons or the top floor with the elves. According to Tukor, White Hand are in the Hill and are the shock troops that will respond in force as soon as the shooting starts. There is a small contingent of White Hand in the bottom floors of City Hall as security for the elves as well. The 287 highway overpass offers high ground right next to all three objectives. Red Arrow, Tukor's people, are in the B & GC. Tukor, what are they going to do when we go loud?"

Tukor considered for a moment as he finished rumbling the human's words to Panchok. "If we arrive first as if we are returning from our patrol, we can be inside the wall before they know something's wrong. I will speak to them from a position of strength; I do not know what they will choose. That may mean the difference between victory and defeat." He paused for a moment, considering the map. "There is another problem we have not discussed, roving patrols. These patrols are either four-elf teams or elf and orc squads, and they could be an unpleasant surprise once the fighting begins. We will not know where they are or how many until we begin."

Lowell grinned. "Not exactly. Our neighborhood watch keeps tabs on the patrols. There are three patrols out right now in the city, two combined forces and an elven squad. The elves are making a nuisance of themselves at Bombshells strip-club right now and are likely to be there for another hour or two. We have a few friends who can take care of them quietly once we decide to go. The other two squads are going to be louder to take down, but we have the hardware to do it in one shot. We just need to detail a few of your boys and a few of ours to get it done. After that, it's all about the city center."

Tukor nodded slowly as he finished repeating Lowell's words to his second. "The elves fancy themselves strategists; if you make enough noise on the ground to the south, the elves will order the White Hand to leave their fortifications in The Hill and give chase, and the Hand won't hesitate to crush a weaker foe. I will approach my people to the north and challenge them to remember their forefathers. If I am successful, we will attack City Hall from the ground. As this is happening, we use your heavy weapons and move them onto the raised road and strike the defenders from above. Only the top floor of the building has both the windows and the height to see the surface of the highway, so the weapons squad will need to be aware of that threat from the elves."

Tukor stopped and made eye contact with the humans at the table. "Misty may be on that top floor, so using heavy weapons to destroy the elves there cannot be allowed. If the high ground is taken from us, do not try to hold the road; retreat and join the assault. If you do not, you will die there." He waited for a nod from each of the leaders at the table.

He turned to the graying biker. "War-leader, do you have warriors for those tasks?" Lowell introduced his line leaders, many of whom had brawled with Tukor before. He nodded his approval. "And do you have tested warriors to use the magicked rifles?" Lowell assured him once more. "Then let us begin."

Lowell held up his hand before Tukor could turn

away from the table. "There is one more thing..."

***

Tukor looked down at the motorcycle club patch hastily adhered to his pauldron with the human's sticky magic as he marched. He scratched at it experimentally and the finely hewn image of a motorcycle bearing down on a fanged rodent of some kind stayed firmly in place. Lowell had said the "sticker" was only temporary; the Killers had grown by an Uruk-ki platoon that day. He looked at his orcs and admired their new adornments and the fine weapons the Killers had given them for their part in the "operation." Shotguns all, his orcs had spent a few minutes becoming familiar with the operation of the finely crafted devices. It was unfortunate that "machine guns" and "ARs" fit the orc's hands not at all, though Lowell believed they could adjust the guns to change that in time. They were approaching their fortified camp and had but a short time before the outlying enemy squads would be attacked, starting the fight.

The youngling he had disciplined two days earlier noted their approach and puffed out his chest, challenging the patrol's entry to the camp, as he should. Tukor saluted the skinny orcling in response and sent his troops inside the wall as he stopped to speak to the watcher.

"Go, and find the kezneg leaders, and bring them to me. Tell them I demand their presence." The youngling's eyes grew round at the order, and he knew something important was afoot. He forgot to salute as he left, but Tukor decided it was not the time to stand on ceremony and allowed him to leave uncorrected.

Yelling inside the building told him when the youngling found each of the five other war leaders, and one by one the massive orcs came out into the open area around the cookfires, often followed by their orcs. Each was angry at the peremptory summons by Tukor, their equal. He had a single opportunity to gather them, and it meant demonstrating his strength and commitment.

While not the smallest leader, he wasn't the largest either. The others respected him, but he had never challenged for a promotion to lead them. This was the moment that would bring victory or defeat. He stepped in front of the largest of the war leaders and unsheathed his battle knife. The taller orc stood still in the face of the bared blade, his enormous arms bulging across his chest.

Tukor stared into the big leader's eyes and brought the edge of the knife across the outside of his bicep, cutting deeply enough to allow blood to flow freely. The sting and bite of the cut grounded him in the moment, and he saw surprise in the older orc's eyes. Tukor held his hand by his side until the blood had filled his palm, then brought the palm full of dark liquid up between them. His blood pattered off of the point of his elbow to soak into the dusty pavement.

"I am Tukor of the Blood Water Horde, Third Son of Glortho Drake-Stalker, and I offer blood bond to my fellow war-leaders. I will destroy the elves here this day, and I would have honored warriors of the Red Arrow by my side. I have made an oath to a human maiden," he heard an indrawn breath from the warriors around him as the rumor was confirmed, "and she has been taken by our so-called lords. I would remind them that conquering the Uruk-ki comes at a cost, and today that cost comes due. What say you, Mazorn, Second Son of Dubok Wendig-Hunter? What say you all!" He roared the last, making even the seasoned warrior in front of him flinch a little. He realized he gripped his knife by the blade, its hilt offered to the bigger orc. Blood dripped from his stinging hand as well where he had grasped the blade too tightly in his need.

Mazorn uncrossed his massive arms, looking at each of the other war leaders in turn and placing his enormous hands on his hips. With a jerk, he snatched the knife out of Tukor's hand, accepting his right to ask the question if not agreeing to the proposal. Tukor's heart hammered in his chest, the wounds on his arm and his hand as nothing to the need burning in his guts. If Mazorn chose not to accept Tukor's proposal, that knife was about to be buried in the smaller orc's chest. In the distance, booming shots sounded.

The big orc laughed. "It seems you've agreed to a party with or without us, Tukor." Without another moment's hesitation, he sliced his own bicep and held his arm down to hold the blood, then slapped the cupped hand into the cooling blood in Tukor's; blood splattered, coating them both in dark flecks as intended. He flipped the knife easily and caught it by the tip. "Who else will dance with us?"

The camp roared its approval, and the other war leaders rushed forward to be the first to join. The Red Arrow made ready to be loosed against their ancient enemies.

***

The outlying squads had gone down cleanly; it was

unfortunate that the mixed groups were Red Arrow orcs, but such was the fickleness of battle. Lowell's people in the city spoke through their strange 'telephones' and gave the Killer's leader and his runners updates as the battle began. Lowell, in turn, sent his runners to Tukor to provide him with the situation. Once Mazorn made it clear that he would follow Tukor into the fray, the rest of their keznegs willingly submitted to his authority. So it was that his orcs provided "stickers" to the rest of the Red Arrow to identify them to their human allies, and they gathered behind their berm to await the signal.

To the south came a mighty roar as dozens of the Killers' two-wheeled steeds howled in on the barracks of the White Hand. Gunshots increased in tempo as battle was joined, and the screams of orcs and humans sang to Tukor's waiting horde like a siren's call. Battle was being done, and they did nothing; orcs did not "patience" well. It was sobering to remember that all of their plans would have been for naught if the elves considered Wichita Falls an important posting. The lack of dragons for the elves was the only thing that gave his smaller forces a chance. That, and surprise.

Finally, the gunfire slackened and the roar of the Killer's machines sped away into the distance, followed closely by the howls of a bloodied White Hand. At last, it was time and Tukor led his people over the rubble wall and across the street toward the elven stronghold of City Hall. On the highway above them, three yellow buses from the teaching centers of the humans squealed to a halt in their elevated positions to provide "fire support" for the assaulting orcs. Tukor's personal orcs assaulted the double doors closest to the rubble wall, while other keznegs went left and right to attack other entrances. From above came the chatter of one of the human machine guns and the sound of crashing glass in the brick building before them.

Tukor stopped worrying about the rest of the battle and focused on the orcs around him, and his world shrank. The metal and glass doors original to the building had been replaced with solid wood after the invasion, and his orcs struck the heavy door like a rampaging troll. Axes rose and fell frantically as the teams attacked the outside hinges and the doors were ripped from the frame in moments. His warriors met the first resistance just inside the hallway to what had been offices before the White Hand had gotten to them.

Two of his orcs went down with axes in their skulls as his shock troops entered the building with a howl. His orc's shotguns boomed in response, knocking the defending Hands down in screams and curses. Turok's warriors rushed forward, axes flashing, and a half-dozen White Hand were left twitching in death as his orcs crowded past. Howls and crashing farther inside the building told of the other war leaders' entry elsewhere. He reminded one of his warriors to rack another round into his weapon and turned the corner into the open lobby at the front of his warriors. His life almost ended right there.

Two arrows thwacked into his chest like war hammers, the magically improved missiles penetrating a short distance into his poorly enchanted armor and the dense muscle below. Sparks and heat flew from the impact as the enchantment failed and Tukor was thrown bodily back into his warriors. With a roar he righted himself and snapped the arrows off at the root, charging back through the door low and fast. He heard a grunt behind him as one of the new arrows meant for him struck another orc instead, and Bertha found the first of the elven defenders.

While the pellets of his mighty weapon were unable to penetrate elven magic, their fury was sufficient to prevent the overbred voog-fuckers from firing back effectively. More shots rang out as his orcs gained the open space and the two archers were overwhelmed and left in a pile of dismembered parts in short order. His orcs kept moving up the stairs, not even stopping to loot the elves on the way by. Tukor was proud of their newfound discipline.

Lowell had described the elevators in the center of the building and emphasized that they were sudden death waiting to happen, as if Tukor had never fought in close battle before. His goal was the top floor, and the stairwells adjacent to the core elevators were the key. He found the doors Lowell had described and took the final piece of armor Lowell had provided, a "SWAT shield", from Panchok. As he made the first turn up the stairwell, it was good that he had.

A hail of projectiles, arrows and spears alike, pounded on the shield, and Tukor hunkered his broad shoulders behind the thick metal. Impressively, some of the elves' arrows were sticking into the metal shield, including one that pinned Tukor's wrist painfully in place. Onward he pressed, and the defenders were forced to retreat in the face of the black shield and the ricocheting pellets from the orc shotguns. Tukor came to believe that he would never be able to hear again over the vicious pounding of the guns on his ears in the human-stone stairwell. Tukor's orcs stepped over the bodies of elves and enemy orcs alike, and defensive fire slacked in the face of their onslaught. After an eternity in the hellish funnel of death, he and his surviving troops gained the last door at the top of the stairs. The door slammed shut in front of them, neatly severing a fallen elf's head that lay in the way. The inside of the stairwell was an abattoir, blood and other vicious bodily substances coating every surface and dripping in streamers down the center of the space.

Tukor reached for the door and stopped, his mind finally re-engaging after the insanity of the battle of the stairs. Why had the elves not used wands in the stair? What were they waiting for? The elves had learned hard lessons during the conquest about their use of magic, and Tukor wondered if the use of wands in enclosed spaces was one of those lessons. The door, on the other hand, led to an open hallway and what had been offices beyond. Opening that door would be offering himself up to death; but it was the only way forward. In the dimness of the foul-smelling space, he saw a ladder to his left. He looked up and smiled.

***

The two terrified elf magisters warily pointed their wands at the sealed doorway to hell. It shouldn't have been a surprise that the orcs had lost their minds, they were roughly equivalent to dangerous animals, and they walked around armed, for the gods' sake. Both of the young elves had unidentifiable things coating their robes from the splatter inside the stairs as they retreated upward, and never in their centuries of study and practice had they been so horrified.

From inside the stairwell came a rhythmic thumping, then repeated clangs rose up the wall as if... The roof! They were loose on the roof! Boots thumped this way and that overhead, and the elves babbled to each other as they tried to track where the horrible creatures would be coming from. In their excitement, they forgot about the door to the stairway to hell entirely.

***

Tukor stood over the corpses of the robed Fae, their visages frozen in horror as they realized their mistakes too late. He had lost another of his people to their magic, but Panchok had not left Earth's plane before sinking the spike of his ax into the throat of one of the elven magisters. He closed his friend's eyes and tucked Panchok's favorite knife behind his belt. "May you find victory and honor, my friend."

His remaining orcs were clustered around finely carved heavy wooden doors, the portal to the only remaining space on the top floor his warriors hadn't been able to enter. From within sounded panicked elven voices arguing with someone on the other end of a magic mirror.

"Father, Lyridas and I are going to die if you don't send help now. The White Hand were useless, and our vassals just as much so. The traitorous orcs even killed our friends! They're right outside the door. What do we do?" Tukor's smile would have shamed a warg. He recognized that name, those voices. These were the honorless animated corpses that had touched Misty.

The weeping fraukanak's sniveling was cut off by a stern voice, one used to command. "Open the door, you cowards, and face them. Show me to them and I will save your worthless carcasses." It took more commands and threats before the terrified elves opened the door. Tukor stood before them, calmly.

"My father wishes to speak to you, orc." Even under such dire circumstances, the lordling couldn't keep the sneer out of his voice. Tukor couldn't have cared less. Chained to the wall was a battered and bleeding Misty, alive. He pushed the elves out of the way, heedless of their bared blades and enchanted armor. They kept trying to speak to him, but he couldn't hear anything the soon to be dead elves were saying to him. He found the pins keeping her manacles together and gently disengaged the mechanism. She was not conscious, and her breathing was shallow, gasping. As he lowered her to the ground, he felt ribs shift sickeningly, and her belly was taught as a drum. Nothing he could do would save her now. He held her face and willed her to wake up, to see life in her eyes for just one more moment. She moaned in agony, and he watched as if from a distance as his vision narrowed to a point, her battered visage the only thing remaining in his world.

The next moment he was aware of himself, he held each of the elves aloft by their scrawny throats, their feet kicking feebly as they fought for air. He brought their faces so close to his that his tusks drew blood from the soft flesh beneath their chins. In his peripheral vision he was vaguely aware of his remaining orcs backing slowly away from him.

"You each have a single chance to live, though you will not remain whole. The first who can assure me they can save the woman's life will survive this day, and the other will suffer until they greet death as the sweet release it truly is. Who will save the maiden?" The words slid from his throat like a caress, an offer of unknowable mercy.

One of the elves began trying to speak, to assure Tukor of his intentions. The other simply raised a glowing hand and reached out for the maiden. Tukor threw the orator to his orcs and the screams that followed spoke of good works starting. He moved quickly to Misty's side and dropped the winning elf to the floor next to her.

The flat words that came from him seemed to come from someone else. "She's dying, work as if your life depends upon the result." The elf turned white and began to frantically mutter to himself over glowing hands. He placed one palm on her forehead and drew the other slowly above her chest and belly. When he reached her belly he glanced at Tukor in terror and sweat instantly popped out on his forehead.

"A moment, good sir, just a moment!" the panicked elf mumbled as he placed both hands upon her abdomen, and the glow returned, shaded differently this time. He leaned over her as if to press her back to health, and his sweat dripped in a steady rhythm upon her tattered t-shirt. Tukor realized her undergarments were partially exposed and felt a flash of embarrassment. He averted his eyes and focused on the elf.

The pointy-eared fop was breathing hard, laboring mightily in his efforts to stem the damage he and his cousin had wreaked upon the maiden. His eyes were glazed as he looked inwardly, either into Misty or into his arts Tukor knew not. The light from the elf's hands spread to surround Misty's core, blending and seeming to come from her rather than the elf himself. Her back arched and spasmed, and her eyes and mouth opened wide as if she were trying to scream, but no sound escaped. After a few unending moments, the light faded, and Misty collapsed back into stillness upon the thick carpet.

The elf fell backward as the light disappeared, his chest heaving and his open eyes staring unseeing at the ceiling. After a few agonal breaths, his chest slowly sagged and a keening moan escaped his lips. When the keening ended, the elf moved no more. Tukor couldn't fault the lordling's efforts, he supposed.

Dismissing the elf from his mind, he turned to Misty, his hands gentle upon her belly. Her breath, while shallow, no longer seemed to be verging on her last, and her belly no longer felt like a too-full wineskin. Color had returned to her face, and she seemed peacefully resting, though he imagined only time would tell if the elf's life-magic had been sufficient. He gathered her gently in his arms, dared to brush his cheek next to hers, and left the remains of his kezneg to their fun. The magic mirror continued to issue screamed oaths and demands as he stepped carefully down the blood-soaked stairs.

***

Tukor sat next to Lowell at the bar, the orc's new plus-size leather vest with the Roadkillers emblem and both surrounding rockers cool against his bare skin. Orc-At-Arms adorned his left chest, and his name, also in human, adorned the right. The elves had bigger problems than a tiny human city in North Texas that had thrown off their yoke, especially when that city continued to ship its region's grain and cattle to the elven capital in Oklahoma City. Without the troops to make a thing of it in the face of all of their other troubles, the elves had chosen to apply something the humans called "realpolitik." As long as the town walked small and kept the capital city elves in ale and kibble, the polite fiction that their little rebellion had been a momentary lapse was allowed to stand.

The lord in Oklahoma City had put a bounty on Tukor's head; a rather flattering one, if he was one to think of such things. That was to be expected for an orc that had tortured his son to death after scaring the other into burning himself out of the plane with his own magic. No one expected to see it paid out any time soon, but the occasional extra-planar bounty hunter had come calling. A number of new and rather deep graves had been dug recently out in the scrub of the desert; Tukor appreciated the distractions.

Misty was still recovering from her ordeal, but her spirit was even stronger than he'd thought. She'd asked him to visit her daily, and he'd finally gotten a response from a matron in California who would be visiting in the near future. Misty still hadn't told him her mother's name, but he knew he was getting close. He sighed contentedly. It was a strange position he had carved out in Wichita Falls, but it was working. Orcs and humans working together, fighting together? It had potential, and he knew she approved, though she claimed to want to stay out of politics.

Politics? Tukor grunted to himself with a smile. Combat by any other name...

Tukor eventually rose from his seat and left the roadhouse through the front door, ignoring the greetings he got from the orcish and human patrons alike. No one took it personally. He stepped out into the dusk and looked to the north, and considered what might one day be. The humans had some odd wisdom; he especially liked one day at a time.

When she'd woken for the first time, two days after the fight at City Hall, she'd listened to his tale of her survival impassively. Nodding slowly at the end, she'd struggled to reach something around her neck. When he offered to help, he'd found a silver pendant on a finely wrought steel necklace, long enough that the medallion had nestled between her breasts. She'd had him unclasp it from her neck before she laboriously attached it around his. Her arms around his cheeks and her breath upon his face still heated his face when he thought of it, though not so much as the promise her gift held within. He knew little of this Saint Michael, only that he watched over warriors in this plane; the honor of her gift humbled him.

After a few minutes, Lowell joined him in the night air and stood for a while in companionable silence. After a time, he looked up at the big orc, "What's next, son?"

A flicker of warmth in the darkness, a reminder that here he belonged to something beyond even her. There were many things still to do, and Misty didn't believe in standing still when there was work to be done. It was time to get up and back into the fight.

"Next, Lowell? Freedom and victory. Freedom and victory, or death."

Brian Gifford is a US Air Veteran and up and coming writer. Look for more of his stuff in the future!

The Fae Wars

What would you do if America and the world were invaded tomorrow by a relentless and brutal enemy?

In an alternate 2015, a US Army Special Forces Team, part of the legendary black ops unit "Delta", is in midtown Manhattan to take out a Chinese spy and his handlers, sending a message short of outright conflict. All goes smoothly until they find themselves in a full blown shooting war through the canyons of the City. Portals from another world have opened in Central Park, making a way for figures out of historical nightmare to invade. The Fae, creatures banished from Earth thousands of years ago and now only part of our legends, have returned with Dragon fire, spell and sword to conquer and take revenge.

The first volume of The Fae Wars covers Team Three, G squadron, Special Forces Detachment (Delta) as they fight their way off Manhattan and then join the defense of the refugees as the Fae assault the bridges. The fabled 69th Infantry puts up an epic fight against superior weaponry and then the war descends into the asymmetric hell that the Delta Operators know so well. Along the way they find new allies and old powers that come to their aid.

FALLEN EMPIRE

The Terran Union has spent five centuries under the control of the alien Grausians, like a barbarian tribe under the thumb of Rome. Now, after almost two decades of civil war and succession struggles, the formerly subject races have settled back in their ancient territories to lick their wounds and rearm, leaving hundreds of settled planets to exist in a political vacuum. Into that space steps the free companies, mercenary units that fight for gold, honor, power and glory. Veterans who can't get the wars out of their souls, new recruits looking for adventure, corporations with their own agenda.

The Thin Dead Line

On a hot July day on the plains of Kansas a US Army mechanized infantry company from the 1st Infantry Division gets a very vague warning order and the young troopers saddle up on their steel beasts to go try to control "civil unrest", whatever that means. Police in a small town start firing on people in self defense, people who seem to have gone violently insane. A prisoner at Fort Leavenworth out on work detail sees a strange murder and is forced to make a run for it. As the situation starts to descend into chaos, confused orders are given, old sins are forgiven in exchange for needed help and the Bradleys and Abrams soldiers fight a desperate battle using every weapon on hand. Chaos reigns in the heartland of America, spreading ever outward.

The Apocalypse written as only a veteran infantryman can, The Thin Dead Line is set as a companion series to the best selling Irregular Scout Team One by J.F. Holmes.

www.cannonpublishing.us

Made in United States
North Haven, CT
08 December 2023